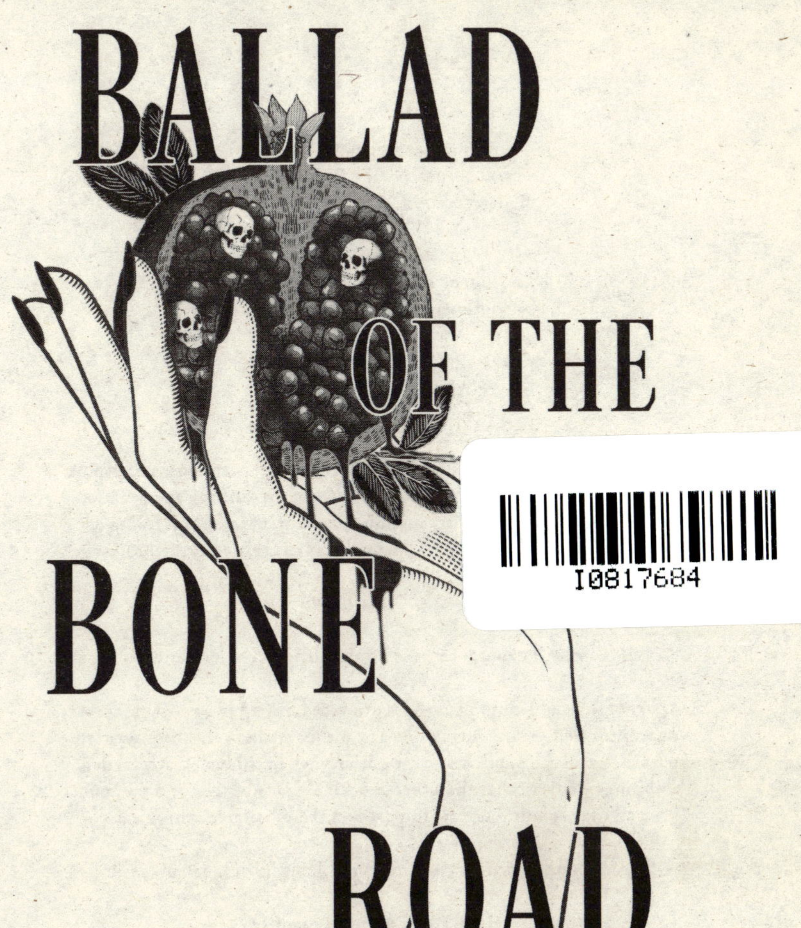

BALLAD OF THE BONE ROAD

A.C. WISE

TITAN BOOKS

Ballad of the Bone Road
Print edition ISBN: 9781835413784
E-book edition ISBN: 9781835413791

Published by Titan Books
A division of Titan Publishing Group Ltd
144 Southwark Street, London SE1 0UP
www.titanbooks.com

First edition: January 2026
10 9 8 7 6 5 4 3 2 1

A CIP catalogue record for this title is available from the British Library.

EU RP (for authorities only)
eucomply OÜ, Pärnu mnt. 139b-14, 11317 Tallinn, Estonia
hello@eucompliancepartner.com, +3375690241

Typeset in Tribute by Richard Mason.

Printed and bound by CPI Group (UK) Ltd, Croydon, CR0 4YY.

Praise for

BALLAD OF THE BONE ROAD

"The ultimate ghost story, many-layered and highly original. *Ballad of the Bone Road* is both terrifying and irresistible."

JULIET MARILLIER, award-winning author of the Sevenwaters and Blackthorn & Grim series

"A new A. C. Wise book is always something to celebrate. A ghostly heartthrob, a hollow queen, a vanishing hotel room and haunted protagonists – what's not to love? Ethereal, wild and liminal, *Ballad of the Bone Road* is a fabulous intersection between weird crime and the next wave of the paranormal. Not to be missed."

ANGELA 'A. G.' SLATTER, award-winning author of *The Crimson Road*

"A breathtakingly beautiful and chilling ghost story, *Ballad of the Bone Road* is like nothing you've ever read before. In these pages, you'll find phantoms, fae, one very glamorous hotel, and so much more. Without a doubt, A. C. Wise is one of the best literary voices of our time, which makes this book a must-read for fans of horror and dark fantasy."

GWENDOLYN KISTE, four-time Bram Stoker Award®-winning author of *The Haunting of Velkwood* and *Reluctant Immortals*

"A. C. Wise has created a lush and lyrical world that draws you in and devastates you. I was captivated."

RYM KECHACHA, author of *The Apple and the Pearl*

Also by A. C. Wise
and available from Titan Books

Wendy, Darling

Hooked

Out of the Drowning Deep

For everyone who grew up on fairy tales
and liked the dark and bloody parts the best.

1

Eight Months Ago

It begins in a hotel room.

Two kids who aren't really kids – old enough to know better, but young enough not to care – believing they will live forever and playing with magic they don't understand. They are stupidly in love. Their pockets are flush with cash for once, and they are determined to spend it all in one glorious weekend at the Peony Hotel.

It isn't sensible, but it's romantic and luxurious and selfish, which is exactly the point. Soon enough, the world will expect them to act like adults, buckle down and get serious about their lives; this is their last hurrah.

And what better place for it than the once-glittering jewel in Port Astor's crown? There's a faded glory here. The ghosts of the past, both literal and figurative, linger only a breath away. In its heyday, movie stars and politicians, poets and dukes alike graced the Peony's halls. The Oleander King and his Silver Stag once took a room for an entire glorious summer that lasted well into fall. Tallulah Bankhead caused a scandal dancing in the Grand Ballroom with the King of Sweden, who was rumored to be half fae himself.

Back then, the Morgans and Rockefellers and Astors regularly rubbed elbows with the High Courts, and the fae still roamed the city streets freely. Nymphs and vodyanoy and all manner of mers haunted the tiled baths and steam rooms. Shadowy wolves tested their voices in the subway tunnels connecting the hotel to the rest of the city. Anybody who was anybody had at least one relative stolen away to the world beneath the world – often right from the Peony Hotel itself – never to be seen again.

Then, the fae vanished. No one knows why, or where they went. It happened just long enough ago that the city is beginning to forget they were ever there – though the Peony remembers.

All this history crowds around Virgil and Leonie in their hotel room. Even faded, the Peony is still the poshest place either of them have ever been. They feel its hauntings and its glamour deep in their bones.

Neither of them is from Port Astor. Hardly anyone is. Port Astor is the place people run to when they're chasing their dreams or fleeing their nightmares, unless they go out west to Hollywoodland. Virgil came to the city from a small farming town, one of seven children, crowded against his siblings like too many seeds in too little soil. Leonie, an only child, ran to escape the unpredictable storms living inside her parents' skins.

They've been living in Port Astor for almost a year now, both working at Oberwager's Department Store. This weekend, they will reinvent themselves as disgraced royalty and louche poets belonging to another age. Already one bottle down, they've been toasting each other since they arrived, picturing themselves dripping jet beads and pearls, just like the guests in the framed illustrations lining the halls.

The wallpaper in their room is a riot of color – a jungle of silky green-black leaves and scandalously blooming flowers. Virgil can't stop running his fingertips over them, smelling their heady scent and feeling velvet when he touches the petals – pink at their ruffled edges, darkening to red in their secret hearts.

There are birds hidden among the greenery, and Virgil wonders what else the leaves might conceal among their dense shadows: watchful golden eyes and sharpened claws. The thought gives him a delicious thrill. *Something terrible is coming*, and in the next heartbeat, *isn't that wonderful?*

There's a thrum, like a storm building, electricity caged behind dark clouds. The room smells like ozone, like everything about to happen. Virgil reaches for a second bottle, digging the cork free to pour them each another glass, feeling wild and powerful, like he could do anything at all.

"To us," he says. "To the movie stars and kings and queens in whose footsteps we're following, and whose bedsheets we're about to despoil."

Leonie smacks him on the arm, light and playful. "A place this fancy washes the sheets every day, you know."

"I know," he says.

They give the bed a furtive glance, heat creeping up the back of Virgil's neck and fizzing pleasantly in his belly along with the alcohol. Neither of them moves to those fabled sheets just yet. It's not like they've never seen each other naked before, but the bed is too large for just the two of them, almost intimidating, and besides, the night is young.

They settle on the floor instead, smokes and snacks and yet more alcohol spread around them. On the opposite wall, above an old-fashioned writing desk, a mirror tilts just so to watch over them.

"You know who I always wanted to meet?" Leonie says, her tone wistful. She leans back against the foot of the bed, legs sprawled out straight, black-clad in wide trousers. Her suspenders, formerly pulled up over a white collared shirt, hang loose at her waist. Her low-heeled boots rest next to Virgil's head, the mess of his black curls smashed flat against the floor.

"Who?" Virgil's position is the inverse of hers, legs kicked up onto the bed, lying with his head near Leonie's feet. There's a hole in one of his socks, toe poking through, and he wiggles it as he waits for Leonie's answer.

"Jimmy Valentine."

The thick shag of her black fringe nearly hides her kohl-lined eyes. Together, make-up and hair give the effect of a mask. She shakes the fringe out of her eyes to look at Virgil properly, revealing the shine of excitement; her mask is for the rest of the world, never him.

Virgil lifts his head. "The movie star?"

"Movie star and singer-songwriter-musician," she corrects. "He started off in music. The movies came afterward."

"Sure, right." Virgil laces his hands over his stomach and looks up at the ceiling. "My grandmother took me to a couple of his pictures. My siblings and I were each allowed one special day a year where we got to pick what we wanted to do and wouldn't have to share it with anyone. I always asked to go to the cinema, I never even cared what was playing. Gran would take me to the lunch counter and the ice cream parlor, too. That little town only had one main street, but it was the biggest place I'd ever been, back then."

He glances at Leonie, the memories warm inside of him, but shadows gnaw at the corners of her expression. Virgil quickly steers away from family, back to Jimmy Valentine.

"I only remember one picture. Jimmy played a poor kid who worked in the mines with his father until he moved to the big city and became a star – just like his real life, I guess. Did you ever see that one?"

Leonie shakes her head. "I listened to his records more than I ever watched his films."

Virgil remembers the record player that used to be in Leonie's dorm room, along with a stack of records in well-worn sleeves. He wonders whatever happened to it, whether it's tucked away in some corner of their apartment or in a box somewhere they just haven't unpacked yet. He's almost sure, now that he thinks about it, that they must have listened to at least one of Jimmy Valentine's songs together. They might have even tried to dance, knocking into the furniture and each other in the tiny space before falling into Leonie's bed together, laughing while hushing each other and trying not to wake her neighbors. Neither of them lasted at Ember College long, though they still have to worry about waking their neighbors sometimes.

"Jimmy sang in that movie about the mines. I think there was a bit where his father made a deal with a devil he met deep in the tunnels. Jimmy had to trade the devil a song to set his father free before he left for the city, but he'd never be able to sing that particular song again and his father wouldn't ever remember what Jimmy had done for him."

Virgil thinks of a voice like summer sunshine, like bees droning around an apple tree. He can almost smell the cider-scent in the air now, overwhelming the flowers. "Now you've got me wishing I could have met him, too."

Leonie captures one of the open bottles and pours herself another glass. "All that fame and fortune, all the songs he never got the chance to write, just because of a stupid car accident."

Virgil can't help thinking how beautiful she looks, talking about Jimmy Valentine like he was somebody she knew, even though neither of them could have been more than five or six years old when he died.

It isn't just Leonie. Every newspaper and magazine cover right across Arcadia carried pictures of him after he died. Movie theaters showed a film of his funeral, and people sat in the dark crying together like they'd known Jimmy Valentine, too. They left flowers and cards and pictures in every place Jimmy ever lived or played a show.

"He used to stay at the Peony all the time," Leonie

continues, more wistful now than melancholy. "He might even have stayed in this very room. Did you know he wrote 'Winter Velvet' about a girl who used to work here? Everyone thinks it's a love song, but it's a tragedy. Her fiancé died in the war. She was mourning him, but Jimmy helped her forget for a while."

"Did he make love to her?"

"Probably. Jimmy made love to everyone."

"Well, then, darlin', I reckon I'd be even more pleased to meet him." Virgil affects his best Jimmy Valentine drawl.

"That was truly awful." Leonie smacks him on the arm again. Virgil is relieved to see her smile.

"I'll work on it." He lays his head back against the floor, his gaze tracing the molded flourishes on the ceiling.

The world is so thin here.

He isn't sure where the notion comes from, except he knows it's true. He isn't even properly drunk yet, but his thoughts move thick and slow as honey. It doesn't seem like such a stretch; he could reach out and find Jimmy Valentine, take his hand, and invite him in for a while. Now that he's thought of it, he wants to do it, more than he's ever wanted anything before. It would chase away the sadness in Leonie's eyes, and on top of that, Virgil wants prove to himself that he can.

Why not? Why shouldn't he? Possibility and energy crackle within him. This is what he was made to do. All he needs is to—

Leonie pokes him in the stomach. "Where did you go?"

He blinks. Leonie's face is inches from his, leaning over

him. Her breath and the ends of her hair tickle his skin. Her forehead touches his own. "Come back."

"I'm here," Virgil says, though he wonders if it's true.

Leonie's eyes are a blue that is almost grey, or a grey that is almost blue, a ring of slate around their lighter interior.

"Good." Her lips brush his. The hair rises on the back of his neck and all along his arms.

She shifts until she's straddling him. Virgil rests his hands on her waist, and when she tugs her shirt free from her trousers, he slides his hands beneath it, her skin pebbling under his touch. The promise in the room shifts until it's centered in Virgil's body. Leonie retrieves the tin of tobacco and rolling papers she carries with her everywhere. For as long as Virgil has known her, she's insisted on hand-rolling her own cigarettes, and she gives it the same care and attention each time, like she's performing a ritual.

She balances the tin and paper on Virgil's chest, using him as the surface to work her magic. He watches her face, enraptured, the tip of her tongue poking from the corner of her lips as she rolls the paper tight, then dampens it with her spit, sealing the tobacco inside.

As they pass the cigarette back and forth, watching each other's fingers and mouths, a new urgency grips them – a storm breaking. Virgil fumbles to get his trousers undone, only managing to get them and his underwear partway down his legs before she lowers herself onto him.

Leonie throws her head back, exposing the column of her throat. Virgil holds on to her waist as she jerks her hips hard, clenching around him as she comes. The swiftness of it, the beauty of it, startles an orgasm from Virgil too, though he'd intended to hold on.

She rolls off him, curling around him and plucking the cigarette from his lips to put it back between her own. His hand drifts to the small of her back as she pillows her head against his chest – careful to keep any ash from dropping on him.

The curtains are drawn against Port Astor's glow, so he has no idea of the time – not that it matters in the city anyway. Stars barely fight through the glare of all the mirrored skyscrapers reflecting each other, the blinking marquee bulbs smearing so beautifully in the puddles any time it rains. It's the most gorgeous city in the world, Virgil thinks. No wonder the fae adored it; no wonder its ghosts never want to leave.

"We could, you know," he says. He's half-dreaming, uncertain whether he's said the words aloud until Leonie raises her head to look at him.

"Could what?"

Virgil absently traces a hand over the line of his ribs. "Call Jimmy Valentine."

There's something there, a whole other world inside him. When he tries to picture it, he sees a white road tucked behind his bones. It looks like crushed-up sticks of classroom chalk. The trees on either side are pale, and beyond them there's grass – each blade sharply defined in its own shadow.

He doesn't know where the road goes, but he's certain the dust there is softer than anything in this world. Somewhere along that road, he'll find Jimmy Valentine.

"I really think we could do it," he says.

"You're serious?" Leonie sits up. After a moment, the beginnings of a smile crease the corners of her mouth.

If Leonie believes in him, Virgil can do absolutely anything. He bounces to his feet, yanking up his trousers, no longer the slightest bit tired. His enthusiasm is like a wildfire, catching as he paces around the room. "Why not? Why shouldn't we?"

He whirls around and comes back to the end of the bed, holding out a hand for Leonie. She takes it, and he pulls her to her feet.

"What do you say? Wanna give it a try?"

"Yes." Leonie breathes her answer against his lips, sealing it there with a kiss. "I really, really do."

Roasted notes of caramel and sugar trailed after Brix as he left the bright copper gleam of the cozy café, returning to the merciless sidewalks of Port Astor. Car horns blared along the street and the flow of pedestrian traffic never slowed, leaving him weaving and dodging to preserve the paper cups of coffee held aloft in either hand. Both were strong and black, his sweetened with sugar, which he probably didn't need given the paper bag of almond pastries tucked under his arm, but he'd barely slept last night and so he'd decided to indulge.

Non-specific and restless dreams had kept him awake, but Belle was waiting on him, and she'd be annoyed if he was late when it was his turn to supply the caffeine. She'd left the outer door of their office open, knowing he would have his hands full. He nudged it with his hip and stepped into the entryway.

"All right, luv? I brought coffee."

"In here," she called.

In the office proper, he found Belle leaning against the large rosewood desk, which dominated the crowded space. Stained glass accents in the bay window scattered colored light across the stacks of books and paper covering every surface. Neither of them had ever used the desk for anything other than storage. Brix found a rare clear spot to set the pastries down and handed Belle her coffee.

"What's on the docket today?" He leaned beside her, digging a pastry out of the bag and scattering crumbs.

Belle glanced up disapprovingly. Brix took a second unapologetic bite. If the crumbs attracted mice, he'd just let one of the cats that liked to sun itself in the back courtyard inside. Problem solved.

Belle didn't go so far as to chide him, paging back through her leatherbound casebook to read aloud to him from the list of recent inquiries.

Despite the growing backlash against spiritualism – and indeed all things occult – that dominated the opinion pages of Port Astor's newspapers these days, they never seemed to lack for work. The fae had only been gone forty-odd years, well within many people's lifetimes, but it was as though everyone had collectively chosen to forget the way magic had once flowed through the streets. But it wasn't as if the city had stopped being haunted. If anything, it had grown even more so. Maybe precisely *because* people had already chosen to forget the old ways; it left them more vulnerable. They no longer knew how to protect themselves.

When the fae vanished, the last of the great robber baron families had claimed it had always been their plan –

to retake the city by sealing the ways between worlds with iron, not to mention claiming that they knew where every single one of those ways was located. They called it a victory, but it struck Brix as remarkably short-sighted. The fae had always had their own unknowable reasons for everything they did; their departure without explanation wasn't entirely uncharacteristic, but it seemed that at least one great industrialist or politician ought to be concerned. What if the fae came back? What if they never did? And what if something worse took their place? A vanishing like that, all at once... It was the kind of thing that left scars.

"An apartment building on 20th and Park. The superintendent's been receiving complaints of odd noises, banging on the walls, things creaking and bumping in the night."

"Sounds like a problem with the pipes."

"A manager at Oberwager's called about items going missing, merchandise mysteriously shifting around."

"Probably underpaid employees having a bit of fun," Brix said. "Nothing else?"

A better quality of inquiries ought to be piling up at their door. Things had gotten worse in the last year or so, though he didn't like to think on the timeline too closely. Those old scars were reopening, and it left him with a desire to distract himself with a proper case. Something real and something sufficiently complex to keep him occupied for a while.

He finished the last bite of his pastry and glanced at the bag, which Belle hadn't touched. He contented himself with a sip of his coffee instead, trying not to fidget. He'd been hoping for a something like the demon-haunted warehouse they'd cleansed for the Carmichael siblings, or the Sutcliffe girl who'd vanished right before her sister's eyes. Strange noises and missing merchandise sounded more like a job for a building superintendent and a night watchman than specialists like him and Belle.

Belle flipped over a page, giving him a measured look, and kept reading.

"Ghostly music from a church on 9th. That one might actually be real, if not terribly exciting."

She found a scrap of paper to mark her page and snapped the book closed. Brix tried to hide his disappointment. It felt wrong to want something a little dangerous – or at least absorbing. Something to keep him out of the house and away from the silences that gathered with increasing thickness each day, stretching themselves longer every time they came to fill up the gaps between the sound of Abby's voice.

Belle set the casebook aside, finally reaching for her coffee. It might have been Brix's imagination, but he caught the faintest hint of a smile. The off-hand way she spoke, as if in afterthought, suggested she'd deliberately been holding out on him.

"There was one more call," she said. "A young woman let go from her job a few months back. A room went missing from the hotel where she worked, completely vanished midway through her shift. She told her boss, but he accused her of causing a scene and fired her on the spot."

Brix stood up straighter. "Oh? Which hotel?"

"The Peony." Belle consulted her notes, no recognition in her voice at the name.

"You're serious? The most haunted hotel in all of Port Astor and you didn't mention it right off?"

The look she returned was guileless.

"Holcombe's Folly? Nothing? Not ringing even one bell?"

"If you say so." She watched him over the rim of her cup. Brix gave into the urge to pace – fully awake now – despite the fact that there was scarcely any room.

"It's the most famous hotel in the city. John Jacobs Astor commissioned it for the express purposes of holding seances after his fiancée vanished. Some hack of a medium convinced him to spend his entire fortune on it. He ruined what was left of his family name and ended up killing himself in one of the suites. I can't believe you've never heard any of this."

"I didn't grow up here," she reminded him with the slightest of frowns.

"Neither did I, luv, but we've both been here long enough now that surely some of the history must have permeated."

"Hmm." Belle made a non-committal sound, but Brix caught the note beneath it. Her interest had been piqued.

"Peony it is, then." He clapped his hands together and rubbed them, nervous energy building between his palms. He wanted to be there already, gone, working, but even so his mouth ran away with him as if Belle needed more convincing. "They've got a whole indoor garden – a gift from some fae queen or other, it still blooms year-round. The Red Rose Girls came up from Cogslea and held an impromptu residency there for a week. A real wonder. I'm surprised we've never gotten a call from there before. What else did the woman say?"

"Not much, but I told her she could stop by if—"

A knock on the door interrupted her.

"Speak of the devil?"

Belle shot him a look, a faint rind the color of blood circling her irises, then called into the hallway. "It's open."

A young woman peeked her head around the door, looking like she might change her mind and take flight at any moment. "Brix and Bellefeather?"

"That's us." Brix gestured her in. "I'm sorry there isn't anywhere to sit."

"It's alright." Her gaze drifted between the two of them, startling slightly at Belle's attire – lilac silk, a skirt that reached the floor and a fitted jacket to match, gloves covering her hands, curls drawn back primly, all of it suggesting she'd stepped into the room from another age.

"Pastry?" Brix held out the bag, hoping to set her at ease, but the young woman shook her head.

She turned her attention to Belle. "I called earlier?"

"Calliope, yes?" Belle folded her hands neatly in front of her, making no move to shake the young woman's hand.

"Yes," she said, but she sounded doubtful.

"Sydney Brix." Brix held out his hand. "How can we help?"

It wasn't uncommon for those who found their way to the office to second-guess whether they should even have come. Brix was used to clients who refused to believe the evidence of their own senses, as well as those who believed fully, but had already lost hope. There were few enough people who could do what he did, especially these days, and Belle was even rarer. Many would-be clients talked themselves out of presenting their cases before they ever stepped foot in the door. It was easier to believe the two of them were con artists, or at the very least, delusional. More comfortable to think that anything that couldn't be touched, tasted, or held in the hand wasn't real.

"You worked at the Peony?" Brix tried to keep his tone level, not to sound over eager. The pain that should have lessened this last year seemed only to have grown, a bruise deep under the skin that ached every time he pressed on it. He longed to sink into a job.

"Yes, I..." Calliope looked down, studying her shoes. "It's going to sound unbelievable."

"Unbelievable is our line of work."

That brought her head up, a small measure of relief crossing her features.

"Why don't you tell us everything from the start?" Belle suggested.

She hadn't moved from the desk, but Brix noted the straight line of her back and shoulders. He checked her eyes. There was no telltale sign of rust-red now. She held her demon in check, but Brix imagined they were restless, too.

"I was a maid," Calliope said. "During my last shift, I was turning over rooms like usual. Everything seemed perfectly ordinary, then one of the rooms was just... gone."

"How do you mean?" Brix asked.

"Well, there are twelve rooms on each floor, six on either side – except that afternoon, there were only eleven rooms on the fourteenth floor, and the spot where the twelfth room should have been felt... wrong."

Calliope glanced between them again, like she was expecting to be called a liar.

"After you found the room missing, what then?" he asked.

"I went to Mr. Gustav – he's the manager. He accused me of making the whole thing up for attention." Calliope shook her head. "I tried to show him, but he wouldn't hear of it. He ordered me to leave, or else security would escort me out."

"That seems like a pretty extreme reaction." Belle stiffened with clear irritation on Calliope's behalf.

"He was afraid of losing business. Anyway, I found another job, a better one. But the thing is, I know I wasn't wrong. Except..." Uncertainty crept back into her voice.

"Go on," Belle said.

"Well, I spoke to some of the other girls, and not one of them remembers there being a twelfth room on that floor. They say there've only ever been eleven, but I know that's not right. Fergus..." Calliope blushed. "He's one of the bellhops... We looked at the blueprints together, and there's clearly supposed to be twelve rooms on the fourteenth floor. Fergus is the only one who believes me. It's like something made everyone else forget." She looked briefly embarrassed. "I even forgot. All of this happened a few months ago."

"But something changed," Brix said. "What?"

He wasn't entirely able to keep the eagerness out of his voice this time. This, whatever it was, *this* was what he'd been waiting for. A shift in the wind, a storm bringing the scent of damp earth to the air. A fae season, his grandmother used to call it – one season slipping into the midst of another where it clearly didn't belong.

"I don't know," Calliope said, sounding genuinely distressed. "I woke up this morning with a feeling something bad is about to happen. Something's coming or..."

"It's alright," Brix told her. "We'll take a look, see if we can't find some answers."

"Gustav still works there. He might not let you investigate. He hates anything that looks even a little bit like scandal, anything he thinks will hurt the hotel's bottom line."

"Well, then." Brix caught himself grinning, unable to help it now that the thing he'd been waiting for had finally arrived. "We'll just have to find a way to look around without him knowing, won't we?"

The look Belle shot him wasn't exactly approval, but it wasn't disapproval either.

Calliope's distress melted into a look of mischief. "Some of the girls like to smoke around back by the laundry room door. They keep it wedged open so they don't have to clock in and out through the lobby."

"Very understandable." Brix patted his jacket pocket. "I'm rather partial to a smoke myself, and I'm feeling like a walk just about now to enjoy one."

He tilted his head toward the door, and Belle pushed away from the desk. Calliope looked surprised at the ease with which they'd taken the case, but hurried out after them.

"Good luck." She held out her hand for Brix to shake. Belle kept her hands wrapped firmly around her beaded clutch. "And thank you for believing me."

Belle felt the wrongness as soon as the building came in sight. More precisely, Belizial felt it, her demon tensing inside her, like a cat arching its back, fur spiking all along its spine.

"What is it?" she asked aloud.

Brix glanced at her, but only briefly, understanding she wasn't talking to him. Belizial curled around her bones.

There are ghosts here, but something else. It's… Distress rose in their tone, fear making them wind themself even closer.

Tightness answered in Belle's chest, as if the corset under her jacket had been laced too hard, cinching her ribs until they creaked and making it difficult to breathe.

Shhhh, she soothed without words, trying to keep her own heart rate even.

The speed of their guilty retreat only left her more on edge. Normally, Belizial would press close to her skin, ready to transform her, ready to devour anything that posed a threat. They rarely made themself this small. Unless—

"Everything alright?" Brix asked.

She reached after Belizial, a question without specific words. The fae who had hurt them was long gone, but what else would make them shrink as if salt-stung, pulling back even from her touch? It was subtle enough, but it still struck at her pride. Didn't they trust her to keep them safe, after all these years?

"I don't know." She addressed Brix, then spoke again internally. *Let me know if you feel anything specific.*

Her tone, even within the confines of her thoughts, sounded petty, but it was impossible to hide bitterness from someone who shared her skin. Belizial agreed without words and settled within her, which only made her feel worse. They were both overreacting.

Brix dropped the last of his cigarette, crushing it under his heel. "Ready?" He tipped his head toward the narrow alleyway between buildings, and the metal door, which had indeed been wedged open.

From behind the Peony, Port Astor's sky was a ribbon divided by buildings. The façade was much more impressive, but even here the strange mix of Gothic and Art Deco stood out. Belle couldn't shake the feeling of space, as if the interior had been folded to contain more than the comparatively drab buildings to either side should allow.

Fae magic. Even now it persisted. The past wasn't the past at all within the hotel. On the walk over, Brix had told her how during the Great Blackout that had smothered the entire city, the Peony alone continued to shine, foxfire and spirit lights in every window. Perhaps that was all Belizial felt, echoes clinging to the place. The Hollow Queen had vanished along with the rest of the fae; she wasn't here. She couldn't be here, regardless of what Belizial felt.

The idea reassured her, but her demon neither agreed nor expressed doubt, as if they weren't even listening. Fine, if they wanted to hide, let them. She and Brix could handle this on their own.

"Ready." Belle tugged at the sleeves of her jacket, making sure no gap existed between them and her gloves. She pulled open the door. Belizial prickled again, but the sense of wrongness remained non-specific. Unhelpful, but it made Belle feel justified in ignoring their unease, at least until she had more information. Gently, but pointedly, she pulled her consciousness from theirs and narrowed her focus.

They turned left, away from the scent of laundry soap and the sound of voices muffled behind a set of double doors. At the end of the corridor, another door let onto a set of stairs, winding upward.

"Fourteenth floor?" Brix didn't sound enthusiastic.

"Fourteenth floor." Belle gathered her skirt and set to climbing.

The stairwell was empty, but sooner or later a staff member or a guest was bound to spot them. Not to mention that even if they weren't caught, they didn't have a clear plan. They hadn't officially been invited to investigate; what exactly could they do?

Gloom pervaded the stairwell, dim and heavy in a way

that had nothing to do with the lack of windows. Belle felt it in her back teeth, a sharp, aching cold, a taste like metal.

We should leave. Belizial squeezed at her from within, rising panic making them careless.

It felt like before, like being closed in the dark, the Hollow Queen hurting them again and again.

"What do you make of that, luv?" Brix stopped just short of touching her arm, drawing her attention.

Two floors farther up the stairwell, a stain spread across the wall. Belle gripped the railing, leaning outward for a better look. "I don't think that's mold."

She ignored the tightness in her ribs. The stain made her think of a spreading bruise, blurred and smudgy. Belizial shuddered, their thoughts humming against her own.

It shouldn't be here. We shouldn't be here.

Brix's dark curls stirred even though there was no wind in the stairwell, the sheen of rust and plum that marked him as ghost-touched gleaming even in the dull light.

"It's just a haunting," Belle murmured, trying to soothe Belizial.

A haunting, but certainly not the kind she was used to, and from Brix's expression, not the kind he was used to either. She leaned farther over the railing, trying to get a better look. Gravity tugged at her, but so did the smudged shadow. The taste of salt and iron lingered at the back of her throat, and with it came the feeling of a knife plied against her skin. Not her skin, Belizial's. Not their skin, but the very essence of themself, layers peeled away as the Hollow Queen took them apart, over and over again.

Don't– Their voice rose, then fractured; they dug in, as if something might pull them away from her.

It wasn't just the shadow, but something inside it, or behind it. The dizzying sensation of the entire hotel turning to peer at her and Belizial swept over Belle. A shuddering ripple, like a stone dropped into a pond.

"You felt it too," Brix said.

Belle let go of the railing to wrap an arm around her midsection, fighting to control her breath. Something cracked deeper within the hotel, a seam splitting somewhere below them.

"Something's wrong." Belle fought to get the words out, then nearly lost her balance, startling at the sound of a door opening above them.

She caught Brix's eye, and as quietly as possible, they hurried back the way they'd come. A new wrongness tugged at Belle's awareness. She never should have brought Belizial into such a fae-haunted place. No wonder they were panicking – and now that they were, where did that leave her?

The door leading back to the alleyway wasn't where Belle remembered it. She'd gotten turned around and Brix had followed her, pushing open a door into a room that smelled of rust and heat. A boiler squatted against the back wall, pipes snaking across the ceiling.

"What happened back there?" Brix asked.

"I'm not sure." Belle opened her eyes, keeping her hands pressed against her aching ribs. "Belizial felt something, but I don't know what. What did you feel?"

"There's a haunting, but..." He shook his head.

Too big. Too much. Curiosity demanded a closer look, but Belle never wanted to look at anything like the shadow in that stairwell again. *Hungry* – that was the word that came to mind, but not for food. A feeling like something with delicate fingers picking at the deepest parts of her, trying to unravel her.

"I think we have more than just a disappearing room on our hands," Brix said. His hair no longer stirred in winds that weren't there, and his curls had returned to their usual brown-black color. He ran a hand through them, sweeping the residual energy and flicking it away like drops of water.

"That mark on the wall. It felt like it wanted—"

The skin at the back of Belle's neck tightened, and she went still, holding out a hand. To warn against what, she didn't know.

"Behind me." She kept her voice low, the words terse.

To his credit, Brix didn't question her, moving so she stood between him and whatever else shared the room with them. Nothing human; a moment later, the stench of sulfur confirmed it.

A small and starveling shape crept from behind the boiler. It was wrong, twisted – somewhere between a hairless cat and a feral child. Naked and sexless, thin enough that every one of its ribs and all the knobs of its spine were visible through its near-translucent skin.

The tearing she'd felt, when the entire hotel shuddered – a demon had come through.

Crouched on all fours, it glared at Belle, its eyes red and baleful, speaking without words of horrible unfairness. It felt Belizial inside her skin and hated that they were there, free while it was not. The desire to bite and rend rolled from it in palpable waves. Belle could almost taste the hot spit filling its mouth, its longing to carry the tattered shreds of her demon back to whatever hell it had emerged from so they could suffer, too.

Without her having to ask, Brix turned away, giving her privacy. Belizial didn't resist her or shrink away this time, already so close to the surface, all spikes of anxiety inflamed by the pure rage pouring from the demon in front of them, minor though it might be.

The thing hissed, baring needle teeth. Belizial flowed over and through Belle, peeling away into a halo of darkness around her, snapping her bones and making her larger. Not a full transformation, but enough.

The pale demon arched its back. Fear gleamed in eyes the color of old coins. Yet it didn't flee, drawn like a magnet to Belizial. Belle might have felt pity – if it hadn't lunged first, if she didn't want to pounce on something weaker than her and crunch it between her jaws, to be feared instead of fearful, and give all the restlessness and distress she'd been feeling since they entered the hotel somewhere useful to go.

A shrieking sound cut off, the hunt over too quickly. For a moment, it wasn't enough. Belle wanted to rake claws down the metal of the boiler and hear it scream as well. Rip the pipes from the wall for the sheer joy of destruction.

Belizial drew back and she let go, reining herself in and folding them back inside of her. Their relief washed through her, the strength of it leaving her ashamed of herself. And even so, some measure of the hunger remained.

Belle smoothed a gloved hand over a new tear in her jacket. Some of the pale demon's blood had spattered across her skirt as well, but not so much that it couldn't be salvaged.

"It's alright. You can turn around now," she said.

"Where in the hells did that thing come from?" Brix came to stand beside her.

"Exactly."

She crouched, placing a hand against the wall behind the boiler while Brix looked over her shoulder. The energy that throbbed beneath her palm, already fading, felt nothing like the shadow in the stairwell. There was no lingering tang of iron, no incessant pull – or rather, the pull was in the wrong direction, as if the demon had merely been passing by, minding its own business, when something compelled it to come here.

"You said John Jacobs Astor built this place specifically to hold seances?" She looked at Brix over her shoulder. "Whether or not that medium was a quack, Astor still hit on something. This place is thin, like a crossroads."

"Yeah, I'm getting that."

There was a note of strain in his voice. Just being here would wear at Brix like a tide, all those ghosts tugging at him and demanding his attention. She straightened, drawing her hand away from the wall.

"That thing..." Brix indicated the wall.

"Believe it or not, I think it was just bad luck," she said. "All of us were in the wrong place at the wrong time. It felt us, or Belizial, and got pulled through. No wonder it was angry."

"It can't be a complete coincidence though, surely?"

Belle brushed her hands off, one against the other, as if

soot stained them from touching the wall, though her gloves remained perfectly clean. Now that the immediate danger had passed, exhaustion gnawed her, too, but the kind that left her itchy and unsettled rather than wanting sleep.

"No. Like you said, this place is thin, and whatever it was we saw in the stairwell is making it thinner."

The Hollow Queen.

"There's no immediate danger," Belle went on, brushing past Belizial's concerns. She'd always kept them safe; she'd continue to do so now. "The tear that demon came through is already closing, and I'm not sure there's much more we can do here right now."

"You're probably right." Brix glanced back at the wall. Belle caught the reluctance in his voice, like part of him hoped the tear would open again and give them an excuse to stay.

It lasted only a moment. "Right, then."

Belle moved to check the coast was clear before leading them into the hall and back outside. The metal door was exactly where it should be, and she wondered how they'd ever gotten turned around. The minute they were in the alleyway, Brix lit a cigarette. He squinted up at the slice of sky above them, and Belle could almost see the thoughts turning, worrying the question of the haunting like a dog with a bone.

The door opened behind them, and two women in maid's uniforms gave them a startled look. Brix touched two fingers to his forehead, tossing them a salute, and before either could question their presence, he strolled away as if he and Belle being in this alleyway, her in blood-splattered clothes, was the most natural thing in the world.

"Until tomorrow, then?" Brix said as they reached the sidewalk.

Belle sensed his hesitation, but she badly needed a change of clothes and the opportunity to talk to Belizial alone. "Tomorrow."

"Your turn to bring the coffee." His smile attempted to project ease, but didn't entirely hide the strain.

But a moment later, he straightened his shoulders as if he didn't have a care in the world, and gave her the same salute he'd offered the maids as they parted ways.

Belle watched him go for a moment. Brix had a talent for smoothing a mask over any grief or pain. It was one of the many things she appreciated about him.

And the fact that he'd let it slip for even a moment unsettled her. Belizial's fear, the flickering glimpses of memory that the smudged darkness in the stairwell had drawn to the surface – all of it left Belle with the impression of the Peony sitting like a scab on the surface of a deep wound. Once they started picking at it, what exactly would they find?

4

Eight months ago

Virgil folds the carpet back and tucks it under a leg of the bed, revealing wooden floorboards. They gleam, despite the Peony's age, making him think of the deepest hours of night. The wood is utterly the wrong color, but it's the feel of it, secret and warm, like being safe under a pile of blankets in the midst of a storm.

Candles flicker around the room. Virgil holds a cork in one of the flames, then uses the charred end to trace letters on the floor. He's never used a talking board himself, but he saw a medium use one at a fair once. It didn't look so hard.

"It's crude, but it will do." He bounces to his feet, tucking a cigarette into the corner of his mouth as he fizzes about the room. He has no idea what he's doing, but just so long as he never stops for even a moment to acknowledge the unease nipping at his heels, he'll be fine.

He promised Leonie Jimmy Valentine; he intends to deliver.

He grabs a bottle as he spins past, fidgeting with the curtains, adjusting the mirror, stalling without admitting to himself that's what he's doing. He steals a sip, whiskey – not the most expensive, nor the cheapest – and sets the bottle down.

It's emptied considerably, but he made sure to set aside a full glass for their guest of honor. Like the idea of the talking board, making offerings to the spirits feels *right*. He's operating on instinct, and the thrumming behind his ribs tells him he's on the right track. The bone-white road is unfurling inside him, Jimmy Valentine waiting at its end.

Virgil lifts the dome from the plate delivered by room service along with the whiskey. It's a grand presentation for a simple meal: peanut butter and jam on white bread, the crusts removed. Leonie read in a magazine that it was Jimmy Valentine's favorite thing to eat in the whole wide world.

The kitchen thoughtfully included a slim vase containing a single peony. There's a whole hothouse of them somewhere in the hotel, blooming through every season. Loretta Hayes did a photoshoot for *Here + Now* right after she won her first Columbia Award, posing coyly behind the ruffled petals in such a way that her strapless gown was hidden, making it look like she wore nothing at all. Maybe after they've had their chat with Jimmy Valentine, he and Leonie can take a stroll through that greenhouse and call her up as well.

"I think we're ready."

Holding the plate with the sandwich, he turns a half-pirouette and folds himself gracefully until he's cross-legged on the floor in front of the makeshift talking board. Leonie straightens her suspenders over her white work shirt, brushes non-existent lint from her trousers.

"You look perfect," he says. "You'll knock him dead. Deader, even."

He pats the space beside him on the floor. She sits, and Virgil sets the plate beside the talking board. He adjusts the glass with its measure of whiskey one last time, then lights a cigarette, balancing it carefully on the edge of an ashtray.

"Food and smoke and liquor for the dead," he says.

He sets his hand, palm up, in the space between them. After a moment, Leonie takes it, and he curls his fingers around hers. There's strength in this, like they're part of something larger. Virgil sees and feels the bone-white road more clearly than ever now. It's only meant to be walked in one direction, but just this once, why not? Jimmy Valentine died so young. Who knows what pictures he would have made, what songs he would have sung, if his life hadn't been cut tragically short? Virgil can fix all that, put things right.

It's like there's a hand pressed to the small of his back, urging him onward, lips right up against his ear whispering, *This is what you were meant to do.*

He takes the second spare glass that room service sent along and up-ends it on the talking board. Placing two fingers lightly atop it, he gestures for Leonie to do the same. Her fingers touch down beside his, making a closed circuit.

“We call to the spirit of Jimmy Valentine,” Virgil says. “We invite him to join us, accept our offerings, and grace us with his presence.”

Candlelight wobbles. Shadows flutter in the room’s corners, then fall still again.

“Please?” Leonie adds tentatively after a moment of silence. “We’d really like to say hi.”

Virgil feels the thinness of the walls between worlds. The white road presses against his ribs.

A figure stands silhouetted against the chalk-colored sky, tooled leather boots leaving perfect prints in the oh-so-soft dust. Jimmy Valentine raises a hand to shade his eyes, the tense line of his shoulders betraying surprise, as if he isn’t quite certain how he found himself here.

And then… oh. Virgil’s breath catches and the motion ripples all along the white road, because Jimmy Valentine looks right at him. Warmth floods him as a slow smile like molasses in summertime spreads across Jimmy’s face. Virgil knows he’s done the right thing for certain now. He’s called Jimmy Valentine home.

Jimmy walks from the horizon toward them, whistling a tune, a guitar slung across his back. His stride is easy, hands in his pockets, like he has all the time in the world. His outline wavers against the road, the sky, the bone-white trees, and the too-sharp blades of grass.

The glass jerks under their fingers, startling Virgil, drawing his attention back to the room, away from the vision. It darts over the floorboards, scraping across the char-written letters. Leonie lets out a small gasp.

"It's okay," Virgil says, squeezing her hand. "We did it. We really did it."

The glass wobbles to a stop. "H-E." Virgil reads out each letter as the glass shrieks across the floor. "L-L-O. Hello! He said hello!"

"Are you here?" Leonie asks. "In this room? Can you see us?"

S-E-E, the board agrees.

Leonie whips her head around. "Where?"

The curtains stir, belling outward. They settle, and there's a shape behind them, the suggestion of a body, the outline of a face glimpsed beneath a shroud, there and then gone.

The vision of the road tries to slip away. One of Virgil's hands remains atop the glass and the other holds Leonie, so he reaches for it with a deeper part of himself.

"We got this sandwich for you. Heard it was your favorite," he says, careful not to lose his cigarette. "The whiskey's yours too, and the smoke. We'd be honored if you wanted to join us."

Virgil's ribs creak. A hand knocks on a door; all he has to do is open it. The lightning-strike thrill of the knowledge fills him, his skin tingling, the tiny hairs on the back of his neck standing on end.

Yes, this is right. This is exactly how it should be.

Leonie watches him across the talking board, her eyes shining with wonder. The up-ended glass shivers under their fingertips. Promise. *Purpose.* Something so much bigger than either of them.

An extra shadow stretches through the room. Virgil holds his breath, feels the pressure shift as a door opens. Everything is waiting and wanting to happen.

Virgil lets his held breath go.

An empty bottle tips from the nightstand onto the floor, rolling toward them. Leonie jerks her fingers back from the upturned glass and covers her mouth. Laughter, mixing nerves and excitement, leaks from behind her hand. The fallen bottle stops rolling, pointing perfectly between her and Virgil.

"Would you look at that?" Virgil says. "Just like spin the bottle. The question is, which one of us does Jimmy Valentine want to kiss?"

He winks at Leonie. She places her fingers on the glass again, her other hand still holding his, and leans forward to kiss him – deep and hungry.

"Both of us, I hope," she says, when she breaks free.

Electricity rills its way up and down Virgil's spine. There's a swooping sensation in his stomach, like missing a step and starting to fall. Something deep and vast stirs through the room. There is a cracking sound, like ice sheets that have existed for millennia calving away.

A door opens. All around its edges there is light, sharp-edged and terrible. Not just a door, but a tear, a hole. Panic grabs hold of Virgil. He's made a mistake. This isn't what he meant at all—

But it's too late. Everything is already in motion. Stars wheel. Virgil feels the entirety of the Peony shift beneath him.

He turns his head. In the corner, between the bed and the wall, a faint, silvery outline appears.

Jimmy Valentine.

"Is it...?" Leonie asks.

"Well, I'll be damned," Virgil says.

His fear melts away, forgotten, soothed by the incredible, magical thing that he and Leonie have done.

Jimmy doesn't move, silent and watchful. He doesn't disappear, either.

Leonie runs her hands over her trousers, then unfolds herself carefully, not making any sudden moves. She peeks at Jimmy Valentine from beneath her dark fringe and offers him the smallest of smiles. "I'm Leonie, and this is Virgil. We're so happy to meet you."

Virgil bounces up beside her and sweeps into a low bow. They're in a haunted hotel room, but it might as well be a glittering fae hall, and Jimmy Valentine is its prince. He deserves courtly manners.

The ghost's smile is the sweetest, most heartbreaking and heartbroken thing Virgil has ever seen. His lips move, but no sound emerges. He touches his throat, his pained expression intensifying. His voice was his instrument, the one he used to enchant the world.

"I'm sorry," Virgil says in a tumbling rush. "We'll figure out a way to fix it, I promise."

He has no idea how, but in this moment, he would do anything to bring back that smile like slow molasses, to hear Jimmy's voice like a summer day, droning with bees.

Jimmy's skin, his clothes, his hair, are all shades of moonlight and shadow. He looks like he stepped right off the silver screen. Too flat, too beautiful, not quite real. The floral wallpaper is visible through and behind him. He is Jimmy Valentine, absolutely, in every way. All Virgil has to do is figure out how to pull him all the way through into this world. It must be possible. He aches to hold Jimmy and Leonie both in his arms.

"I wish we could hear you," Leonie says, wistful. A blush creeps up her cheeks. "I wish we could... touch you."

"We'll figure it out. Maybe the food would help? The smoke?" Virgil gestures, sweeping one arm to indicate the meal.

Something between hope, hunger, and curiosity flickers in Jimmy's eyes. He moves slowly at first, not quite walking, not quite drifting, like he's remembering how to be human as he goes. He bends at the waist, reaching out a tentative hand. His fingers pass through the plate, and he looks like he wants to howl with sorrow, as if a peanut butter sandwich and a glass of whiskey is the most precious meal imaginable.

"It's okay," Virgil says. He tries to keep his smile and every line of his posture easy and reassuring. "There's no rush."

Jimmy continues to look mournfully at the sandwich and drink.

"Why don't you try the smoke first?" Virgil suggests. "That might be easier, being less substantial and all."

Virgil sits on the edge of the bed, smoking his own cigarette, giving Jimmy plenty of room. Leonie comes to stand beside him, squeezing his hand, and watches Jimmy.

He bends in a way no living human body could and puts his face close to the rising threads of smoke. He breathes, deep, deep, deep. The smoke shifts toward him, the faintest movement, as if he really is drawing it in. When he straightens, Jimmy looks a little more solid than he did a moment before. He beams.

"There, you see?" Virgil crows. "I knew we'd figure it out. Don't worry, there's plenty more where that came from. We'll work the rest out as we go. Relax and make yourself comfortable, why don't you?"

Virgil taps free another cigarette, lights it, and holds it out. A smile spreads across Jimmy's face as he leans close. Virgil very much wants to brush his fingers over those lips and drink the smoke back from his lungs, but he needs to take his own advice and be patient. Slow, like taming a skittish horse.

Leonie fairly vibrates beside him. Virgil takes her other hand, holding her next to him – he can feel her wanting to lunge at Jimmy and swallow him whole.

"It's okay," Virgil says. The words are true, or they will be if he believes them hard enough. "We have all the time in the world."

Brix finished another cigarette standing on the curb outside the brownstone. He'd lost count after about the third, but Abby wasn't overly fond of him bringing his habit inside the house.

After leaving Belle, he'd spent some time walking without a particular destination in mind, smoking and trying and failing to think about nothing at all. Killing time and delaying the inevitable. The sky had turned the color of melting orange sherbet, streaked with cream and gold. It was a beautiful day, which seemed vastly unfair. Once upon a time, he and Abby would have sat out on the steps together, watched the sun set, listened to the sounds of the city. One year, three months, twenty-one days, and it still hurt as much as the first night he'd spent in the house alone. He hauled himself up the steps to the front door.

A brief glance into the dining room to the right of the door before heading to the second floor to shuck off his clothes and run a bath. Belle had taken the worst of it, but he still felt battered, with the need to wash invisible grime from his skin. The sky darkened beyond the windows, silence stretching around him to reveal every little tick and shift and sigh of the wood. The Peony nagged at him – not a simple haunting, but haunted nonetheless.

Enough to let a starving demon slip through. When the Morgans and Rockefellers had set about sealing all the ways they knew about, they'd been more concerned about the fae than the hells, but one was a pathway to another. And the mortal world sat atop or beside or within them all, depending on which direction you wanted to look at it, but either way, closer than most people were willing to admit.

The hotel's history didn't seem to fully account for what he'd felt though, or the way Belle's demon had reacted. She'd never been too specific about what they'd been through before they met her, and he didn't want to pry. It was for her to sort out. Ghosts were his area of expertise. So why couldn't he tell what exactly haunted the hotel?

The scent of aftershave followed him back down the stairs and into the kitchen. He cut vegetables, drizzled them in oil and set them to roast. Now that he'd run a straight razor over his skin and a comb through his hair, he felt almost presentable. Someone in whose company Abby wouldn't be embarrassed to be seen.

Brix switched on the small radio that had belonged to Abigail's uncle, from whom she'd inherited the house. He hummed along to the music, something soft and instrumental.

When he'd first moved to Port Astor, he'd frequented a few of the jazz clubs and piano bars around the apartment he'd had at the time. It seemed to be the expected thing to do, but he'd ultimately decided it wasn't his scene. He'd much rather listen to the radio or records in the comfort of his own home.

A cast iron pan went onto the stove, the heat turned up high to give the filet a good sear, and he opened the wine to breathe.

He hated the way the shadows clustered in the dining room. Using a long taper, he lit candles down the center of the table, smelling faintly of honey and beeswax, but not enough to interfere with the scents of the meal. Oddly, drawing the curtains made the dark feel less intrusive, rendering the space private and cozy, hiding the view of the street – their own little world.

The pan of roasted vegetables came out of the oven – small potatoes perfectly crisped and golden-brown on the outside, creamy on the inside; carrots, mushrooms, and sprouts. He plated them on the good china and slid his steak into place – pink and juicy, with a perfect charred crust.

In the dining room, Abigail's plate sat empty at the far end of the table, her glass as well. He checked the line of salt meticulously drawn around her chair and set his food down.

A shallow bowl containing a silver ring, twin to his own, sat in the middle of the table. He slipped his off – not a wedding ring, but a promise. It made a soft chiming sound as he dropped it into the bowl to nestle against Abby's.

There would have been a wedding, if Abigail hadn't died.

He rested his hands, palm down, on the table and concentrated on the empty chair, holding the door open like a gentleman this time – as he had every time since the first. Brix made himself smile, half genuine, and hoped that half was enough to hide the edges which ground together like broken glass.

"Abby? Care to join me, love?"

Love. The word was always different in his mouth when paired with her name. Brix couldn't have explained it aloud, but he could taste it, feel it. It had quality and weight, like good chocolate and fine wine, melting together on his tongue.

The air at the far end of the table thickened. A breeze passed like a sigh through the room, stirring the curtains, but left the salt circle intact. The hair on the back of Brix's neck stood on end, gooseflesh breaking out all over his arms and their inked protective markings.

Abby wasn't just any ghost. He didn't need protection from her. Except...

His heart tripped over its next beat, the same as the first time he'd seen her. It didn't matter that the carved back of the chair showed right through her moon-tinted skin and clothes. She wore the dress she'd been buried in, but she was still his Abby. Nothing could change that.

"Hello, love." Something like relief melted around his bones. His smile was all genuine this time. "I've missed you."

"I've missed you, too," Abby said.

Brix heard the catch in her voice and chose to ignore it. Chose to ignore the panic it engendered. He took up his knife and fork, focusing on his meal for somewhere else to look and something else to do with his hands than reaching for Abby across the table. His touch would sink right through her. Instead, he sliced his meat into unnecessarily small bites, sectioned each vegetable precisely. As he did, he let forth a tumble of words to wash over the pause, the *but* he'd sensed and not given Abby a chance to say aloud.

"Hell of a case today. A young woman came to us. She'd been fired from her job at the Peony Hotel after reporting a room that just up and vanished. Met a demon in the basement, but Belle took care of it quick enough. I wish we'd seen more than just the service tunnels and a stairwell, though. We always meant to stay there, didn't we? Just for a night or two, to spoil ourselves."

He didn't say the word *honeymoon*, swallowing around it instead. His first visit to the hotel should have been with Abby on his arm, walking her across the lobby under the famed Tiffany glass into the greenhouse where they'd have had tea or champagne, or whatever it was people who could actually afford to stay at the Peony did.

"Syd," Abby said.

The hook in her voice made him lift his head. It brought a chill with it, a new stuttering trip-beat to the rhythm of his heart. He held her gaze, letting her longing – tinged with sorrow – soak through him. Would this be the time she finally said it aloud?

Any number of protests rose to his tongue. He wasn't ready, he never would be, but Abby only sighed. Her gaze skated over his meal with a suppressed shudder of hunger. "It looks delicious," she said. "You should eat before it gets cold."

Brix skewered a bloody slice of meat, put it in his mouth. He chewed so he wouldn't have to think for a while. Abby closed her eyes as if tasting the meal along with him, the brittle edge easing from her smile.

"How's the wine?" she asked, eyes still closed.

Brix sipped, rolling it across his tongue. Abby had always been the one with the finer palate, able to pick apart the complex flavors in each glass. He knew which varietals to pair with what, which years were worth paying for, but that was where it ended. He might be able to pick out a citrusy note from time to time, but smoke or birch bark or whatever ridiculous flavors Abby claimed to taste always eluded him.

"Wet stone," he said.

She opened her eyes, arching a brow. "You taste no such thing." Her cheeks dimpled, her smile slightly higher on the left side.

Gods, but he loved that crooked smile.

"You shouldn't be dining alone," she said after a moment.

"I'm not alone. You're here." He tried to project bravado, ease, as if he could sweep Abby's feelings away.

"Syd—"

"No." The word was too quick; he fought to bring evenness back to his tone. "Please, Abby, we'll talk about it after dinner if you want, but not yet."

What he wanted to say was *not ever.*

But he didn't have to say it for her to read it in his eyes. She knew him too damned well.

"Alright." She let hurt sit under the brightness in her eyes, just veiled enough that he could pretend not to see. Which made him an utter ass, and he didn't care. Except he did.

"Promise," Brix said, and tried to mean it.

He tilted his glass toward Abby, taking another sip, holding the wine behind what he hoped was a reassuring smile.

They both tasted the lie, thick in the air between them.

Abby, stronger than he could ever be, let it go – for the moment. She let him chatter about nothing as he ate. Maybe he'd put some planters on the front step to add color, and what did she think of repainting the spare bedroom?

He tried not to see the way Abby sat very straight through it all, holding herself together. Her answers grew briefer, her voice thinner as she frayed at the edges. Brix desperately wanted her to stay, trying to make all those things be just his imagination.

Like the weight of her hand growing more insubstantial in his every day.

It's okay. We'll try another doctor, a different hospital.

Syd, I can't do this anymore.

Brix couldn't remember what he'd said to her back then, what comforting words he'd offered. Maybe she hadn't even said that at all. She'd been scared, so had he, but then he'd fixed it all, brought her back, given them a second chance. Not forever, of course not, but a period of grace, to make things easier for both of them.

He'd made it safe for her to be here, made it so it wouldn't hurt being pulled between two worlds. She couldn't touch him, he couldn't touch her, but they could speak, they could be in the same room, and that was something.

"You should invite Belle over for dinner sometime," Abby said.

Brix nearly knocked over his wine. "Belle? Why?"

The horrible thought occurred that Abby might be trying to set him up. Horrible for many reasons, not the least of which was the stupid, awful kindness of her not wanting him to be alone. But Belle? "I don't want—"

He must have looked panicked. Abby's lips curved in silent laughter. "Dear gods, no, I didn't think you did. You *do* need a friend though, and Belle is that. Think about it, please? I'm sure she'd love a home-cooked meal. Have you ever cooked for her before?"

"No." It was a strange thought. He remembered the stale tin of biscuits she'd offered the first time he came to her office – their office now – to meet with her. It had taken a whole pot of tea to wash the damned things down. Properly cooked food would do her a world of good.

She'd never even been inside his home, nor he inside hers, now that he thought about it. With everything they'd been through together, with all that he knew about her and she about him, why that last barrier between them?

His plate was clean, but he kept a death grip on his knife and fork. The moment he put them down, they'd have to acknowledge that the meal was done.

"Syd." Abigail's voice was soft, but it still landed like a blow.

Brix made himself uncurl his fingers and set his knife and fork down across his plate with a sound like the final closing of a door.

"It doesn't have to be tonight, Syd. But it has to be soon."

She tried to be gentle. That only made it worse. Brix's eyes stung. He tried not to look away and failed.

"Syd, promise me." A sharp note rang in Abigail's voice.

He'd promised her already, and he'd broken that promise. Given the chance, he would keep breaking his promises forever. Just one more night. One more dinner.

"Syd." Her voice gripped him like a hand on his chin, digging in, turning his head when he resisted.

"I promise," he said, the words emerging from surprise than anything else.

The hand that wasn't really there – except it was – let go. Abigail looked stunned. "I'm sorry. I didn't mean... I didn't know I could."

She shouldn't be able to. Even from where he sat, Brix could see the salt circle around her remained unbroken.

He'd been careful, he knew what he was doing. He'd followed the rules – but he'd pushed.

"Something's wrong. Syd—" Abby's voice wavered, and between one breath and the next, she frayed. Bruising traced the veins in her smoky skin, her eyes blank and frozen. At any moment, they would shatter, crack, and let terrible things come through.

Brix stood, took a half step toward her. "Abby, I'm—"

Her hands pressed flat to the table – *pressed*, like they had weight.

Frost spread from beneath her palms, fractal patterns across the polished wood. Brix stared in horror. Cold wrapped lovingly around his bones.

Abby jerked away, and air rushed back into the room. But the outline of her hands remained, like condensation on cold glass. When her eyes met his, her expression was stricken.

"I didn't..." Her voice broke. "I couldn't..."

Gods, he wished he could hold her, stroke her hair. "Shhh. I know. It's my fault. It'll be okay, I promise. Rest now. Go back to sleep."

He let her go – not a full quieting, but no longer holding her in the room. Abby was too afraid, or too upset, to argue. She vanished immediately, taking his heart with her, her face a picture of misery. Brix slammed a hand against the empty table, making the plates jump.

"Fuck." He swore into the silence, into the absence left in Abigail's wake.

He leaned forward to extinguish the candles, dragged a toe through the circle of salt, then retrieved his ring from the dish and slipped it back on, leaving the darkened room and the plate and the smoking candles behind. No matter how he worried at it as he climbed the stairs, the silver refused to warm against his skin.

Belle turned the topmost lock, the third and final securing her apartment door, then removed her jacket and hung it on the rack. She peeled off her gloves and dropped them onto the halfmoon table next to the coatrack. The scars circling her wrist itched, but she resisted the urge to rub at them. She left the lights off. It was easier on her eyes, which, when she chanced to catch them in the mirror, had a ring the rusted color of old blood around the edges, hemming a black pupil sheened like crude oil.

"What happened today?" Now that she was alone, she could talk to Belizial aloud without looking like she was talking to herself.

Pain. Their voice thrummed directly against the bones of her skull.

Fear rippled through them. Belle's pulse spiked in response.

"You're safe here—"

No.

The word clattered against her. Belizial collided with her ribs – fight and flight at once, as her demon tried to hide from the cascade of memories and grow big enough to fight them.

"I'm sorry, I—" Her words cut off in a gasp, and Belle braced a hand against the table where she'd left her gloves. Their distress hurt, squeezing everything tight inside of her.

I'm sorry.

She couldn't speak the words aloud with Belizial's grip on her, but hopefully they could still feel what she meant, even as her legs threatened to buckle to the floor. Belizial unwound themself, slinking guiltily away, only now realizing how tightly they'd been holding on. Air flooded back and Belle shuddered with it.

She felt them settle, but their unease remained.

I'm sorry. I didn't mean to hurt you.

"You never have to apologize to me. Not for that."

She withdrew her hand from the wall, shaking out the pins-and-needles sensation that had lodged there. Her scars itched and she gave into the urge to rub at them.

What she'd felt at the hotel wasn't pain exactly, but the memory of pain. That, she understood – how recalling something or anticipating it could tighten every muscle in your body, lock you up with fear and make you feel like you were under threat when you were perfectly safe. How could she convince Belizial, though?

And how much truly was simple memory, anticipation of being hurt again, rather than the thing itself?

If I remember it, I'm there again. I'm always there. Belizial spoke directly to her thought, a reminder with just a hint of sharpness to it.

The scattered bits of memory they'd shared back when they first met left her breathless, her skin burning, every one of her bones grinding together at the faintest movement as though they'd shattered. For Belizial, those memories were a raw, screaming wound. Not just remembering what had happened, but reliving it as if it had never ended, as if it never would. Was it any wonder what they'd felt in the hotel had been enough to bring it all back. They'd escaped the place where they'd been imprisoned, but nowhere could ever truly be far enough. Even worlds away, even tucked safe inside Belle's skin.

She tried to tamp down the hurt that wanted to rise, the feeling of not being enough. She'd done everything she could to protect Belizial, hadn't she? But this wasn't about her; it was about them, and what they'd suffered at the hands of the Hollow Queen. They had every right to their pain.

Belle took a steadying breath. Later, there would be time to convince them they were safe here. The ways between the worlds had been closed, and the fae hadn't been seen in Port Astor for nearly forty years. Whatever haunted the Peony could only be an echo.

"Would you like to join me?" Belle stepped away from the glass.

Her fingers and voice steadied as she got her skirt undone, letting it pool on the floor. One more night of letting the stains set wouldn't be the end of the world. Her clothing had seen worse, and she'd gotten remarkably good at repairs. She hoped

Belizial didn't notice the remaining tremor under her words; she didn't want them to feel worse than they already did.

Just as she'd stepped free of her skirt, Belizial stepped free of her. Strands of blackness pulled away from her skin like tar. She unbuttoned her blouse, cast it aside, and slumped onto the chesterfield, draping an arm over her eyes. Belizial leaned over her, peering down.

"What?" she asked without moving her arm.

It's your business if you want to dress like something out of a history book while you're at work, but you're home now. At least undo the laces.

Standing outside her skin, the demon spoke both aloud and within her head, a buzzing double echo. Belle had long since learned the trick of hearing Belizial in both spaces without getting dizzy. The voices overlapped, sliding like wind through fallen leaves, silk rustling on skin, comforting her. Both held gentle notes of chiding. Good. Selfish as it might feel, if Belizial was focused on her, they might forget their pain.

Belle lifted her arm from her eyes. Belizial regarded her upside down; she knew they wouldn't move until she obliged them. It never ceased to amaze her how they could feel things so sharply, how their hurt could be so raw in one moment, and how they could seemingly step away from it in the next. Perhaps it was the only way they could survive.

She half sat, picking at the laces of the corset. Outside of her, Belizial seemed calmer. Or calm enough, at least.

"I'll do it in a moment."

Belizial didn't move.

You need to eat.

"I'm not hungry."

No, but your body needs fuel.

Those who praised the patience of angels had clearly never met a demon. Belle grumbled, dragging herself upright.

"Fine. I'll make toast."

She moved to the kitchenette, putting the kettle on, finding jam and butter and setting them on the counter so Belizial wouldn't nag. They made no sound as they moved closer, melting against her, chin notched in the space between her neck and her shoulder, letting their essence flow through the corset's eyelets. The laces slithered free, no longer cinched tight.

Belizial relaxed behind her, and Belle let herself sink back into them, letting them take her weight. It was easier to simply take comfort in their body against her own than to dwell on the ways they'd both been hurt. When Belle had first found them, they'd been lost, broken, alone. She'd offered them a home inside of her, something they both needed. Couldn't that be enough? Being here and now together, instead of revisiting everything that had led them to each other?

Barefoot, she padded back to the chesterfield. Belizial followed, taking up their post behind her again, rubbing soothing circles into her shoulders and along the back of her neck as she took neat bites of toast followed by precise swallows of tea.

They seemed content to distract her, and she was inclined to let them. She put her head back against the arm of the chesterfield. Belizial massaged her temples, threaded bits of themself through her hair, loosening the pins holding it back and setting her curls free.

She finished her toast and set her plate aside. Belizial leaned closer, their touch moving lower, tracing Belle's collarbone, circling her throat. The demon's eyes were infinite pools. Stars and the birth and death of universes, the torment of burning souls and perfect, infinite love, all contained in the black that went from edge to edge, leaving no hint of iris or white.

Belizial's attentions returned to her temples, her brow, brushing over her cheeks. Belle settled deeper into the cushions. The pressure of their touch changed. Belle allowed a soft noise of contentment to emerge, threaded with need as heat spread across her skin.

If Belizial didn't want to probe the shadows or what had happened to them at the hotel, that was just fine. Belle was more than willing to let the past go, especially as Belizial's hunger caught and echoed her own like a mirror, rising. Belle stretched her arms up, pulling the demon down to flow over her. Teeth that were and were not teeth grazed her throat as she arched her body up into theirs. Tendrils slid beneath her chemise, down from her collarbones, up from the shirt's hem, meeting to circle her nipples and draw out a gasp.

Belle freed one hand to push her underclothes down. Belizial caught the waistband, tugging them lower still, but not all the way off – too urgent and eager for that now. She parted her legs, another low, whimpering sound of need emerging as Belizial sucked her into themself, pushed inside her, their want perfectly matching her own.

Belle let go of the last of the tension, the worry. This wasn't like Belizial occupying her skin, sharing space inside her, or transforming her. This was fucking, pure and simple.

Pleasure taken and given in an endless feedback loop, burning everything else away as Belle and her demon took each other apart and put each other back together again.

It was still dark when Belle woke, the sky deep blue through the window, lit by the city's perpetual glow. Her thoughts were slow, muddled; she had the vague impression she'd been dreaming about a bird drumming its beak against a tree. The sound resolved into quiet but insistent knocking.

Belle pulled herself upright and raked a hand through her hair. There was a kink in her neck from falling asleep on the chesterfield, but Belizial, sated and safely tucked beneath her skin, helped ease the ache.

She tugged her underclothes and chemise into place but didn't bother with a robe before yanking open the door, ready to let her irritation be known. It wouldn't be the first time Walter from down the hall came slinking home well past midnight, drunk and trying to gain entrance to the wrong apartment.

"Dee?"

Cordelia, Dee – her sister – startled as if she hadn't expected the door to open. She looked like she might bolt. Belle peered down the hallway, habit making her check for pursuit. What else but the direst trouble on her sister's heels would bring her here, to Belle's door, in the middle of the night?

Only the empty hallway greeted her, electric bulbs accentuating the dark circles under her sister's eyes. Had she taken the train all the way into the city? Had someone brought her? The sudden image came to Belle's mind of Dee walking dusty country roads until they gave way to city streets, making the entire journey from Morgansville to Port Astor on foot – which was absurd.

"What happened?" Belle asked.

Their parents were long dead, and even if they weren't, her sister wouldn't come all the way here to tell her in person. There would be little point. Dee knew full well that Belle didn't care.

Dee flicked a gaze over Belle's attire, or lack thereof, her expression pinched and sour. In the next moment, guilt crumbled her prim resolve, and she looked away. Belle's state of undress left the scars on her wrists and ankles fully visible. There were more on her chest, stomach and back that Dee couldn't see, but her sister knew well enough that they were there.

"Can I come in?" she asked, voice small. Whatever was wrong was enough for her to put aside her general disapproval for everything Belle did and was, along with whatever guilt she felt.

Belle bit down on the word *why*, moving aside to let Dee enter. Small things added to her worry: a bobby pin slipping from her sister's hair, one of the buttons on her coat misaligned. Dee carried no bag, only her purse. Not only had she left in a hurry, it was possible she hadn't intended to leave home – her home, but once Belle's too – at all.

Dee's shoulders slumped. Belle could see she wanted to chew on the skin at the edge of her thumbnail the way she had as a child. The sharp sound of slapped hands, their mother's chosen method of breaking the habit, rang in Belle's ears. Dee held her hands deliberately at her side, fingers flexing to remind herself to keep them there, rather than letting them creep up to her mouth.

"It's Clarence." Dee put her shoulders back, chin up, as she said her husband's name.

Belle studied her sister in the hall light. "Did he hurt you?"

Belizial stirred beneath her skin, hackles rising. Belle peered close, making certain the smudges under her sister's eyes really were exhaustion, not bruises. If he had hurt her sister, Belle would tear him apart.

"No." Dee shook her head, alarmed, stepping back from the violence in Belle. "Not... like that, anyway."

"Let me guess. He cheated on you." The words were out before Belle could stop them, needlessly cruel.

Dee's shoulders curled inward. "Yes," she said. "At least, I think so."

Belle watched her sister give in to the urge to chew on the side of her thumb. Belle took her hands and held them – there was blood from where she'd already gnawed the skin smeared around the cuticle of one thumb.

The shine in her sister's eyes was almost unbearable. "Jess—"

"Don't," Belle snapped. Her grip tightened reflexively on Dee's hands, and Dee pulled away. Even in her regret, Belle still bristled. She wouldn't let her sister speak the name her parents had given her, not here, in this life she'd built for herself.

"Fine. *Belle.*" Dee's sour expression returned. A beat, a breath, then—

"The girl is pregnant."

"Oh." She needed something to do with her hands, somewhere to look other than at the cracking mask of her sister's pride. "I'll make tea."

Dee followed her into the kitchen, holding on to her silence.

"I assume you need more than somewhere to stay, though you're welcome to that," Belle said.

She kept her tone even, business-like, as if discussing terms with a client. She wished Syd were here. He was so much better at this sort of thing. It didn't matter that he'd never met Dee; he would immediately know what to say. He would charm her, put her at ease, comfort her. All the things that she herself seemed incapable of doing.

She'd never blamed Dee for what their parents had done, but it meant love could never be easy between them. There were too many walls in the way; family could never simply mean safety, comfort, home.

She steered them toward the kitchen. There was more Dee hadn't said yet, and Belle wasn't sure how to break through the last of her reserve. They were too alike, and too different.

"Do you need help leaving him?" She poured tea, turning with two mugs in hand, letting her eyebrow quirk upwards. "Or disposing of him, perhaps?"

When Dee made no move to take either cup, Belle stepped past her and set them down on the coffee table. She drew her sister to sit beside her, holding her hands less for comfort and more so she couldn't escape.

Anger seethed just beneath Dee's surface, but it was a thin skin pulled over something else. But the last of her pride hadn't cracked yet. Superiority was closer to Dee's hand, and she pulled it to her as an easy defense, eyes narrowing. "Is *it* listening?" she sneered.

Belle forced herself not to snap. "*I'm* listening, Dee. Why don't you start at the beginning. How did you find out?"

Dee pulled her hands back, gently this time, folded them in her lap.

"It's been going on for a while, but I wasn't sure... I'm still not sure, except everything is getting worse. Clarence's behavior, the girl, Ava. I couldn't pretend anymore that nothing had changed."

She lifted the cup and set it down again, toying with it restlessly rather than sipping her tea. Belle held herself as still as she could; their mother would have displayed annoyance and impatience – telling Dee to sit up straight, not to fidget. Or, more likely, letting Dee's admittedly smaller infractions slide, finding ways to blame and criticize Belle instead.

Belizial held her without making any part of themself visible outside her skin. She let a measure of gratitude flow their way, but kept her attention on Dee.

"Last Sunday morning, Clarence didn't open up the church." Dee lifted a hand, as if Belle had been on the verge of interrupting her, though she hadn't said a word. "I know that doesn't sound like much, but he's never missed a sermon. Not when he was sick, not even when..."

Dee trailed off, shaking her head. "He never wanted to let his congregation down. He never wanted them to feel as though he wasn't there for them, no matter what was going on in his own life."

A note of bitterness crept into Dee's tone, but she shook it off. "The last thing I remember from the night before was Clarence making a pot of tea after dinner. He wouldn't let me help. At the time, I thought maybe it was a kind of peace offering to make up for the way he'd been acting, some of the things he said to me. I let myself believe things were finally going back to the way they used to be, except now I think..."

Distress took over Dee's tone, mixed with something like shame, as she let the words trail. Belle tensed, ready to... she didn't know what exactly. Spring into action to defend Dee, even though Clarence wasn't in the room?

"I think Clarence put something in my tea to make me sleep. When I came downstairs in the morning, I felt groggy and awful. I was certain Clarence would already be gone, but he was sitting at the kitchen table.

"He said there was no need to deliver his sermon. That, in fact, he wouldn't be returning to the church at all, because a new truth had been revealed to him. The way he said it... I can't even explain. It was like Clarence was gone, like something else was inside him and speaking through him, but I was sure I could still reach him. I'm his wife, and I thought—"

Dee's voice broke. More than simple misery, she seemed embarrassed that she'd cared enough to give her husband the benefit of the doubt.

"It's not your fault, Dee." The words felt inadequate, but Dee scarcely seemed to hear them anyway.

"I asked Clarence to explain. If I understood what he was

going through, I thought I could help. He looked at me with pity at first, then just like that, it became contempt. This blank expression, like he wasn't even there anymore came over him, and he told me to stay out of his way. He said he'd been chosen to bring his brothers and sisters into the light of the new dawn."

"What does that even mean?"

"I don't know, but when he said it..." Dee put her hands over her face and took a shuddering breath. "His expression, his tone, I just knew deep down he didn't love me anymore. If he saw me at all, it was as a *thing*, standing in his way."

Dee put her shoulders back, dropping her hands and lifting her head, but it was only a moment before her resolve broke again. She balled her hands, slamming them against her thighs, and when she tipped her head back this time, she was blinking rapidly against tears.

"Fuck."

She said it quietly, but the word might as well have been a glass dropped to shatter in a thousand pieces on the floor. Belle stifled a laugh of sheer startlement. The last time she'd heard her sister say anything close to an impolite word, she'd been eight years old and testing out the mildest of curses, saying *the damn chickens got out through the fence again.* Even then, instead of giggling, bold and rebellious, her eyes had immediately prickled with tears, convinced hellfire would swallow her whole. When it didn't, she voluntarily assigned herself extra chores as penance, something Belle would never in a million years have done.

She bit her lip until she was certain she had her expression under control. "Did my sister just swear?"

Dee didn't answer. Her eyes shone, but there were no tears, only an expression of hollow defeat.

"That's when I decided to leave," she said. "I went to our neighbors first. I kept thinking Clarence would change his mind, come to his senses, but he never even tried to find me. It's like he'd already forgotten me. When my neighbors Cady and Rob told me they were going to join Clarence, I walked out. I didn't even ask them what they meant, what they were joining. I didn't even say goodbye or thank them for their hospitality, I just left."

Belle pictured her sister, red-eyed and sleepless, with nothing but her purse and the clothes on her back, spending the night in the train station, navigating an unfamiliar city, and finally washing up at her door. Belle was her last resort.

"It's not me I'm worried about, or divorce, or any of that. I don't even care anymore," Dee said all in a rush, like a floodgate opening. "It's the girl he... I think she's in trouble. Or they both are. Like I said, he isn't himself and she isn't either. Even if she did... if they did... she's a sweet girl. She doesn't deserve to be hurt. Despite everything, Clarence doesn't, either."

She paused for a breath and her eyes shone even brighter. Dee seemed determined to invite even more pain upon herself. How could she continue to hold her heart out like that, worrying about Ava and Clarence when they'd betrayed her?

Belle couldn't fathom it. At the same time, a petty voice that had nothing to do with Belizial echoed in her mind, saying that Dee had never shown that much care for her. She'd stayed, let Belle run, and why? Was she so monstrous, so unworthy of her sister's seemingly boundless love?

"I need your help, Belle."

That – Dee saying her true name without even stumbling over it or rolling her eyes – cut through the bitterness and washed it away.

"Of course, Dee." Belle covered her wrists with her hands, hiding her scars away as best as she could. "I'll do everything I can."

7

Eight months ago

An hour passes. Maybe two. Maybe a lifetime.

They've been at it for moments, or possibly days, testing the limits of Jimmy's solidity, pushing beyond the bounds of what should be possible a little bit at a time.

"Do you want to try the glass again?" Virgil asks. He can't help bouncing on his toes a little as Jimmy offers a game smile. His fingers pass right through the whiskey glass, but the alcohol within shivers at his touch.

Virgil claps in delight. "That's it. We're getting closer."

Jimmy puts his fingers in his mouth, an expression of pure bliss crossing his face like he can really taste the amber liquid clinging to his skin.

Jimmy laughs, and Virgil hears it. A delicious shiver runs up his spine.

Leonie's mouth drops open. "Did you...?"

"I heard it, too."

Jimmy's laughter becomes deeper and richer. His eyes glitter as he opens his mouth again. "Well, I'll be."

Jimmy's voice is soft – his tone and the feel of it, like Virgil could rub right up against the velvet in it that made him a star.

"Wow," is all he manages aloud, too struck for anything more elegant.

"Wow," Leonie echoes.

"Virgil. Leonie." Jimmy turns to each of them in turn, drinking them into the deep, soulfulness of his eyes. "Thank you."

Jimmy no longer looks as if the slightest breeze will swirl him away, and it reflects in his expression. He looks confident; nothing in this world or any other can move him if he doesn't want to be moved. He is every inch the idol, a minor god of the concert stage and the silver screen. At the same time, Virgil catches just the faintest hint of fear. Jimmy's been gone from the world for such a long time and now his eyes are full of hunger – for food and smoke and drink, for Virgil and Leonie. Hunger for the whole damn world.

"Go on," Virgil says, gesturing to the pack of cigarettes.

Jimmy moves all at once, like a cat pouncing on a mouse. His fingers don't sink through the cardboard this time. He lifts the pack, shakes a cigarette free, and lights it himself with a flame conjured from thin air. There's only a moment to appreciate the wonder of it. The sandwich and whiskey are next. Virgil can almost taste it, like ambrosia rolling across his tongue, as Jimmy devours them.

Plate clean and the glass empty, Jimmy shifts his attention back to Virgil and Leonie

"I've been running for so long, I didn't think I'd ever be able to stop."

A shadow passes across his face. Virgil wants to ask what Jimmy was running from, where he was before, so that Jimmy might explain the white road to him – but if he does, the delicate spell holding them all together will break.

"Well, we're sure glad you did. We want to know absolutely everything about you."

They talk past the thing crackling in the air between them, the questions Virgil is afraid to ask.

"Did you really learn to play the guitar before you learned to walk?" Leonie asks.

They're all cross-legged on the bed now, close enough that their knees touch, but not so close any of them feel crowded. Jimmy's weight dents the mattress and creases the covers, just the same as Virgil's and Leonie's.

"That one's almost true." Jimmy's warm chuckle reaches out to caress the back of Virgil's neck as he favors Leonie with a smile.

She's been quizzing him for what feels like hours. He never seems to run out of patience. The candles around them burn lower without ever going out. Virgil's supply of smokes is endless, and the alcohol, too. When they're hungry, they eat, and there always seems to be food enough to go around, though none of them have called room service for a second time.

If Virgil squints just so and lets his vision go soft, there's a cart – except now it's as long as a table, piled high with oysters on ice. There's cheese and bread, all drizzled with honey, slices of fruit and roasted chicken. It's all so real, he can almost taste it. He can even taste the things he's never eaten in his life – pomegranate and candied lemon peels, caviar and goose-liver pâté and some kind of jellied meat he thinks might be peacock tongue. He doesn't look at any of those too closely, keeping his mind fixed on the safety of peanut butter sandwiches whenever the mood to eat strikes him.

"I learned to play the piano first," Jimmy says. "I could walk, but barely. My mama held me by the hand and took me down to the local church. She didn't like to accept charity, but they paid her a few coins to clean up every other day. There was an old, upright piano down in the basement, and I taught myself how to play while she worked. The first time she heard me, she thought the building was haunted. She nearly fainted right away when she saw it was me playing, being so young and never having a bit of training. She said I must have been fae-touched."

Virgil catches that shadow again, a shivering flicker, but it dissipates as Jimmy shrugs it away.

"What about your father? Your siblings?" Leonie asks, ravenous to know every single thing.

"My daddy worked in the same mine as his daddy before him. As for brothers and sisters, my mama had three other babies before me, but none of them survived. Even when grief wore them down and the mine closed and we had to go without just about everything, my mama and daddy always made sure there was laughter in our home. And my mama made sure I got the chance to play that piano as often as she could. She said music was the one thing no one could take away from me."

Leonie drinks in Jimmy's words, leaning toward him. Virgil finds himself canting in Jimmy's direction as well. He wants to fall right into him and go to sleep. As soon as the thought crosses his mind, he's stretched out with his head on one of the pillows, Leonie's head on the other. Jimmy sits between them, leaning up against the headboard. Ghosts don't sleep, Virgil guesses. The thought makes him smile as Jimmy's fingers pass softly through his hair.

He's still talking, telling them how his parents died, how he left that small town before it could swallow him up. How he came to Port Astor, but lived just about every place in the world, making pictures and playing shows. Virgil sees it like a movie up on a screen: Jimmy walking along a dark and lonely road with a guitar slung over his back, chasing his dreams. He gets to a crossroad, and there's a beautiful woman there, holding something glowing in the palm of her hand. *A star*, Virgil thinks, and in the next moment, with sudden, terrible certainty he knows that it's the crossroads where Jimmy dies. His car is speeding toward a collision, and Virgil wants to shout a warning, but he startles awake instead.

His pulse rabbits. He runs his hands over the covers, assuring himself the bed is real. The candles flicker; none of them have burned any lower. Leonie lies beside him, face mashed into the pillow, dark hair covering it so only glimpses of her sleeping features peek through.

Virgil sits up and the shadows in the corner of the room

coalesce. His pulse slows with relief to see Jimmy sitting in the chair next to the bed, his body curled around the guitar on his lap. There's a cigarette at the corner of his mouth, smoke threading upward. He strums lightly, unaware of Virgil watching him and wanting to fall into him.

Then he lifts his head. Eyes the color of moonlight steal the breath from Virgil's lungs.

"Sorry, darlin', I hope I didn't wake you."

Jimmy's smile is as easy as his voice. The cigarette vanishes, but smoke continues to leak from his lips. He leans forward, slinging the guitar behind his back so that it folds into somewhere that isn't here and leans his elbows on his knees to give Virgil his full attention.

"What were you playing?"

"Something new I've been working on."

"Can I hear a bit more?"

"It's not ready yet, but soon." Jimmy glances past Virgil to Leonie's sleeping form. "It's a gift for you both, a kind of thank you for bringing me here."

The tips of Virgil's ears warm. No one's ever written a song for him before.

Jimmy's gaze fixes Virgil. His eyes are dark, but there's a pinpoint of light in the center. It's like looking along the length of a tunnel, or sitting at the bottom of a deep hole peering up at the sky. Virgil can't get a sense of how things are oriented, where he is in space. He's here in the hotel room, but he's also on the white road stretched inside of him.

The road. That's what it's like looking into Jimmy's eyes.

He pushes himself from the bed to kneel in front of Jimmy's

chair so his face is almost level with Jimmy's. "Where were you, before you were here?"

He knows he shouldn't ask, but he can't help himself. Even knowing Jimmy is dead, he feels so real, solid beneath Virgil's anchoring touch.

"Oh, here and there," Jimmy says. That easy smile again, but there's an edge beneath his words, like everything could slip out if Virgil pushes too hard. "I did a stint down in Siegleville singing at the lounge in the Flamingo Hotel for a whole year, and before that, I lived in Hollywoodland making pictures for RKO then MGM. I traveled to Constantinople and Queensland and the Western Empire, everywhere making my music, and then..."

Jimmy stops, his gaze distant for a moment, before he shakes himself, his smile returning.

"It's blurry sometimes, like looking through a window when it's pouring rain. I remember my life, but sometimes it's like it belonged to someone else. When I died..." Jimmy's frown deepens. "Sometimes I think that happened to someone else, too. There's something inside me that says things were supposed to be different, and I can feel it all, the life I was meant to live just wanting to pour out of me. There's so much of it. I was meant to live forever."

The words spark something in Virgil, a feeling behind his breastbone, the white road inside of him shivering in an unsettled way.

"You did. I mean, your songs, all those movies you made. People still listen to them and watch them all the time. That keeps you alive in a way, doesn't it?"

"Hmm," Jimmy says. "Maybe it does."

He doesn't seem fully satisfied, but instead of turning the question over further, he leans forward and cups a hand beneath Virgil's chin.

Virgil forgets to breathe. None of his wonderings matter, especially not when Jimmy runs a thumb across his lower lip and the shuddering pleasure of it goes all the way through him.

"I'd rather focus on the here and now. Wouldn't you?" Jimmy places a kiss atop the still-tingling memory of his thumb. "Let's wake Leonie. She'd never forgive us if she missed all the fun."

Virgil doesn't trust his legs to hold him. Whatever he was meant to be afraid of doesn't seem as important as the fact that Jimmy Valentine just kissed him.

"Hey, darlin'." Jimmy leans over the bed, brushing the hair away from Leonie's face.

Virgil manages to stand as Leonie raises her head, favoring them both with a sleepy smile. He finds himself transfixed by the way her shirt, with its first few buttons undone, frames her collar bones.

"What have you two been up to?"

"Nothin' much. Just talkin'." Jimmy leans into his accent, softens his words. It's as good as a finger dragged along Virgil's spine. The heat travels all through the rest of his body, drawing a shiver. "Mind if we join you?"

Leonie's smile is the most beautiful thing in the world, like sunshine breaking through clouds. Jimmy crawls onto the bed, nudging Leonie over to make space. Virgil slots himself in on the other side. The size of the bed makes sense now, a puzzle piece slipping into place.

Leonie leans over Jimmy, sliding her hand up to his shoulder and leaning close to kiss him. When she breaks off the kiss, she turns to Virgil, inviting him in.

Virgil feels something within him reach outward and *pull*, closing a door, sealing them away from the outside world. They'll be safe here inside the Peony Hotel.

Jimmy's lips nuzzle against his throat, and Virgil traces a path with his mouth from just behind Leonie's ear down to her collarbone. Gently, reverently he undoes the remaining buttons of her shirt. This isn't like their urgent fucking when they first arrived – this is sacred, a ritual to be observed with care.

It's like he's undressing her for the first time.

When he takes hold of her unbuttoned shirt, Jimmy puts his hands over – through – Virgil's. He remembers a childhood that doesn't belong to him: watching from the window of a house whose rooms are mere suggestions, divided by sheets and blankets hung from the ceiling, waiting for his father to come walking down the long, rutted dirt road, swinging a metal lunchpail at his side and whistling off-key.

It's a dizzying sensation, but not entirely unpleasant. Virgil peels his thoughts away, feeling Jimmy's memories like tacky, silver-sweet strands of sugar, stretching before they snap and let go.

He focuses on Leonie's pulse. On his hands, on Jimmy's hands, which become one pair with a multitude of oddly jointed fingers, both undressing Leonie together.

Virgil unbuttons his own shirt, undoes his trousers. Jimmy's hands remain enmeshed with his, sending a shivering thrill straight to Virgil's core. Everything blurs and at the same time, the tiniest details are startlingly clear. Leonie's lips are faintly chapped. There's a salt-sweat taste at the hollow of her throat.

Jimmy's hands – Virgil's hands – slide around Leonie's waist. All three of them become one new thing together. Virgil loses all sense of himself. He is Jimmy. He is Leonie. It doesn't matter where one of them ends or the other begins. Leonie parts her lips and whispers, "Please."

Or maybe it's Virgil himself.

Leonie wraps her legs around him. Virgil enters her, and Jimmy does too, sinking right into her body, sharing her blood and her breath and her bones.

Virgil feels it the moment Jimmy slips from Leonie's skin into his, filling him, trading body for body, pleasure for pleasure. He shudders with it, what little control he has shredding and slipping away in an uncareful erasing of boundaries.

Help, he thinks, and just as quickly, the thought flies from his head as pleasure subsumes him.

Leonie throws an arm back over her head to grasp the headboard. It fragments, two forearms sprouting from a single elbow. Her skin is translucent, the network of her veins showing right through. She arches her hips upward, a cry breaking from her throat. She comes, and Virgil comes, and Jimmy comes, and they are all one and the same, tumbling through a sky of shattering stars, falling deep beneath the earth where magic is raw and unpredictable and wild.

Life and death are not separate things; they, too, are one and the same.

"There's been a complication. Coffee's over there." Belle followed one statement with the other, as if both held equal weight, as if either were a reasonable greeting as Brix entered the office.

"Good morning to you, too." Brix retrieved the cup she'd indicated, and Belle looked up.

"My sister arrived unexpectedly last night."

He'd been dreading telling her about Abigail; his first reaction was selfish gratitude he wouldn't have to, despite the dark circles under Belle's eyes that said she'd barely slept. Brix didn't imagine he looked much better; he'd spent another night tossing and turning before giving up and going back downstairs to scrub the kitchen and clean up the dining room. He'd tried to settle on the couch with a book about the Astors, hoping it might touch on their relationship with the Peony Hotel. If it had, he hadn't absorbed a word.

"Cordelia?" Brix dredged the name from his memory. Belle didn't get along with her sister, he knew that much. If she had come to Belle for help, that could mean nothing good.

"Her husband cheated on her."

Conversing with Belle could be like pulling teeth at times, but it gave him an excuse to avoid the problem of Abby, and so Brix was content to coax the information from her one piece at a time.

"Sorry to hear that. But I'm guessing there's more to it?"

"It might be nothing, but Dee says they're both acting strange, Clarence and the other woman. As if they're under the influence of something."

"Do you need to..." Brix gestured toward the door.

"No. I left Dee sleeping. She can wait." Left unsaid was that she also wanted a distraction. Clearly, she didn't want to dwell on the question of her sister, and Brix didn't blame her in the least. Family was a personal matter; he would deal with Abigail on his own when the time came, but for now, it was nothing he couldn't handle.

"I think we should go back to the Peony, but through the front door this time, speak to this Gustav directly and see if we can't convince him to give us access to the fourteenth floor."

"I agree." Belle adjusted her gloves, like putting on armor, and retrieved her bag.

"Are you sure Cordelia will—"

"She's fine." Belle swept past him, effectively ending the conversation, and Brix followed her out the door.

The weather felt as unsettled as it had yesterday, a restless wind making him glad for his jacket. It felt oddly like it could storm, but the sky remained clear as they walked uptown.

Neither of them looked like they belonged in the hotel's polished lobby, so Brix made a point of walking with purpose, as if they had an appointment to keep. A few heads turned, gazes following them – Belle especially – to the reception desk.

"I wish we had more time to look around," Brix said.

He at least allowed himself a slower pace as he passed under the massive glass garden suspended from multiple chains over the center of the lobby. Ethan Holcombe had commissioned it from the Tiffany Studio, and he was fairly certain he'd read somewhere that it took nearly a full year to cut, assemble, and ensure the piece didn't collapse under its own weight, all while maintaining the illusion that the whole thing floated effortlessly. All told, there were thousands of individual pieces of glass in every shade of pink and green imaginable, lit by dozens of bulbs, leaving the whole thing glowing softly. Abby would have loved it.

"Unfortunately, we don't have that luxury," Belle said.

They did, in fact; it wasn't as though they were on a strict client-dictated timeline, but Brix didn't correct her. The haunting was undeniable, whether they'd formally been invited to investigate it or not, and that was reason enough not to dally.

The thrum of energy he'd felt when they'd slipped into the stairwell yesterday was less urgent here in the brightly lit lobby. There were too many people in the way, too much living energy, but that brought tension of its own. A nervous edge lay beneath the buzz of voices, and the lobby itself felt more crowded than it should – as if people had instinctively sought safety in numbers and no one wanted to be caught alone within the hotel.

Belle rang for service, and a moment later, a man emerged from a narrow office.

"May I help you?" His look and tone both bordered on disdain, leaving Brix wondering if it was hotel policy, trying to add to the exclusive air by suggesting that no one was good enough to stay here.

The man wore a single peony bud in the buttonhole of his lapel, just on the point of blooming. The nametag below it read *Gustav*; Brix wasn't surprised, given Calliope's account of him. Rather than coming at it sideways, he decided to dive straight in.

"I'm Sydney Brix. This is my partner, Bellefeather. We're here about the missing room on your fourteenth floor."

Brix slid a card across the desk identifying their specialty in dealing with the supernatural, enjoying the way Gustav immediately blanched. His lips pressed into a thin line beneath his neat mustache. He moved them as little as possible when he spoke, keeping his voice a tight whisper.

"I haven't the faintest idea what you're talking about. If you'll excuse me, I have paying guests to attend."

When neither of them moved, Gustav came around the desk, trying to usher them back toward the revolving door.

"One of your former employees, Calliope, came to us for help."

Gustav flinched. "I don't—"

"But you do." Brix kept his voice similarly low. Despite taking a certain amount of pleasure in the manager's discomfort, he had no desire to cause a scene. "You need our help. There's something very wrong in your hotel. Surely even you can feel it. Your guests certainly can."

Brix indicated a man and woman hurrying toward the door, throwing glances over their shoulders. He could only imagine how Gustav would react if he mentioned the demon in the boiler room, but that would also necessitate explaining Belle and how they'd dispatched it. She seemed tense enough as it was, glaring at a young man standing next to a table full of brochures when he made a move to approach. Best to stick to what he knew for certain – ghosts.

"How much longer do you think it will be before word spreads, before guests start cutting short or cancelling their stays?"

This, at last, seemed to register with Gustav – the threat of lost profit. Brix caught Belle's disapproving look. The manager didn't care for the safety of his guests, only for their wallets.

"If there is a problem, I'm sure we're more than capable of handling it on our own."

He tried again to usher them toward the door. Brix planted himself.

"Not this kind of problem, luv."

It felt underhanded, but Brix shifted his awareness, opening himself up to the hotel and letting his presence be known. The haunting existed already; all he was doing was giving it a little nudge, so that Gustav couldn't reasonably ignore it anymore.

As if a dozen pairs of eyes throughout the room had turned toward him all at once, Brix felt the air thicken and grow heavy. Belle tensed beside him, ready for whatever might happen.

The ink warding tingled along his arms. Brix pinched a measure of salt from the bag he always carried in his satchel and scattered it around him. Then, he reached as far as he could and pulled.

A breeze stirred, touching only him. A woman who had just entered the lobby paused near a cluster of chairs, suddenly jumpy and uncertain. She braced one hand on the back of the nearest chair, digging her fingers in. There were fragments of ghosts, tattered things that more likely than not had simply gotten caught up in the larger tide of whatever was happening, just like the demon yesterday. Brix seized on those, and as they swarmed toward him, he let himself feel the haunting fully. The wrongness of it clung to him like a viscous substance he wished he could wipe off. These weren't even ghosts, but mere wisps, as if they'd already stepped onto the bone road, and something had drawn them back.

Their confusion and hunger swirled around him. Brix clenched his jaw. The stained glass hanging over the lobby shivered, the echoes attaching themselves to the flowers, drawn to the light and the memory of something beautiful. They were starved, but had no idea for what, had no ideas at all, only wanting. The entire piece swayed on its chains; a single flower detached itself, tumbling free to shatter on the floor.

The woman who'd been standing by the chair jumped back with a startled yelp.

"What did you do?" Gustav rounded on Brix, glare accusing.

"I've been right here beside you the whole time," Brix said. "I'm not the problem."

Even as he spoke, Brix sharpened his attention, gathering as much of the restless, hurting energy as he could before the entire Tiffany garden came crashing down. The ghosts, or what remained of them, rushed toward him. He barely had time to throw open the door, to brace himself. Insubstantial as they were, the ghosts shredded even more, catching on his ribs in their eagerness to get away. It hurt, and it was unlike any quieting he'd experienced before.

He swayed on his feet. Belle held out a hand, ready to catch him. "Syd?"

Steadying himself, he waved her off. He didn't miss the relief as she dropped her hand, smoothing the fingers of one glove over the other as if they might have slipped at the mere suggestion of touch.

"It's alright." He turned back to Gustav with a pointed look. "What you just saw is only a small part of a bigger problem."

"Fine." Gustav looked shaken and defeated. "Follow me."

Brix dragged a toe through the line of salt, regretting that some poor staff member would have to clean it up along with the broken glass. At least no one had been hurt.

Weariness settled around his bones as Gustav led them past the gleaming bank of elevators down a corridor lined with framed photographs, some of them signed.

Loretta Hayes, Charlie Chaplin, Senator Archibold Warren, Marion Shaw, all famous guests who'd stayed at the

Peony over the years. Gustav unlocked a door and ushered them into a private office, waving them toward a group of chairs in front of an unlit fireplace. Brix spotted an ashtray on the coffee table.

He dug out his lighter. "May I?"

"Go ahead."

Belle took the chair across from his, perching on the edge with her back straight and her hands resting on her knees. Brix let himself slump. The chair was surprisingly comfortable, and helping the dead move on always left him drained. It felt as though each ghost took a tiny piece of him with them when they moved on, imperceptible when looked at individually, but in the aggregate...

Gustav set two leather-bound folios on the table and took the chair next to Brix. He accepted a cigarette when Brix offered, looking slightly guilty. It was the first human thing he'd seen the man do, and it made Brix dislike him just a tiny bit less.

"These are the floorplans for the hotel." Gustav opened one of the folios. "The layout of each floor is the same. Except the fourteenth." He tapped a spot marked by absence. "There was never a room here, by design..."

Brix caught the uncertainty in the man's voice. "Except?"

"There is one now. Sometimes." Gustav sighed, exhaling a cloud of smoke.

"You fired Calliope for trying to tell you as much." Belle's tone indicated she hadn't warmed to Gustav at all. At least he had the grace to look chagrined.

Reluctantly, Brix sat up straighter to take a closer look.

The blueprint shifted. Faint lines indicating a room just like all the others surfaced through the page, there, then gone. An ache made itself known behind his eyes, like he was trying to focus on something at once too close and too far away. The spot was blank; the spot was filled.

"This is the guestbook?" Belle indicated the second folio on the table. She flipped through the pages, not waiting on Gustav's answer. "The missing room has been occupied by a number of guests over the years."

"Those pages were blank, up until a few days ago." Gustav sounded miserable.

Brix glanced at the page; a handful of the names even matched the portraits he'd just seen in the hallway.

"The record stops roughly eight months ago," Belle said.

Brix turned to Gustav. "Who was the last person to check in?"

"It... isn't clear." He looked as upset by the lapse in record keeping as anything else.

The last entry for the room was indeed blurred, as if water had made the ink run. The ache Brix felt looking at the blueprints returned, doubled now. He could almost make out the name, but it resisted him. The harder he tried to bring it into focus, the more the ink smudged, corrupting strands of mold spreading rapidly across the page.

Like the stain he and Belle had glimpsed in the stairway. Something trying to stay hidden, protect itself and keep from being seen.

Brix set the stray thought aside and pinched the bridge of his nose, letting his gaze wander across the artwork on

Gustav's walls until the pain receded. Framed sketches showed the Peony's grand ballroom populated by guests in formal gowns and tailcoats, a crowded dining room where waitstaff navigated between tables with trays of champagne, and the famed greenhouse, filled with blooms.

"We've moved all the guests off of the fourteenth floor," Gustav said. "It's highly inconvenient as we have a convention renting space in the hotel this weekend."

"Have you attempted to investigate the room yourself?" Belle asked.

Brix let his attention linger on the greenhouse.

"The room, even when it's visible, isn't exactly accessible." Gustav's tone was defensive.

Brix let their words wash over him. He was listening to a different sound entirely – the gentle splash of a fountain nestled somewhere in the maze of blooms. The scent of flowers overwhelmed him, that particular odd smell of peonies – not quite sweet, but not unpleasant, either. Abigail's arm was tucked beneath his own, a strangely old-fashioned and courtly way of walking. A memory of something that had never happened, a promise of something that never could, but her warmth against him was real and—

"Syd." The urgency in Belle's voice shook him.

The overwhelming perfume faded, and she sat back in her chair. Brix noted the furled bud tucked into Gustav's buttonhole had turned brown and withered. The manager scowled at it and dropped it into the ashtray.

"Sorry, I must have drifted there for a moment."

Doubt lingered in Belle's eyes, the faintest ring of rust-red circled the cornflower blue of her irises. "We should take a look at the room, or the lack of one, for ourselves."

"Right." Brix pushed himself up. Gustav stood as well, looking eager to be rid of them.

"Is there a key?"

"You won't need one. As I was telling your associate, there's no longer a lock on the door. There's no way into the room from the outside."

"But someone is in there. A guest who checked in and never checked out."

Gustav flushed at Brix's tone, moving them toward the door and locking the office behind them.

"I will concede that this problem is beyond me, but do you really think you and Miss Bellefeather—"

"Just Bellefeather," she corrected.

"Do you really think you can do any better?"

"I don't know." Brix held the manager's gaze. "But that doesn't mean we aren't going to try. And it certainly doesn't mean we're going to walk away and hope the problem solves itself on its own."

"Very well. I won't stand in your way." Gustav gestured along the hall, as though he were the one doing them a favor.

It struck Brix that he wanted them to fail. It would justify the fact that he'd fired Calliope, refused to see the problem, and remained steadfast in his denial for so long. It never ceased to amaze him how people could twist just about anything around in their minds if it meant they wouldn't have to admit they were wrong.

"Much obliged." Brix strode past and made himself keep

walking rather than grabbing the man by the lapels and marching him up to the fourteenth floor, forcing him to confront the haunting himself. As satisfying as it would be to watch the blood drain from the man's face as his nerve left him, it wouldn't exactly be professional.

"Can I interest you in a brochure?" The same earnest young man who'd tried to approach her earlier stepped into Belle's path as they neared the elevators. "We're offering information sessions throughout the weekend."

"Thank you, no." Belle tried to go around him, but he refused to be put off this time.

"We've had several new members join us already. We're offering a better way to live. Freedom from sin by embracing the light."

The guileless way the young man said the words only made them worse. Belle ground her molars together to keep from snapping. "I suggest you try someone else." She put frost in her tone and hoped it was enough to cool his enthusiasm.

Belizial had been restless since they'd entered the hotel, not as panicked as yesterday, but clearly unhappy at returning. Belle's attention was frayed from trying to calm them while worrying about Dee. Then, back in Gustav's office, she'd lost Syd. He'd been there in the chair across from hers one moment and the next – it was like looking at the blueprint or the guest register, a flickering translucence where two contrasting truths overlapped.

"If you'd just give me a—" The young man tried one last time, putting a hand on Belle's arm.

She caught herself on the verge of slapping him away. He had no right to touch her, infringe on her space, as if what he wanted was more important than her own desire to be left alone.

"I'm sorry, but we're in rather a rush. We'll just take these for later." Brix plucked two of the brochures from the man's hand, positioning himself between them in such a way that the man was forced to step back.

He did it smoothly, but Belle could see he was ready to fight as well, if needed. It left her grateful and annoyed all at once. She owed Belizial better self-control if she was going to protect them; she owed herself better, too.

She glanced past the young man, taking a centering breath. A sign propped on an easel stood next to a table stacked with brochures. Sketched in concentric, broken circles, an orb rose above skinny trees with bare, reaching branches. Or were the branches hands, fingers crooked and stretching up to pull the oddly fragmented sun from the sky?

See the New Dawn. The words and the image were also printed on the brochures in Brix's hand.

The new dawn – Clarence's words.

It could be a coincidence, but what if it wasn't? Belle

snatched one of the brochures from Brix's hand, ignoring his look of confusion.

Don't, Belizial urged, rising as if to shield her.

She ignored them as well, flipping the brochure over. Dee's address, printed along the bottom of the page, glared up at her. Belizial drew back, slinking away.

Belle hadn't doubted any part of Dee's story, or Clarence's capacity for getting wrapped up in some kind of religious fervor, but how had he moved so quickly? Unless whatever this was had been going on for far longer than Dee had allowed herself to see. Now that she was gone, Clarence had, what? Turned their house into the headquarters for a cult? Sent his parishioners into the city to recruit for his new movement?

"Your leader," Belle wheeled on the young man, shaking the brochure in his face. "Is he in the hotel?"

"No, he's... tending the flock." He wasn't even a young man, really – a boy, barely old enough to grow a beard, but she caught the scent of aftershave as she leaned in. There was a rawness to his skin, and his dark hair was parted neatly, with enough Brylcreem that the comb dragged through it had left furrows behind.

"What did he tell you to do here?"

"I'm just supposed to hand out brochures." The boy looked confused and frightened in equal parts. Belle took vicious pleasure in it as he cringed away, though Belle hadn't touched him.

Oh, but she wanted to. She ached to let Belizial crack every one of her bones and change her so thoroughly, she could never go back.

Gustav's footsteps clattered across the floor. "Mr. Brix, would you please control your associate?"

She was causing a scene. Good.

"She's not my associate, luv, she's the boss. I answer to her." Brix sounded as if he was enjoying himself.

That, finally, brought her back and let her reel in her shaking anger. She'd stepped to the edge, but hadn't gone too far; Brix still trusted and believed in her. She wasn't utterly lost.

The elevator door slid shut with a ding. Belle felt her ears pop, as if surfacing from underwater, the hotel rushing in to fill the spaces around her again.

"It's alright." Brix interposed himself again, this time to put a reassuring hand on the young man's arm. "She won't bite. Probably. Even so, maybe take a break and go have a smoke?"

The boy scurried off. Gustav remained behind, using Brix's body as a shield between himself and Belle.

"Care to explain what's going on?" Brix asked.

Belle held up the brochure. "This is my sister's address."

"What do you want to do?" Brix asked.

"What do you mean? We're in the middle of a case. I can't just leave."

It was precisely what she wanted to do, Belizial's eagerness to be away from the hotel rising and making it hard to think for herself. Weariness gnawed at her, and with it the unshakable feeling of wrongness. Caught in his religious mania, would Clarence go so far as to send someone to hunt her down? Better to go on the offensive then, before Clarence found her and Dee both. Unless...

The horrible thought struck her that Clarence had sent Dee – that this whole thing was a ruse to draw her back for some unfathomable reason, though he'd wanted her gone from his land as much as Belle had wanted to leave. It made no sense. She needed to talk to Dee.

Belle strode across the lobby toward the bank of glass-enclosed phones tucked against the wall.

"Where are you going?" Gustav called, but Belle didn't slow.

She slid the door of the cubby shut, fished a coin from her purse, and dialed with shaking fingers. The phone, pressed to her ear, rang and rang. Dee might not feel comfortable answering Belle's phone. It was a reasonable explanation, but a new fear gripped her. What if Dee had woken to find Belle gone, and come to the conclusion that her sister had abandoned her? Again.

She should have left a note. She'd meant to, but she'd escaped instead – to work, to take her mind off Dee and her problems.

She slammed the phone back into the receiver. Would Dee go back to Clarence if she felt she had nowhere else to go? Gods, why couldn't her sister have waited, had a little faith in her? It wasn't as if she hadn't asked – begged – Dee to run away with her when she'd left at sixteen years old.

Brix met her halfway across the lobby.

"I think I need to go," she said, at the same time he said, "I think you should be with your sister."

After a moment, Brix added, "Ghosts are really more my specialty anyway."

She knew he meant his smile to relieve her of any guilt she might feel, but she felt it nonetheless, made worse by the fact that it was mixed with a small measure of relief. Belle wasn't eager to keep exposing Belizial to the Peony's haunting. It wasn't fair to Brix, but it wasn't fair to her either that – whether he intended to or not – Clarence was about to succeed in dragging her back to the house where she'd grown up.

"I promise I'll give you a call if I run into more trouble than I can handle, just so long as you promise to come running if I do."

"Deal," Belle said.

It felt like giving in, being irresponsible. She might be giving Clarence exactly what he wanted, walking right into a trap, but she couldn't leave Dee alone. Not again. Belle took the brochure Brix still held, quickly scrawling her sister's number across its face before handing it back.

"I'll give you a call as soon as I've had a look. Promise." Brix could sense her stalling. "Besides, you'll only be in my way if you stay."

"Thank you," she said quietly.

Brix looked surprised. Was it really that uncommon for her to express gratitude? Something else she needed to work on. Later.

For now, she needed to focus on... going back. For Dee. It wasn't home, never that, but it was still a part of her. It might be a part she hated, that she never wanted to look at again, but it meant something to her sister. Belle couldn't just let Clarence take that away.

10

Eight months ago

It's a selfish thing, when the preacher asks God for a miracle.

The whole point of faith is belief without proof, without reciprocation, asking for nothing, but he's struggling. In his heart, he has sinned. He's shaken. All he needs is one little sign.

Which is why he's on his knees in the hayloft above the old barn. The space below the rafters, used primarily for storage now, smells like dust and the memory of animals. The boards are hard, and his body aches. He's been here for over an hour, hands clasped, nearing desperation.

The open door of the hayloft gives him a perfect view over the rolling fields, the blue-purple dark of the starless sky, and the faint outline of trees beyond. The wind whispers as it stirs across the grasses. A bitter man might think it was mocking him.

He still has hope that he was made for something greater. All his life, he's felt that he can help people, lead them to a good path, save their souls. He saved his wife from her past, but he can do more.

Deep down, he fears it is his own weakness holding him back. He's plagued by visions. Vivid images assault him every time he closes his eyes. A woman whose form shifts and writhes and refuses to settle walks through cold, empty halls past a feast-table covered in rotten food.

Her mouth is blood and pomegranates, her teeth impossibly sharp. She wears a crown of glass that grows straight out of her skull. Her feet are bare; the hem of her dress makes a horrid sound as it slithers against the floor.

Too often in the mornings he wakes freezing, all the covers kicked off his body, his breath hanging condensed in the air, though winter is months away. There are stories of unholy things that ride men in the night, steal them from their beds and drive them to exhaustion, weakening them and leaving them open to sin.

The Good Book itself has stories of prophets who cast out demons, who were chosen to lead their people to a better life. Is it so unreasonable to believe that he could be one of those men? If only God would answer him, then he might know that he is blessed, and not cursed.

But in the cold hours, when night bleeds slowly from the sky and the sun hasn't yet risen, his dreams linger. He cannot get warm. In those hours, he knows that the woman with the glass crown and horrible mouth has chewed away his love and left a hollow in its place.

It is the reason, it must be, that he does not love his wife anymore. She is a good woman, his partner, his helpmeet. It is as true now as when he first asked for her hand. He should be grateful – but he doesn't *feel* it anymore.

At the same time, his flock, no matter how close-knit, no matter how faithful, is dwindling. The town's population is aging, and the children who should replace them move away, seduced by the city.

And then, there is Ava.

Ava, Ava, Ava.

He is filled with her. She is the antithesis of the woman in his dreams. At times, the preacher wonders whether she is the miracle he's asked for.

Ava has grown ever closer to his church, despite the sorrows life has heaped upon her. She used to attend with her parents, then her older sister after her mother fell ill and her father left. Now, she comes alone. Her trials have only deepened Ava's faith, and grief has made her lovely.

In the privacy of his mind, sitting in the darkness of the confessional booth waiting for parishioners who rarely seek him out anymore, he's done terrible things to her. He's torn the buttons from her blue mourning dress. Rucked her skirts up and taken her against the pulpit. Ravished her between the pews and in the neat iron-bound boneyard, penetrating her with his fingers and his tongue, leaving her nails to gouge furrows in the earth between the cold, silent graves.

This is the woman's doing as well, with her hungry mouth and jagged glass crown. Her long, white fingers creep and seek, testing for chinks in his faith, gaps in his armor.

When he turns away from one temptation, she offers another, searching for a way in.

If God does not answer him soon, the preacher is afraid of what he might do. How long before he falls? How long before he lashes out and takes from those around him to feed the terrible ache inside?

Wind hisses over the grass. There is a crick in his neck from keeping his head bowed. His voice is hoarse, lips cracked and dry.

"Please, God," he says. "If you're there, if you're listening, give me this, I need this. Now."

His words betray him. He means to say, *I know you're there, God, I know you're listening. I know I don't deserve your grace or your mercy, but I humbly beg it anyway.*

His heart thuds, beating as if to shatter his ribs. Surely God must see how desperate his servant has become.

"Please," he whispers.

At last, something answers him.

Above the low murmur of the wind, there's a rustling, crackling, like flames burning in a fireplace, and brilliance follows.

The preacher raises a hand to shield his eyes. Above the trees hangs an orb like the sun, only paler, lower, closer to the ground. The topmost branches almost touch it, like hands raised in prayer. The light continues to grow – then he understands that it's because the orb is speeding toward him. He throws himself flat against the hayloft floor in a moment of pure panic, of which he is immediately ashamed.

The barn shudders, a soundless clap of thunder shaking

dirt and bird shit and feathers from the rafters. The preacher covers his head, squeezes his eyes closed. For the first time in a very long time, he is not thinking about Ava. He is not thinking about too-long teeth and a red-stained mouth.

When the shaking stops, he raises his head. Everything is terribly still, terribly alive. He's aware of the grass in the fields, roots stretching into the earth, leaves yearning toward the sky. He feels the warmth of the animals in the newer barn and his wife asleep in the farmhouse. All he has to do is reach out and he will feel every soul in every house, every fallen and lapsed parishioner, waiting for him to gather them.

The preacher pushes himself upright and hurries to the ladder, half tumbles, half climbs down into the barn. Just inside the open doors, his sun, his sign, his prayed-for miracle, lies nestled on the ground.

The light is silvery-gold, ice and pearls; it is no shade he can name. It is every color and no color at once, warm and cool. It hums, ever so faintly. Not quite music yet, but something joyous that wants to become a song.

It is everything.

He can just make out what looks like feathers, like a dozen or more doves all nested together. Even as he looks, it changes – a tangle of vines, a crown of thorns, a shallow bowl. It is a chalice filled with clear water, a hissing ball of snakes, a seed. He kneels and stretches out his hands, ready to be burned to ash, if that is God's will.

Tears shine on his cheeks. The preacher bows his head, thanking God, and listens with every ounce of his being, to hear what his miracle will say.

Brix rattled the elevator's gate closed. A soft chime sounded, the car descending, leaving him alone on the haunted floor. Despite the chill, he shucked his coat off and draped it over his arm. Even if Gustav hadn't told them the rest of the floor was empty, he would have felt it – absence all around. Unoccupied hotel rooms were a haunting of their own. Liminal spaces, waiting and wanting to be filled.

The stain they'd glimpsed in the stairwell looked so much worse from this side. Even the air seemed thicker toward the end of the hall, smudged and filled with smoke. Beneath the creeping dark, he caught a glimpse of an outline, more like the memory of a door than the thing itself. A ghost.

It gave Brix the same feeling as the blueprint in Gustav's office, two layers of reality lying one atop the other. He concentrated on the layer beneath, the one that didn't want to be seen. He kept his body angled as he moved down the hall, so the door sat in his peripheral vision. It hurt less that way, and there was less chance of startling whatever lay on the other side. Hauntings, he'd found, could be like skittish horses; it was best to approach them easy and slow to show you meant no harm.

A pressure, weight leaning against his bones, made him want to wrap his arms protectively around his torso. This haunting didn't seem the sort to politely step onto the bone road and be on its way. It would more likely rip the doors of Brix's ribs wide so that the gate barring the road would never close again.

"What are you, then?" He didn't expect an answer, nor did he receive one.

How aware was this haunting? It was entirely possible the wispy ghosts he'd encountered in the lobby were the equivalent of a leak – a tap left inadvertently open, spilling everywhere.

He set his jacket aside and pushed up his sleeves. Even in the hallway's dim, flickering light, the ink on his arms shimmered, wet and fresh, though he'd had the markings done years ago. His hair stirred, the edges of the haunting tugging at him and testing his resolve.

Most hauntings wanted to be let go, even if some needed a little help realizing it. This one, though? This one felt different.

He would help it if he could, but he also wouldn't hesitate to put it down hard, if it came to that.

"Hello? Anyone home?"

A thump answered from the other side of the door,

followed by a silence full of strained listening. He thought of a horse again, blowing gently from flared nostrils, getting his scent.

He could see what Gustav meant about the door. There was nowhere to fit a key even if he'd had one. Tendrils of black crept across the wood, pulsing slightly, like something breathing. Against his better judgement, he brushed his fingers against the wood, then rested them on the doorknob.

It clunked as he turned it. Before he had the chance to let go, the knob wrenched in the other direction. An ear-piercing scream, the shriek of nothing human, rang in his skull. He jumped back, yanking his hand away. The door seethed, its watchfulness doubled. The scream didn't repeat, but the message was clear: Brix wasn't welcome.

He rubbed his hands against the fabric of his trousers. That had been stupid, reckless. Belle would have chided him.

He turned back to the idea that whatever occupied the room had sealed up the door, hidden itself away. It could have easily spread through the whole hotel long before now. It hadn't. Maybe the door reappearing was a cry for help.

"All right, luv. I'm sorry, that was rude. We haven't even been properly introduced. My name is Sydney Brix."

He stepped back, giving the haunting space, and thought he heard faint shuffling.

"If you'll tell me what you need, I'm here to listen."

There was whispering, voices distant and static-scratched, like a needle poorly placed on a record or a radio improperly tuned. Brix couldn't make out the words, but they weren't for him. Ghosts talking among themselves.

Brix turned his back to the door, letting it know he wouldn't be easily intimidated, but also giving it a measure of trust. It didn't push him away. He dug in his satchel and pulled out the first paper that came to hand, the pamphlet from the *Order of the New Dawn*. He found a pencil, flipped the brochure over and wrote his name out in full. It was risky, a declaration of intent. Beneath, he wrote: *I want to help.*

He considered the words for a moment. He'd already said that. Fuck it. Time to go all in.

> *My wife is a ghost. I know loss, and I know pain. I've spent more than half my life trying to understand hauntings of every kind. If I don't understand you yet, it isn't because I don't want to. Please just give me a chance.*

He stuffed the brochure under the door, hoping to hear the lock disengage, but it didn't. There was only the un-sound of listening again, the sense of *want* slipping out from beneath the door. The faintest of noises, like a caught breath, but nothing more.

Then, a torn page from the brochure slid out from under the door. There was something almost childish about the scrawl, like it had been written by someone too impatient for penmanship.

> *Please, don't give up. Come back later. Help them.*

12

Dee looked impossibly small against the vastness of Grand Plaza Station. She hadn't even made it as far as the outbound platforms yet, gawping up at the deep blue ceiling overhead, flecked with golden stars. Belle couldn't blame her; she'd likely been too exhausted to appreciate it all when she first arrived. Even with the number of times Belle had been through the station, it was hard not to be awed by the arched ceilings, the massive, gauze-clad figures of fae kings and queens guarding each branching hallway.

"Dee." Belle caught her sister's arm as gently as she could, pulling her away from the flow of irritated travelers parting around her.

"You left." Dee blinked, as if needing a moment to recognize Belle. "I woke up, and you were gone."

"It didn't occur to you that I was coming back? Here." Belle shoved a hastily packed bag into her sister's arms.

She'd only stopped at her apartment long enough to confirm Dee was gone. Unlike Belle, Dee had left a note: *Noon train. Follow me, or don't.*

It cut at Belle, like her sister's expression now. She could only answer it with exasperation; otherwise, she would break down entirely.

"You'll have to make do with borrowing my clothes until we get to the farm. There's a bathroom over there. Go change. You've been wearing the same clothes for at least three days."

She nudged Dee toward the painted doors. Dee hugged the travel bag against her chest, but let herself be directed. A few moments later, she emerged, having scrubbed her face and re-braided her hair.

"Your clothes are ridiculous," she said, without any venom.

On Dee, they did look absurd, long and fussy and not at all her sister's style.

"I could barely even get them done up. Do you eat at all?"

"Only when necessary." Belle took the bag and her sister's hand, leading her toward the platforms, passing under the carved stone gazes of the fae.

"What about the gloves?" Dee asked. "Do you always wear those, too?"

"Yes, and you know very well why."

Dee's expression crumbled. If she'd meant to tease, then she'd failed miserably. She followed Belle in silence, almost meekly, as they boarded the train and found an empty carriage. Belle handed over cash for both of their tickets; Dee hadn't even gotten that far, it seemed.

"Were you really just planning on running off like a sulking child?" Belle knew she should hold her tongue, leave it alone, but she couldn't help herself.

Belizial hushed against her thoughts, wordlessly urging her to let it go. She didn't miss their eagerness to leave the Peony and the city behind either. She ignored both feelings.

"Why shouldn't I? You certainly did." Dee's tone was sullen.

Belle pressed the tips of her fingers hard against her forehead. It was that or slap her sister across the face. Dee might as well have slid a knife directly into Belle's midsection and twisted it. The worst of it was, she didn't even seem to know how badly her words hurt. Or, she didn't care.

Gods, they were grown women, both of them, and they couldn't seem to behave around each other. Every conversation devolved into sniping, because it was easier that way. Easier, certainly, than asking why Dee had largely been spared, while Belle had become their parents' scapegoat. Than asking whether there was truly something wrong with her – then, or now – that made her deserve the way they'd treated her. The pain, the...

Belle lowered her hand. "Try to get some sleep."

Dee turned her head, resting it against the window, but she didn't close her eyes. A few moments later, the brakes hissed and the train jerked into motion, pulling out of the station.

Belle folded her hands in her lap, keeping her back straight. Across from her, Dee watched the city glide past and then eventually, fields. When she couldn't stand the silence any longer, Belle walked to the café car and purchased them each a paper-wrapped sandwich. Belizial let their approval flow through to her, even knowing Belle wouldn't take more than a few bites, if that.

"I may have learned a bit more about Clarence's plans." Belle resumed her seat, unwrapping her sandwich and looking at it in dismay. She should at least have bought tea as well to wash it down.

"How?" Dee asked.

She inspected her own sandwich and took an experimental bite, finishing the rest quickly as Belle summarized the encounter with the young man in the hotel.

"I don't suppose Clarence mentioned any of this to you?"

Mouth full, Dee let her expression speak for her. She crumpled her wrapper, then pointed to Belle's sandwich. "Are you even going to pretend to eat that?"

"No." Belle handed it over, and Dee polished it off as well as if to make a point.

Be nice, Belizial said.

Belle caught herself before snapping *I don't know how* aloud. She had no idea what a safe topic might be, what wouldn't set one or the other of them off. Had they ever known how to be sisters, or had they only ever been two people who shared the same house? Their experiences in that house had been so vastly different; perhaps it was no wonder they were practically strangers to each other now. Except Dee had come to her for help. Belle hadn't been her first choice, but even so, didn't it count for something?

"Tell me more about Ava. You said you thought she might be in danger. Why?"

Dee pulled her gaze away from the window. "Her behavior has changed lately, too. Not as much as Clarence's – or maybe it's only because I've spent less time around her – but she doesn't seem like the person I knew before. Or thought I knew.

"She and her family used to attend church together, but now she's all alone. Vulnerable. I could see how... someone could prey on that, but..." Dee hesitated. "If you'd asked me a year ago whether I thought Clarence could hurt Ava, or hurt me with Ava, I would have said no."

Belle's mouth must have twitched, or something else in her expression gave her away, because Dee's tone sharpened. "You've never even given him a chance. He isn't... wasn't what you think."

Dee's shoulders slumped. She looked away, fidgeting with her skirt, kneading at the fabric like a cat looking for a place to settle. Belle had never told her sister about the ultimatum Clarence had given her. He'd allowed – *allowed* – Belle to stay, to enter his church and see her sister wed on the condition that afterward, she would never set foot on their property again. As if Belle wanted to. As if it hadn't hurt her, going back even long enough to see her sister married.

Perhaps she should have confronted Dee with the truth then, shown her what kind of man she was marrying. But a small voice in the back of her head, one that had nothing to do with Belizial, had stopped her. What if Dee already knew? What if she believed, as Clarence did, that Belle was a bad influence, one she was better off without?

Dee had chosen their parents over Belle. Was it so hard to believe she'd make the same choice again with Clarence?

"He's been... different," Dee said, her voice soft. "He was having bad dreams. I thought they'd stopped. Now, I think he just stopped telling me about them."

"What kind of dreams?"

"About a woman in a long, bleak hall. He could never explain exactly what was so horrible about her, but he always seemed shaken. Some nights, he wouldn't even come to bed at all. He'd set himself up at the kitchen table or in the parlor, saying he was going to work on his sermon or read. I think he was afraid to sleep."

A cold, ticking sensation, all along Belle's spine. Like needle-tipped fingers clicking directly against her vertebrae, counting them one-by-one. Dee's description brought stuttering flashes of memory. A face peering through cold, iron bars, hands wrapped around those bars as if they didn't burn or perhaps precisely because they did, a blood-smeared mouth whispering *again*.

The Hollow Queen.

Belizial flinched, drawing away to the deepest part of her. Belle tried to hush them while still tracking Dee's words, but for a moment, her sister's voice was lost under the tide of her pulse.

She'd first met Belizial on the farm where she'd grown up; the tree they'd stepped through to reach this world, as far as she knew, still stood. But it had never once occurred to her that the door could still be there, a weak place between the worlds where the Hollow Queen might step through.

She'd believed she was carrying Belizial away from danger by going back to the farm – helping her sister and protecting them at the same time. Instead, she might be dragging them both into greater danger.

"I suggested that he see a doctor, but he wouldn't hear of it. He started getting short with me whenever I asked about it, so I stopped asking. I... Are you even listening to me?"

Belle brought her head up quickly, hiding guilt behind an answer that matched Dee's irritated tone. "Of course I'm listening."

Dee chewed on the skin of her thumb. The sharp slap of their mother's correction rang in Belle's ears, the worst punishment Dee had ever suffered at her hand. She caught her fingers clenching, as if her mother's ghost might suddenly possess her to correct her sister.

"Maybe he talked to Ava about the dreams, but he stopped talking to me." Dee's shoulders slumped in defeat.

Belizial shifted, rippling against her skin from the inside, echoing Belle's tension, making sickness rise to the back of her throat.

Shhhh, Belle said. *They might just be dreams. You said she couldn't leave, didn't you? That she was trapped in her hall?*

I don't know. I don't know. Belizial's voice bordered on a howl.

We'll figure it out. I promise. Belle sent the words in a rush and, hating herself for it, tried to tune out the sound of Belizial's fear, focusing on Dee instead.

Some measure of the struggle must be evident on her face, because Dee's expression shifted back toward impatience again. Belle didn't want to lose her, and she wanted to keep Belizial safe. She'd made a promise to help, and it was getting increasingly difficult to do both. Chagrined, she felt her demon tamp their fear as much as they could, drawing back, and that only made her feel worse.

I'll figure this out. I promise.

A wordless humming sensation in response – she took it for agreement, but a note of distraction and unease remained. Even so, she wanted to lean into the sound, curl against them. She could only imagine what Dee would think of her if she gave into that urge; her sister would rather Belle slap her.

"Ava's behavior started to change shortly after Clarence's," Dee went on. "Even after her father left and her mother died, she was always a sweet girl, worrying more about others than she ever did about herself. Now, it's like they're both drunk all the time, but I know for a fact that Ava is a teetotaler. I'm certain she wouldn't do anything to hurt her baby, but..."

Dee's mouth twisted into a pained expression.

Belle had to ask, still hoping for some other mundane explanation, a coincidence that would assure her this wasn't all her fault. "You're sure the baby is Clarence's?"

Dee's head snapped up, but the fire in her eyes faded almost immediately. "I'm not certain about anything, but they've spent so much time together recently. I've not seen Ava spend time with any other man, and Clarence has been so secretive, so impatient. It's like he can't stand to be near me, but when he looks at Ava, he's a different person. He glows."

"What else can you tell me about her?" Belle fought to keep her mind on Dee's words, not jump to conclusions or let her thoughts run wild.

"Like I said, her family came to church together until her mother got sick. Ava left off schooling to care for her. She was going to be a teacher, but she gave up every dream she ever had once her father ran off. She has an older sister, but after their mother died, Bess moved away to the city."

Belle could well imagine that kind of aching loneliness. That kind of loss and wanting could easily attract the attention of the fae, or a demon, intent on offering a deal. Maybe Ava had unwittingly called something – or Clarence had, though Belle didn't want to spend too long thinking about the kinds of things he might want. It didn't have to be the Hollow Queen; no one really knew what had happened to the fae, only that they weren't in Port Astor, or Arcadia at all, much anymore. When Belizial escaped, the Hollow Queen had been unable to follow. If the world remained thin where they'd first stepped through and found Belle, then something else might have found that same doorway.

Whatever the case, even if she wasn't directly at fault, she might still be to blame. Guilt roiled in Belle's stomach. The parallels with Ava were obvious too, and that only made things worse, though their father hadn't left. He'd died shortly after their mother, and Belle had left long before either of them passing.

She'd had every damned right to leave. If she'd stayed... it would have been far worse for all of them.

"I can see how Ava could develop feelings for Clarence," Dee continued softly. "Just having someone to listen to her, to look at her like she means something and is more than just a burden to be carried."

Belle made herself lean across the space between them and place her hand atop her sister's. Did Dee even want that kind of comfort? She didn't pull away. Even through the gloves, Belle could feel her almost feverish warmth.

She searched for something kind, soothing to say, but memory cruelly overlaid itself. She saw Dee at ten years old, peeping around their mother as she stood in Belle's bedroom doorway, back ramrod straight, crucifix and bible clutched in her hands.

Dee's eyes had been so wide, blue-violet like a summer sky at twilight, fringed by damp lashes. She had freckles scattered across her cheeks, her hair more strawberry than Belle's had ever been. Half in terror, half in fascination, she'd watched from behind their mother while their father locked manacles around Belle's wrists and ankles.

Dee had only been a child. She couldn't have done anything to help, and she never even saw the worst of what their parents had done. The heavy bible striking Belle, leaving her covered in bruises. The crucifix heated on the stove and pressed to her skin. All in the name of driving out the devil they believed had possessed their child.

She could forgive Dee for that. What she struggled with, still, was that four years later, she'd slipped into her sister's room with her bag packed and begged Dee to run away to the city with her. Dee had refused.

Belizial spiked inside her again, riled by Belle's pain. Her memories were only memories, not like theirs. She could look back on the torture she'd suffered as a separate thing – but did Belizial feel it, her memories becoming their own? She'd never thought to ask, in all the time they'd been there for her, calming and soothing her.

She willed her pulse to slow. *Strong*. She held the word forcefully at the front of her mind. *Unafraid*.

Dee hadn't pulled away from her. Belle herself maintained the touch without feeling the urge to draw back. The past was the past; she tried to see her sister with fresh eyes. Time had deepened the color of her hair to something more like pale copper, threaded here and there with strands of gray. The freckles once spread across her cheeks and nose had been lost to the weathered skin of a woman who spent hours every day in the sun.

It wasn't that Belle struggled to love her – that would always be there, buried at the core of her. It was that she struggled to understand her. Even now, after so much time, with Dee looking at her through hurt and worried eyes, it was hard.

"The last time I saw Ava," Dee said, "right before I came to find you, it was like she was under some kind of spell. She was walking on the hill above the old barn. She scarcely seemed to know where she was. I called her name at least three times, and when I finally caught up with her, it was like she didn't even recognize me."

Dee paused, looked down at her hands. "I tried to get her to come into the house. Even if... Even if she's carrying Clarence's baby and he intends to put me aside, it was the right thing to do. I was worried for her. She wouldn't come with me, though, and in the end, I had to leave her there."

"Do you think maybe this New Dawn, whatever it is that Clarence is involved with, could explain some of it? Maybe he used mesmerism or something and he really does have Ava under a spell?"

"That wouldn't explain the changes in his behavior, though. Unless you think he also mesmerized himself." Dee sounded tired. Her cheeks were dry, but her posture was bowed, guilt gnawing her, as if she could have done something more to stop all of this from happening.

Kind, tenderhearted Dee, always trying to save everyone. Except Belle.

She retrieved a handkerchief from her bag and handed it to her sister. Dee stared at the cloth as if she would refuse, abhorring the pity it represented. After a moment, she took it, twisting it in place of Belle's skirt.

"I tried to talk to Clarence about Ava. I thought if she wouldn't listen to me, she would listen to him. But he screamed at me. He told me I wasn't worthy of touching her. That I was unclean and—" Dee's voice broke. A moment passed before she continued. "It was like he was a stranger. He said such foul things to me, demanded I stay away from him and Ava both."

Dee's shoulders hitched, and Belle felt her own stiffen. Clarence had used almost the exact same words with her, standing outside the church in one of the squares of light falling from the window. *Unclean*. Had Dee ever wondered at her leaving the wedding without saying goodbye? Or had she been too busy dancing, surrounded by her community, her friends?

Belle remembered the floor shaking with all those stomping feet, the laughter and the music. Dee had looked so radiant, her cheeks flushed, strands escaping from the braid Belle herself had woven for her, threading it with flowers to match her bouquet.

She could have fought for her sister, but she hadn't. She'd accepted Clarence's words as coming from both of them, and walked away.

Belle lifted her hand from Dee's. Light traced her profile, harder than Belle remembered it being. Not that her sister had ever been soft. She just hadn't needed to be this before.

Dee shook her head, drew in a breath, let it out slowly. "People make mistakes, but I don't believe marrying Clarence was one of mine. If he needs help, then I want to help him. Ava, too."

The clack and thrum of the train, the thousand little mechanical sounds that propelled them along their journey, filled the silence.

Belle let out a breath of her own. "Dee, look at me. We'll figure it out together."

She held Dee's gaze until she inclined her head. Belle couldn't tell if she was agreeing. She couldn't tell if she believed her. Belle wasn't certain herself whether there was anything in her words, in herself, worthy of Dee's belief.

Six months ago

The preacher doesn't ask for the second miracle; it comes to him unbidden, further proof that God has forgiven him all his sins.

There's evidence already in the swelling numbers of his congregation. He hasn't even shared with them the miracle of the light yet, but they can feel change and promise in the air. When he stands at the pulpit and looks over their faces, turned toward him in rapt attention, they know God works through him, and they are bathed in His reflected glow.

His church has become a locus, his congregation bringing friends and neighbors back into the fold. A few curious strangers have even begun to appear in the pews, like trees yearning toward the sun. The air in the church crackles with promise, like the moments before a storm. It's a struggle, every day, not to burst forth with the good news. But he's being patient. When the moment is right, he will know.

Clarence hears it first in the restless wind. It calls his name, so he leaves Cordelia tying up rows of tomato plants in their garden to follow. The day is bright and clear. A faint sheen of sweat clings to him by the time he reaches the churchyard. Shadows from the old oak twist across the green lawn and he feels, overwhelmingly, that his miracle needs him.

He enters the church to find Ava sitting in the foremost pew, her head bent in prayer. There's something different about her today. The sun is shining a warm gold, but the light falling over Ava reminds him of his miracle, tucked safely inside the barn.

More than simply illuminating her, the light seems to lay a hand against the back of Ava's neck, across the first knob of her spine, visible above the collar of her blue dress, the one he's dreamt of so many times. Without words, his miracle is showing him the way. *Here, this, she is set aside for you. Your dreams, your desires, they are not wrong. They are your destiny.*

Fresh heat prickles beneath his armpits. Ava's braid, the color of winter wheat, snakes down her back. He longs to take it in his hands. He almost backs out through the doorway, startled by his need, but Ava turns, and the smile that breaks across her face is like sunshine through clouds.

"Preacher Warren. I'm so glad to see you."

He's told her to call him Clarence so many times, or

Brother Clarence, if she must be formal, but it never seems to stick.

She rises, steps toward him, and a shadow falls across her features. "Oh, but you're busy. I can come back another time."

Beneath the first, Clarence sees another, deeper shadow: sorrow. The loss of her family. Her heartsick missing of her sister. His fingers land on her wrist almost of their own volition as she ducks her head apologetically and makes to step around him.

"Not at all. You're always welcome here. In fact..."

"Is everything alright?"

Clarence feels her concern like a palpable thing. He shuts his eyes; he needs to be sure. It's there, the voice of his miracle, a joyous clarion call rushing to answer his doubts and sweep them away. *Yes, yes, now. It is time. Go!*

He opens his eyes. Like a hand pressed at the small of his back, he feels himself propelled closer to Ava.

"Yes, thank you," he says, his voice even now. "Everything is quite alright. I'm glad you're here. There's something I'd like to show you."

Her mouth forms an *o* of surprise. Clarence's heart tumbles behind his ribs, but she doesn't pull away. She trusts him.

"Will you come with me?"

Ava nods, shyly. He keeps hold of one of her hands and leads her out into the sunshine. She doesn't question him or ask where they're going. He leads her the long way around Cordelia's family property, far wide of the field where his wife may still be working the soil, rinds of dirt under her nails. They climb the gentle slope of the hill to the old barn. Long grass brushes against their legs.

Clarence squeezes Ava's hand and feels a moment of regret. He was wrong about Cordelia. *Here* is his perfect helpmeet, but that isn't Cordelia's fault. It was his mistake. He should have seen it. Then he could have put her aside gently, found some other place for her, but there's too much happening now, there isn't time.

Five years ago, Cordelia woke to terrible cramps, the sheets beneath her sodden with blood. She hadn't even known she was with child. Clarence sees what he couldn't then – it was a sign.

He doesn't blame her; he never would. Even if he doesn't love his wife anymore, he still feels affection for her. He wishes things could be otherwise. If only he'd listened to his instincts, gone farther instead of staying his hand against Cordelia's sister, Jessamine. He forbade her from returning, but he should have done more. Her memory haunts the land. It soured Cordelia's womb, drove his flock away.

It's all so clear to him, now. The light of his miracle has shown him the way.

He needs to eradicate her completely, drive her and the demon inside of her out of the world all together.

Yes, his miracle agrees. *Together. We will do this work together.*

Together, with Ava by his side.

"Are you ready?" he asks.

The air thrums as they step into the barn. A breeze lifts strands of hair from Ava's face. The smell of dust greets them, along with his miracle. A soft gasp emerges from Ava, and her cheeks flush pink in the miracle's light. It isn't fear he sees in her face – it's awe.

"May I?" she asks.

Clarence lets her fingers slip from his hand. She approaches the miracle, and after a moment, begins to sway. Her hand goes to the back of her neck, her fingers digging into her skin. The miracle isn't just shining on her – the light is inside her as well, just beneath the surface. If she dug her nails deep enough, she could peel her flesh away until only brightness remained.

A faint moan escapes her lips. She lets her head fall back, her hands pressed to her waist now, cradling her belly. She tugs at her clothing, stumbles over the buttons at her collar, getting two undone and peeling the fabric away. Her back arches, eyes closed. There's sweat in the hollow of her throat, illuminated by his miracle's glow.

Clarence watches her, enraptured.

Beyond the barn doors, the sky falls toward twilight. The evening will be cool, but Ava writhes as if caught in the full heat of a midsummer's day. Her body rocks faster, one hand at her throat, the other continuing to tug at her clothes. Ecstasy – Clarence's traitorous body recognizes every sense of the word. Heat pulses at his groin, his cock stiffening, the desire to rut like a base animal threatening the sanctity of this moment.

Ava bunches the fabric of her skirt between her legs. Her body twists impossibly, with a force that seems like it should snap her spine. All at once, she drops to the ground, rolling onto her back, clawing at the fabric of her dress and tearing it, head tossing from side to side, lips moving soundlessly.

Possession, he thinks as she shakes. Her heels drum the floor. *Possession*, but not the kind to be feared.

Clarence drops as well, clasping his hands in prayer. Ava's legs splay wide, like a woman giving birth, like a woman in the act of copulation. Her hips lift upward as the light crawls over her, thin tendrils, branches, roots, wrapping around her, entering her, filling her. Her mouth opens wide, impossibly wide, her whole being shuddering with a silent scream.

Her loneliness, her wanting, answered in a single holy act from his miracle, stitching her back together again and making her whole.

All the lust in Clarence is snuffed in a single breath. He understands, finally. She is the vessel, pure and perfect, that will bring his miracle fully into the world.

Clarence's cheeks are wet with tears as he crawls across the dusty barn floor to Ava's side. He seeks her hand, catches it, and presses it hard between his own. She turns her head toward him. Sweat plasters hair to her cheeks and brow. She looks happy, exhausted. He smooths the hair from her eyes with a gentle touch.

"Yes," she says. "I'm ready."

Together, they will birth a new world.

14

Brix slid from his seat at the bar. He'd been careful to nurse just the one drink, but he felt unsteady nonetheless. The ghosts in this place wore steadily at him.

He'd positioned himself so he could see both the mirror behind the bar and the room itself, and the images didn't match up. Figures moved in the reflection who most definitely were not in the bar, at least not here and now. The glasses and bottles in front of the mirror shivered periodically, chiming softly, even with no one anywhere near them.

Guests and staff both were on edge, snapping at each other, startling as if someone had tapped them on the shoulder, or simply stopping, blank and utterly lost. One server had dropped a full tray and burst into tears; another had quit, stormed out, then returned a moment later, seemingly with no memory of what they'd done. The confusion belonged rightly to the ghosts leaking out of the missing room, and it would only get worse.

He checked his watch as he crossed the lobby. It was well after 6 p.m. He'd been at the Peony nearly all day, doing his best to question members of the staff as gently as he could, but very few were willing to talk to him. After what had happened to Calliope, he couldn't blame them. Gustav hadn't left yet either, and he gave Brix a pinched look as he passed, as if all of this should be sorted and done by now so the hotel could go back to making money. Brix tossed him a mock salute and pressed the button for the elevator.

He wondered how Belle and her sister were getting on; he hadn't checked in with her yet, but he had nothing to report. The table with the New Dawn brochures remained in place, but the young man Belle had frightened earlier was nowhere in sight.

On the fourteenth floor, the shadow staining the walls had spread. The lights were dimmer, and some had burnt out altogether. As Brix stepped off the elevator, a child went careening past him, ribbons flying in her hair, the once-brightly colored balloon tied to her wrist bobbing above her. She seemed oblivious to the fact she was dead, caught in a joyful game of her own, not acknowledging Brix either. The hauntings were growing more tangible, but at least some of them had the good grace to mind their own business, wanting nothing from him.

He couldn't count on them all being so well-behaved though. Brix rolled his shoulders back, making them crack. The closer he drew to room twelve, the more it hurt – cold inside the marrow of his bones, whispering that he would never be warm again.

Even so, he rested his forehead against the black-stained wood before knocking softly, letting himself feel everything. "It's Brix," he said. "Sydney."

Fabric rustled, the sound of a body shifting, the faint creak of wood. He got the sense of someone mirroring his position, their head pressed against the door, keeping their voice low so as not to be heard.

"Tell me about your wife." The voice was male, young. It sounded tired, and like it was traveling from much farther away than just the other side of the door.

"Her name is Abigail," Brix said, throat aching. "She's the best thing that ever happened to me."

He paused. By saying her name, he was dragging her into this mess with him. He'd let his exhaustion get the better of him again, slipping into carelessness. It was like there was something pulling at the frayed edges within him, trying to unravel him and make the holes even bigger. He wanted Abby here with him, the comfort of her presence, someone to talk to about his fear and unease. The wound was scabbed, not scarred, the hurt fresh.

"It's okay, Syd."

Abby's hand on his shoulder, her voice next to his ear. It felt so real, he couldn't help but startle. His head bumped against the door as if he'd nodded off. Gods, what was wrong with him? Letting himself be lulled like that, leaving himself open.

The ink on his arms sheened in the weird light of the hall, the skin beneath it prickling. He needed to be more careful.

This wasn't just a haunting; there was something behind it, waiting for him to let his guard down.

"Are you still there?" The voice from the other side of the door held a plaintive note.

"Yes. Sorry, luv. Got distracted there for a moment."

"You were telling me about Abigail."

"Abby." Despite everything, Brix couldn't help the tug of a smile at her name, as unwise as it might be to invoke it. "I was nineteen the first time we met. She was twenty-three. I was so love-struck and utterly distracted looking at her that I fell right into a duck pond, the one just on the edge of Madeline's Wood in Astor Park. Do you know it?"

No answer, but Brix felt attention from the other side of the door.

"Abby fished me out, laughing the whole time."

Perhaps he should have known back then. Meeting in the haunted wood where Madeline Astor had drowned herself – how could it be anything other than a bad sign?

"We met again when I was twenty-seven," Brix went on. "Abby had just come back from traveling the world with her parents. They were professors, working on archeological digs, she was their assistant. Would you believe when I ran into her again, it was in the very same spot I'd first met her all those years ago?"

Like fate.

Brix didn't expect a response, and didn't get one. But he could tell the person on the other side of the door hadn't moved away.

"I managed to stay out of the duck pond the second time

around, at least." He let out a rough chuckle, dangerously close to becoming tears. "Abby didn't remember me. I joked that she must spend an awful lot of time fishing wet fools out of ponds if I'd made so little impression and that made her smile. It kept her talking long enough to convince her to have coffee with me. I proposed to her at the end of the week."

Now that he'd started, the words spooled out of him. Abby, her hands pressed flat to the dining room table, frost colonizing her eyes. Fuck, but it hurt, talking about her like this. He didn't want to stop.

"She turned me down, of course, like any sensible person would. But for me, it felt like all the time she'd been away, us living our separate lives, I'd just been waiting for her. It took me a full two years to convince her to marry me, and even then, she wasn't in any rush.

"We had five years together before she got sick, two more before she died. Never did manage to get her into a church or in front of a city official. It never seemed as important as spending every moment together we could."

Brix thumped his head softly against the door, deliberately this time. He wanted to smash it much harder, as if physical pain would take the other hurts away.

If he let himself slip again, would Abby put her hand back on his shoulder?

"I thought you said she was your wife," the voice said from the other side of the door.

"She is, in every way that matters. We just never made it official."

"She came back though, after she died?" The hope in the

young man's voice caught Brix's heart, a hook in the meat of it, pulling.

"Something like that, yeah." He ran a hand through his hair, pushing it back and feeling the crackle of all manner of energies raked from between his curls.

The truth – the truth he very rarely chose to hold up to the light and examine – was Brix had dragged Abigail back. Up until then, he'd encountered ghosts by chance, or because he'd been hired to send them on. He'd helped them, every single one. Abby... He hadn't even known it was possible, certainly hadn't discussed it with her before she died. He'd simply wrenched open the door that held the bone road back – a bruising splintering he'd thought might just kill him – and he'd grabbed hold of her and refused to let go.

All the work he'd done over the years, the ink on his skin, the rules he'd set to keep himself safe and to keep the world safe from him, he'd thrown away in an instant. There were nights when he woke with the bone road right behind his ribs, pressed up against his skin. It felt too big, too hard to hold. It was unfair that he could do this thing, that he'd been chosen for it, or that it was simply part of him by random chance. Let the doors swing wide. Let the dead be someone else's problem, coming and going as they pleased, two worlds bleeding into one another. He'd never considered it seriously though; he'd never been truly tempted, until Abby.

He'd called her back, and the world hadn't ended. He'd ripped the door wide, pulled her through, broken the first and most important rule. The universe hadn't risen up to slap him on the wrist. He'd gotten away with it. All he wanted was a little more time; then he would let her rest. He'd been promising her as much for more than half a year now, long enough for him to lose track.

Fuck.

He pushed the urge to confess down as far as it would go. Brix didn't know who he was talking to, didn't even have a name.

"It's not that simple," Brix said, swallowing around the lump in his throat. "Nothing ever is when it comes to missing someone."

The door held almost all his weight now. Brix wasn't certain he could stand up if he tried. He might just go to sleep here, let the sadness in the room take him until he became another part of the Peony's latest haunting.

A click so soft he almost missed it jolted him: the door unlocking. He found reserves of energy and scrambled back just before it opened a crack. At first, all he could see on the other side was darkness.

"You can come in, but you have to be quiet," the young man said.

Brix could just make out a sliver of his face – one dark eye, a strong nose, tousled hair that flopped in unruly curls, much like Brix's own, down to the same sheen of plum and rust hidden among the more natural colors. The young man was ghost-touched. The bone road lay behind his ribs, just as it lay behind Brix's. It shouldn't have surprised him, given how strong the haunting within the room was, but it did. He'd never met anyone who could do what he did before; he only knew they existed from newspaper articles and the books in Belle's library. Most of those accounts were historical. Over half of what he read in the opinion pages, mostly penned by the anti-spiritualist societies, clearly described charlatans. Those who could do what he did, genuinely see and feel and talk to the dead and help them move on, were increasingly rare these days.

Judging by the boy's frightened expression as Brix stepped fully into the room, he had no idea what to do with the road inside him. He might not even know it was there, calling a haunting by accident, and letting it get out of hand.

One thing was painfully clear however, so that even the boy must recognize it: he desperately needed help.

The haunting was so much worse inside the room. Crushing, cold, sucking the memory of existing anywhere other than here right out of Brix. How in the hells had the young man stood against it all this time? Brix struggled to make his mind believe his feet were firm on the ground, that there was a ceiling above him, four walls, a bed. The room kept wanting to be something else – a forest; a long, cold hall; an intimate night club bathed in soft rose-colored light.

Each fragmented image passed by too quickly for Brix to hold, leaving only vague impressions behind. It was like seeing someone else's memories, almost the way he sometimes did when he pulled a ghost through his body. Except he hadn't quieted the haunting here. It existed somewhere within the confines of the room, whose dimensions shifted constantly, leaving him utterly disoriented.

A gunpowder and sulfur smell hit him, accompanied by the hiss of a struck match. The small noises grounded him as light flared, sudden enough that he had to shield his eyes. A moment later, the cherry of a lit cigarette bobbed in the dark.

"Smoke?" the young man asked. "They never seem to run out."

"Thanks, luv," Brix said. "Could use one right about now."

His eyes adjusted slowly, enough to see the young man as he lit a second cigarette from his own and handed it to Brix.

The tiniest gap of light seeped between the curtains, the city's nighttime glow, but even that seemed changed and wrong. It was enough to illuminate a desk to his right, a bed to his left. Between the bed and the dresser, the carpet peeled back, the floor scratched as if dogs with ill-trimmed claws had spent years digging at it. The wood was smeared with char beneath the scratch marks, the faintest suggestion of letters, sending a chill down Brix's spine. Dirty plates, empty bottles, and overflowing ashtrays were littered everywhere – but not enough for a living person who'd been sealed inside a room for eight months.

Other bits of the Peony bled in, flickering in and out of view – the greenhouse rioting with blooms; the grand ballroom dripping with crystal; a soap-scented maze of corridors and laundry rooms; even the subway tunnels that had once connected the Peony to the rest of the city.

"What's your name?" he asked, for something concrete to focus on.

"Virgil." The young man indicated the bed with its heaped covers, and Brix saw what he'd missed before: the other occupants of the room. "And this is Leonie and Jimmy."

Brix looked closer at the figure on the bed, then immediately wished he hadn't.

The young woman lay curled on her side, asleep, but looking by no means comfortable. Naked, with sheets twisted around her body, her face was smushed into the pillow and half-covered by her hair. Her breathing was erratic – shallow, rapid sips of air intermingled with rasping breaths as her lungs struggled to expand.

Brix could see the bones through her skin, the blades of her shoulders and the knobs of her spine. More than that, he could literally see the outline of her skeleton glowing faintly, shining through translucent flesh.

She wasn't alone inside her skin. A second body wound around and through hers. A man whose age it was hard to read – not as solid as Leonie, yet undeniably present.

There was a tugging sense of familiarity at the back of Brix's mind. He knew the man from somewhere. He was silvery dark, like a photograph. A ghost, far more substantial than a ghost had any right to be, but woven so tightly around the fabric of Leonie's being that Brix could barely see where one ended and the other began.

An absurd stab of jealousy caught Brix off guard. What he wouldn't give to hold Abby that way, to shelter her with his own body and keep her in this world. It was utterly the wrong sentiment for the moment, yet he couldn't help the thought, or the longing that came with it.

"Can you help them?" Virgil asked.

Brix turned his focus back to the young man and the hope in his eyes. He knew loss, he knew fear, and even after spending eight months in this room with two other people – one living, one dead – he felt utterly alone.

"I don't know," Brix said, because Virgil deserved honesty. "But I'll sure as hell try."

15

Belle regretted her decision to walk from the station. During the nearly six-hour train ride, clouds had rolled in, leaving the evening air humid, heavy, pregnant with the threat of rain. She'd wanted the time to gather her thoughts, but now her feet hurt, and dirt kicked up from her bootheels clung to her skirts.

"Why do you dress like that, anyway?" Dee asked. She lagged behind Belle, struggling with the weight of her borrowed skirt. Her shoes at least were flat and sensible, but the soles looked thin and Belle imagined her sister's feet hurt as much as hers did.

"Because I can," Belle said.

She could have said, *because clothing is armor*, *because it's a choice I can make for myself*, or any number of other things she wouldn't expect her sister to understand. Even now, her sister favored the type of dress her mother might have worn –

plain, almost severe, old fashioned in a different way from Belle's clothes. They were the kind of dresses that seemed designed to make the person wearing them disappear, as if they had no personality at all. Belle's clothing on the other hand stood out, made people look at her twice, then usually choose to leave her alone, unsure if they could trust someone who so deliberately set apart.

Because you don't want things to be comfortable or easy. Belizial's faint chiding rose inside her. Belle didn't bother to mask the annoyance that rose in return.

So what if she made things deliberately difficult on herself? That was her choice as well – to be strange and unapproachable, so people would leave her alone.

So you can be miserable in turn and wallow in self-pity?

"Shut up." She hadn't meant to say it aloud.

"I didn't say anything." Irritation gave Dee's voice an edge.

The heat was getting to both of them. Belle swiped at the back of her neck, then wiped her sweaty palm against her skirt. Like a spiteful child, she wanted to strip out of her clothes right here, leave them in a dusty pile and march up to the farmhouse naked. Clarence already thought she was a wanton devil. Why not let him see how terrible she truly was?

Belle.

Belizial's voice, soft against her ear, drew her attention. She stopped, seeing where they were, where the demon meant for her to look. All the breath left her lungs.

For a moment, all she could do was stand there, dazed. The oak still stood to the left of the long, winding drive leading up to the farmhouse. Somehow, in all these years, neither her father nor Clarence had thought to cut it down. The tree into which she'd poured so much want; the tree where she'd first met Belizial.

At her weakest, starved and feverish and chained to her bed, Belle had started to believe she'd heard the Devil's voice there. Her parents had repeated the assertions so often that their words began to overwrite whatever truth existed. It wasn't merely that she believed the world was wilder and full of more powers than their singular god. It wasn't that she was loud when they wanted quiet, that she wanted to forge her own path rather than following theirs. She was more than disobedient; she was wicked.

The Devil had stepped from the cleft in the tree's trunk, and she'd allowed him to take possession of her body. More than that, she'd invited him, choosing damnation just to spite her parents' god. If she would only confess, they could save her and set her free.

All of it blurred in Belle's mind, even now. It had never happened – or it had happened, but only later. Belle had poured all her hurt and wanting into that tree like a prayer, and somehow, worlds away, Belizial's own pain had answered hers. And they'd found each other.

The memories colliding in her head left Belle dizzy. It hadn't happened the way her parents believed, but they'd punished her for it anyway, giving themselves an excuse to hurt a child they didn't understand. Or maybe, somehow, they'd always known what she would do one day.

The long grasses around the tree's base were caught in a perpetual winter – pale gold and withered, on the cusp of dying. Belle stepped off the road, ignoring Dee calling out behind her, listening instead to the grass crackle under her heels then shush as she moved closer to the oak. Even now, she couldn't unpick exactly what had happened to her as a child. Time moved differently in the fae realms. Sometimes, even now, it was easy to believe she'd heard voices whispering to her when she was twelve years old. That she hadn't met Belizial in truth until she was sixteen didn't matter.

Other times, she knew with terrible certainty that she'd simply been a willful child. She'd wanted a different life than the one her parents could offer her, and their faith – with its rules about who could speak, who was allowed to want things and who owed strict obedience – had never made sense to her. Belle couldn't remember now who had been the first to raise a hand against her, her mother or her father, but by the end, they'd been a united front, the fervent light of true belief shining in their eyes. Maybe it had been their own sick way of protecting themselves. After they'd hurt her once, they convinced themselves it was for a higher purpose. If they pushed things further, made pain a holy mission, never admitted to having made a mistake in a moment of weakness, then it would all be for the greater good.

They would save her from herself, even if it meant killing her. Better dead than filled with sin, possessed of a mind and heart and voice of her own.

The lightning-struck smell of char and ozone hung in the air, though none had ever hit this tree as far as she knew. It would always smell like this – a scent more intrinsic to her than her mother's cooking or her father's pipe. A scar split the tree crookedly, black as pitch, but it was still, improbably, alive. Or both alive and dead, roots in one world, crown in the other.

Belle lay her hand against the trunk, the rough bark welcome against her skin. This tree, more than the farmhouse itself, was where she'd truly been born. She didn't want to believe – couldn't believe – that its existence was a wound in the world, that her wanting had left a gap the Hollow Queen might use to return. Or if not her, something else.

Her throat tightened. This place, this tree, it had to be a good thing, it had to be—

Home.

The word, in Belizial's voice, held more comfort than any physical place Belle had ever lived. It washed over her, leaving her eyes prickling. She knew they didn't mean the tree, or not just the tree, but her, pressing against her as they said it, yearning toward her and away from something else. They trusted her; they didn't blame her for whatever was happening here now. They agreed with her – the tree was pure and good, and them finding each other was good. If only she could erase everything that had come before.

"Belle?" Dee hadn't left the path.

She turned back to look at her sister, standing uncertainly behind her. Long before she'd ever run away and asked Dee to leave with her, Belle had left her sister behind. The realization hurt. She'd already gone somewhere Dee couldn't follow, giving herself first to the imagined Devil in her mind as a defense against her parents' abuse, then to Belizial when they'd stepped through the oak.

She let her hand fall.

The words *I'm sorry* stuck on her tongue. It felt too late to apologize now, the words too big, too fraught.

Instead, she said, "Let's go." Sweeping past Dee without looking back.

The farmhouse loomed at the far end of the drive against the weird light cast by the storm-laden sky. Wind tugged at Belle's curls and pressed the fabric of her skirt against her legs. The house was both bigger and smaller than she remembered. For a terrible moment, she couldn't even pick out which window had been hers, the one she'd been locked behind at twelve years old. The one she'd climbed from at sixteen when she set herself free.

Dee reached for her hand, surprising Belle. Her fingers were calloused and strong – at once protecting and seeking protection. She should have loved her sister better. She should have done... *something*. What, she didn't know.

"Thank you for being here with me," Dee said. Her eyes picked up the weird storm light, turning them a color Belle couldn't name. She noted Dee hadn't said *thank you for coming home*. It wasn't home, and she wouldn't stay; they both knew that. The knowing hurt, like pressing on a bruise.

They entered the farmhouse together, finding it dark and empty. It was an eerie kind of emptiness; it felt meticulous. The plates had been washed and put away neatly in the cabinets. Upstairs, they found the beds crisply made. Surfaces had been dusted and scrubbed. It was as though the first thing Clarence had done after Dee left was to clean the house from top to bottom.

She remembered her parents setting a small bowl of oil over a candle flame at the foot of her bed after they'd chained her to it. The preacher – the very one whose position Clarence had inherited – had given it to them without question. The stink of it, sputtering within the same bowl her mother used to hold sugar for tea when company came around, assaulted her nose.

Scalding drops spattered against her skin, and the drone of her mother's words. *"By the oil that anointed the Savior's brow, you will be made clean."*

"Do you hear singing?" Dee asked. Belle shook herself, seeing that her sister had opened the door leading out from the kitchen and stood with one foot on the back porch. Belle stepped past her and went to lean against the rail, looking out over the field. Storm-weighted air whipped across her skin, lifting her hair, crackling with the promise of electricity.

"Do you still use the barn?" Belle asked as Dee came to stand beside her.

"Only for storage," Dee said. "We built a new one last year."

"I think that's where the singing is coming from."

Neither of them moved. With the way the grass rose then flattened in the wind, it was easy to imagine they stood on the deck of a schooner. It might pitch and toss at any moment, casting them overboard. Belle tightened her grip on the railing before pushing herself away from it forcefully, descending the two steps to the yard. She didn't immediately drown. Dee followed her, the two of them wading into the grass together.

The wind pushed at them, telling them to turn around. Grass tangled at their ankles. Belle ignored it and the uneasy way Belizial purred against her ear, a nervous sound vibrating the delicate bones in warning. Trusting, but afraid, wanting to flee, but trying to hold themself here and hold themself together for her. Flesh goose-prickled all along her spine.

The sensation only grew the closer they got to the barn, akin to the panic they'd felt at the Peony – not just Belizial's, but her own unease. The two bled together. She should stop, turn around. This was a bad place. But she'd promised Dee; her sister needed her, too. She'd left Dee behind once before, and it didn't matter that it had been Dee's choice. Belle should have tried harder, or been someone different, someone her sister could trust and love enough to run away with her. She couldn't leave Dee behind again.

Just a quick look, then she would turn around. She would keep Belizial safe, but she had to know. The singing grew clearer the closer they got to the barn, but Belle still couldn't make out the words. It wasn't in a language she understood. Maybe not in one ever meant to be spoken by a human tongue. Below the singing came the snap of canvas in the wind.

Belle paused a few feet from the barn, shielding her eyes though the clouds had swallowed all the light. "Are those—"

Dee shifted closer until they stood shoulder to shoulder. "Tents."

They surrounded the barn, some improvised from sheets and tarps, others the kind one would buy to go hunting or camping. They reminded Belle of nothing so much as mushrooms fruiting after a hard rain. She shot a questioning look at her sister, but Dee merely shrugged.

Belizial coiled closer, no longer screaming, but delivering the same warning.

Hush, I know what I'm doing. Belle let the words flow from herself to the demon.

Did she?

Dee moved first, reaching for the barn door.

"Don't." Belle pulled her back, then tilted her head to direct Dee around the side of the barn. "This way."

There were knots in the wood large enough to peek through. Belle pressed her face to one. Light seeped between the gaps, bright and strange enough to rival the storm. All around them, the grass hissed, and tongues joined the chorus – the whole world whispering, making the hairs on the back of Belle's neck stand on end.

Belizial's alarm grew. They wanted to reshape her, snap her bones into new configurations – a dog with its hackles up, all instinct. *Danger. Bad. No.*

A knife touched her skin – not her skin, Belizial's – cutting into her truest self, changing her into something else. Her screams, their screams, twisting up through the shadows in the dark place under the earth. The urge to apologize clogged her tongue, but the Hollow Queen pressed a hand to her – their – mouth, silencing them.

Eyes fathomless and black all the way to the edges, then frost white, then no eyes at all. Just darkness, pits within the thin, sharp planes of a face. Everything good had been scooped from inside of the Hollow Queen with her glass crown. Oh, how she'd starved and been made into a thing capable only of pain. Feeling it. Making others feel the same.

It was all there in those dark eyes, looming over her, boring into her. The knife clattered to the ground. She had cared for them once, hadn't she, the queen? Or she'd claimed to, when they served at her side. When they were—

"Again," the soft word spoken from a bloodied mouth as the Hollow Queen turned away.

Her beaded dress hissed over the prison floor, dragging behind her and smearing the perfect red prints her bare feet left behind.

Belle jerked back, pulling her mind back from Belizial's, taking a moment to come back to herself.

I'm sorry. I'msorryI'msorryI'msorry.

The words became an incoherent stream in her mind. Belizial tried to soothe her, tucking their pain and their memories away, and it was horribly unfair. She should feel the pain, all of it, as deeply as they had. They shouldn't have to carry it alone.

Her sister's hand on her shoulder grounded her, but the touch wasn't meant to steady her. Dee was trying to make room so she could see through the knot in the wood herself.

The barn was packed wall-to-wall with kneeling bodies. They formed concentric circles, faces lifted, hands outstretched, mouths open in song, all basking in the glow of the figure hovering above them.

"Ava." Dee's tone was incredulous.

"What the fuck?"

Weightless, the girl drifted in mid-air above the singers

without visible means of support. No ropes held her aloft; no wings beat at her back. A glow emanated from her, washing over the congregation below. Her feet were bare beneath a white dress that made Belle think of a christening gown. The fabric rippled – either in the breeze or from some other force, the same that lifted the hair around her face as if she floated underwater. When the breeze pressed the dress flat against her body, there was no mistaking the soft roundness of her belly.

And yet something felt off. This was something different, something new.

Belle caught sight of Clarence, half-hidden in shadows against the barn wall, his hands serenely folded in front of him. She willed him to look her way, to see and recognize her watching him. But all his attention remained on Ava, rapt in holy devotion.

There was something tender in the way he watched her. His expression made Belle wonder if she'd blown it all out of proportion over the years. Had Clarence really banished her?

"You'll only end up hurting her again."

But she'd never hurt Dee. Not on purpose. She'd only pushed her away after she'd refused to run, cut her off so she could... *wallow in being alone.*

No. That wasn't right. That couldn't—

Ava's eyes opened. They were bright white like the sun, no iris or pupil visible. She turned her head, looking right at the knothole, right at Belle.

"We have visitors."

"Holy—" Dee stumbled backward.

“Shit.” Belle caught her sister before she tripped over her heels and fell.

They clung to each other amidst the susurrating grass, staring at the barn, at the light seeping out from the twisted miracle within. Then, Belle hauled her sister up, and together, they ran.

"I'm going to step out for a moment and come right back. Do you think you could let me back in when I do?" Brix asked.

He wasn't just asking if Virgil would, but if he *could*, trying to ascertain how much control he had over the room.

Virgil glanced at the bed and nodded uncertainly. "Where are you going?" He kept his voice low, but not low enough to hide his alarm.

"Just down the hall. I need to use a phone, and I don't trust that one."

Honestly, Brix wasn't sure he trusted any of the phones in the hotel. The cream-colored one in here was especially egregious though, smudged as if someone with soot on their hands had picked it up, leaving blackened fingerprints. He also needed a moment to think, free of the direct influence of the haunting. He needed to make sure his head was on straight so he didn't do anything stupid.

Stupider.

He hoped Virgil could see that he wasn't giving up or running out on him. He looked gaunter than when he'd first let Brix into the room. Now that he'd acknowledged its danger, the haunting was wearing him thin.

"Okay, but please don't take long," he said. His gaze drifted back to Leonie. She hadn't moved, as far as Brix could tell, and the pattern of her breathing hadn't changed.

"Ten minutes, tops. I'll be right back." Brix edged toward the door and groped for the handle without looking, thinking the memory of it might be easier to find than the thing itself. The lock clicked and he pushed, backing into the hall. At least, he hoped it was still the hall. He had no sense of how much time had passed, and hated the thought of leaving Virgil and Leonie inside alone. Then again, they'd survived this long.

He trotted to where the black stain didn't reach and ducked into an unlocked room. The sound of wind blowing down the line greeted him as he lifted the handset. He listened for longer than was strictly wise before gritting his teeth and dialing the number Belle had given him.

It rang seven times, eight, then clicked to a stop. It wasn't quite the sound of someone lifting the receiver, and no one spoke or breathed on the other end. Static crackled down the line. Then – voices, rising through the static, fragmented echoes of conversations past.

"...a moment, I'll connect you."

"...the front desk your name, you can come right up."

"Could I order a..."

Echoes of guests who'd stayed at the Peony over the years, not all of whom could have died here, but pieces of them were being called back nonetheless. If John Jacobs Astor could have seen how effective his hotel had become at drawing ghosts, would he be pleased, or merely disappointed that it had drawn all the wrong ones? Brix recognized a senator who notoriously kept a room here where he could meet with his mistresses, girlfriends, and hired companions. The man had died not two months after announcing his candidacy for president, a heart attack. He'd heard recordings of that voice giving speeches dozens of times; hearing it as if it truly spoke on the other end of the line was disorienting.

Whatever Virgil had called into the room at the end of the hall seemed to be attracting other ghosts to itself in turn. Brix thought again of open wounds, thin places in the world. When John Jacobs Astor had built this place, he'd done so at a crossroads, taking a place that was already thin and making it thinner. Was John Jacobs himself among the dead who'd returned to wander here? Or Ethan Holcombe? Although Holcombe had simply vanished. For all Brix knew, he'd merely gone deeper inside the hotel, to the places where the fae realm overlapped with this one, as drawn to Holcombe's Folly as the dead.

All that overlapping power couldn't help but leave a scar, even when the fae went wherever it was they'd gone. The skin of the world might have healed over it, but echoes of the wound remained.

The voices faded into an indistinct slurry. Beneath the storm of electrical sound, he heard an unpleasant noise, uncomfortably like laughter. Brix rubbed at his jaw, then carefully replaced the handset.

Belle and her sister might not have arrived yet. Or they hadn't heard the phone. Or he'd simply dialed wrong. There was no need to try again. Even if he got through, what was there to say? Anything he could report at this point would only worry Belle unnecessarily. Calling and not getting an answer for a second time would only do the same for him.

The urge to call home welled up in him. Abby would answer. He'd be able to hear her voice asking him if he was running late, if he'd be home for dinner. Like she'd never died.

Brix jabbed his finger against the cradle to cut off the number, half-dialed. This place was dangerous; the part of him that wanted to let it get to him was growing stronger.

He called the front desk instead.

"I need you to send a few things up to the fourteenth floor." The static remained; Brix had to shout to be heard. Something lonely howled along the line, a rainstorm long done and gone pouring out its fury. Brix had no idea whether he was making himself understood. He plowed on regardless.

"Four sandwiches. Candles, all you can spare. A few packs of smokes, if you would. Load the cart into the elevator and send it up. Fast as you can. Much appreciated."

He didn't wait for a response, replacing the receiver and stepping away from the phone. He'd already been gone from room twelve for too long. He'd promised Virgil ten minutes.

He stepped back into the hallway to wait, restless and impatient. At least twenty minutes passed before the elevator finally let out a soft chime. He folded back the gate and retrieved the cart, hoping he wasn't too late. Who knew how time worked on the other side of the door.

A silver dome-covered plate held the sandwiches. Everything else he'd asked for had been crammed around the sides, even the smokes. He tucked one pack into his pocket and pushed the cart up to the door. He should have asked for whiskey; too late for that now.

Brix didn't knock this time. "Virgil?"

A faint scuffling sound followed as Virgil struggled with the lock, then the door creaked open. Brix pushed the cart inside. His eyes adjusted more quickly this time. Virgil didn't chide him or ask him where he'd been, possibly because Leonie was awake now and sitting up on the bed. She'd wound the sheet around her body like a shroud. The shag of her hair surrounding her face made it look smaller, the bed vast, leaving her lost in the dark. She blinked at him – luminous eyes, movie idol eyes – and recognition finally dawned on him, putting the name Virgil had given together with the nagging familiarity at the back of his mind.

"Jimmy Valentine." Brix let out a low whistle. "Well, I'll be damned."

"Virgil, what did you—" Leonie started.

"I'm sorry, but this is too big. We need help." Virgil's words rushed atop hers.

Leonie had turned her head partway to look at Virgil, but Jimmy Valentine remained looking at Brix head on. The effect was disorienting, like one of those two-headed eagles printed on an old coin.

"It's alright, darlin'," Jimmy Valentine said. He spoke to

Leonie, but kept looking at Brix. "It's a pleasure to make your acquaintance, Mr. Brix."

It struck him that he hadn't actually introduced himself, meaning the ghost had been listening when he spoke with Virgil earlier.

"Likewise. My… Abby and I caught a couple of your pictures at the Aztec a few years ago. There was a whole festival showing them back-to-back. Loved every one of them."

Flattery seemed like a safe enough course. In truth, he and Abby had spent more time necking like teenagers than paying attention to the screen, but the ghost didn't need to know that.

"It's nice to meet you too, Leonie." Brix wasn't quite sure where to focus when he spoke.

Leonie crossed her arms, scowling at him, but Jimmy smoothed over her expression with his words.

"I'm always happy to meet a fan."

He beamed, sincere in a way that suggested the compliment did indeed mean the world to him, as though he hadn't heard it a million times. Brix could understand why so much swooning adoration had been thrown his way over the years.

It was Leonie's mouth that moved, though the soft drawl that emerged belonged to vinyl records and the silver screen, like velvet brushed against skin, made unnerving as Leonie's lips failed to match the words, lagging or blurring too fast.

"Is that peanut butter?" she asked, and Jimmy said it as well, voices intertwined. "I'm starved."

Leonie crawled toward the end of the bed in a spider-like,

eerie motion that suggested too many limbs for one body, not all of them jointed the right way. He'd seen mediums who claimed to be ghost-ridden; this was something else altogether.

Brix tried to keep his expression neutral as he lifted the cover from the plate. The kitchen had indeed sent up one peanut butter sandwich. He handed it over. "The rest are for later."

A last meal for the condemned seemed only fair. Virgil and Leonie would be hungry once Brix sent Jimmy on his way. Presuming he could extract Jimmy from Leonie, and that the whole fragile haunted ecosystem that had sustained them didn't collapse immediately.

"Don't suppose you want to tell me how all of this came about?"

He used his thumbnail to slit the foil seal on the pack of cigarettes he'd left on the service trolley. Virgil and Leonie exchanged a glance that spoke volumes before their gazes bounced away. Leonie continued shoving peanut butter into her mouth, into her mouths, two sets of lips and two sets of teeth moving asynchronously. She gripped the sandwich in fingers that were too long, wolfing down bites and clutching what remained like it was the most precious thing in the world.

Virgil looked uncomfortable. Brix distracted himself by shaking out four cigarettes, handing one to Virgil and leaving two nearby where Leonie and Jimmy could reach them once they'd done eating. He wondered which, if any of them, would answer his question. He lit his cigarette, making a circuit of the room, trying to ignore the dimensions that shifted as he did.

"I don't need to know all of what went down to help, but it would be nice to get an idea of what I'm dealing with."

"Nothing needs to be dealt with." Leonie's voice rang with tension. "We're just fine."

"Are you sure?" Brix wheeled to face her, Jimmy sitting watchful behind her eyes. "Because from where I'm standing, it looks like you've gotten yourselves into quite the mess."

He resumed pacing, lighting candles this time. Virgil watched him mournfully.

"There are rules," Brix said. "You've broken quite a lot of them."

Hypocrite, his inner voice chided him. Brix tried to ignore it.

"I'm sure you didn't mean to," he went on. "Maybe it started off as just a bit of fun, and things got out of hand."

His foot hit a bottle half tucked under the bed. Brix retrieved it, dug out the cork, and singed its end in one of the flames. The back of his neck itched. Leonie's gaze was on him as he traced symbols of protection across the walls.

He turned to face the bed again. Brix found if he squinted it was easier to hold both Jimmy and Leonie in his mind at once. It didn't hurt quite as much to look at them.

"I've heard quite a few stories about you, luv." He directed his words at Jimmy. Based on the seething resentment he felt from Leonie, she would be the hardest one to crack, but if he could get Jimmy on his side as well as Virgil, maybe they could convince her this was the right thing to do.

"Half of them might even be true," Jimmy said.

Under the charm in his voice, Brix heard the unease. The curtains stirred, a restless breath blowing through the room, and the desk behind Brix vibrated subtly, picking Jimmy's tension and echoing it.

He was skirting the edge of something dangerous, but surely these kids would see sense. If they let him do his work before things got worse, they could leave this place, move on with their lives. It would hurt, but they were young. The wounds would heal.

Hypocrite.

"There's a ballad about you by Northrup Carroll I quite like," Brix said. "I always thought there might be bit of truth to it, how you took a fae lover and she danced you away 'neath the hill."

He didn't have even an ounce of a singing voice, but Brix quoted the song as best he could remember. Instead of a simple car crash ending Jimmy's life, an ill-advised drag race amidst a storm, he'd been fleeing the wild hunt. Twisted metal and shattering glass became the sound of horns and hooves, and Jimmy Valentine had been snatched away in the moment of his death to meet a greater doom.

"I don't want to talk about that," Jimmy said.

The mirror across the room shuddered; the bed did too. Brix held up his hands, as if in surrender. He pushed more gently this time. "If you died with some kind of bargain that tangled up in your soul, it's possible something unintended came along for the ride when Virgil called you back."

"I didn't mean—" Virgil started.

"I'm not blaming you." Brix glanced at him, then turned his attention back to Jimmy. "You, though. I think you know better, don't you, luv?"

It was a risk, and a guess as well, but Brix trusted his gut. There was something in Jimmy's eyes that made him think of stars, distant and cold, shining with unearthly light. They weren't cruel eyes, but more than death haunted them. He'd seen enough in his time to know that something else had touched Jimmy Valentine long before he died. Half-fae himself, whether by nature, or through some bargain he'd made. Looking at him left Brix with the feeling of looking at a body of water that was so still and so perfectly reflected the sky that there was no way to know whether it was deep enough for drowning.

"I said I didn't want to talk about that." Anger edged his voice, but hurt clouded Jimmy's features too, leaving Brix wondering how much he didn't want to say versus how much he couldn't.

The candles went out. Leonie wrapped her arms around her body, making a soft whimpering sound.

"Leonie." Virgil moved to the bed, reaching for her.

"It's alright," she said. "I'm alright, but he has to leave. Now."

Her eyes were like Jimmy's – silvery moonlight, not entirely human as she glared at Brix. "Get out." Her spine hunched like a strung bow. Brix imagined her lunging for him, every line of her body suggesting the capacity for unnatural motion.

"I'm sorry, but Virgil here asked for my help, and I don't intend to leave until I've given it my best shot."

He turned his back on her, which was probably a dangerous thing to do. He moved to re-light the candles, feeling Leonie watching him. He braced himself, but when the attack came it was soft and verbal, and it took the breath right out of him.

"You haven't told us how you quieted her."

Brix's hand jerked. The candle he'd just lit tipped; he caught it before it fell, sucking in air as hot wax spilled over his skin. He righted it carefully, giving himself time to school his expression.

Leonie's gaze pinned him, a chill hand pressed to his heart. She'd been paying more attention than he realized. He wondered if she'd been asleep at all, or if she'd been listening the whole time.

"Who's that?" He was stalling. Leonie was probably aware of that, too.

"Abigail. Your wife." Leonie's lips curled, ugly and predatory. She knew. Gods knew how, but she knew, and she wanted to see if he would tell the truth.

"You told Virgil that you brought her back and how much you love her, but not how you let her go."

Leonie drew her knees up against her chest, her arms wrapped around them and Jimmy's arms wrapped around hers. Despite having two pairs of eyes, nested one inside the other, Leonie never seemed to blink. She waited for his answer. Brix's mouth was unaccountably dry.

"That's what you're here to do, isn't it?" Leonie demanded. "You're here to quiet Jimmy, and we're just supposed to let him go, even though you—"

"Wait a minute," Virgil cut in. "No one said anything about—"

"Of course he's going to send Jimmy away." Leonie

whipped around, glaring at Virgil. "What did you expect when you let him in?"

Virgil blanched, the reality of the situation settling on him. He'd been scared enough to let Brix into the room, to ask for help, but he clearly hadn't thought through fully what that would mean. The fear in his eyes was joined by grief.

Leonie was clearly the more pragmatic of the two. She could only see one end.

Brix was more certain than ever that neither of them – hells, not one of the three of them – had meant harm. The empty bottles, the ash markings on the floor… they were kids playing a game, in over their heads. They'd made a mistake, that was all.

"Look," he said. "I'll do it as kindly as I can, but I can't see a way out that doesn't involve Jimmy moving on."

"I won't let you." Leonie's multi-jointed fingers bunched the fabric beneath her, gripping the sheets like claws.

The flatness of her voice unnerved him. It was a simple declaration of intent, delivered without anger, but she meant it right down to her core. As Brix watched, Jimmy relaxed Leonie's grip, made her let go of the sheets.

"Now, darlin', let's give the man a chance, why don't we? Mr. Brix is here to help. I'm sure he'll figure something out." Jimmy's voice in Leonie's mouth was lazy and assured, designed to soothe. All trace of his earlier anger was gone. It was the voice of someone who was used to things going his way.

"Leonie," Brix said. He wasn't sure how to continue.

What he'd done was far worse, far crueler than anything

these children had. They'd been playing with magic they didn't understand. They were stupid, young, and in love. Brix could only claim two of the three, and he knew *far* better. How could he ask them to do what he himself wasn't willing to?

He braced himself for Leonie to challenge him, but all at once her shoulders went slack. The tension holding her rigid dropped away, like Jimmy had tucked her deep within herself with loving tenderness, moving himself closer to the surface of her skin. It should have been horrifying. Brix felt selfishly relieved. Leonie's words struck too close to home, and her ferocity unnerved him. He had no doubt she would fight to protect what was hers, and right now, she didn't know her own strength.

"What did you do?" Virgil asked, worry coloring his voice.

"It's alright." Jimmy unfolded Leonie's body from the bed, laying a gentle hand alongside Virgil's face, fond and reassuring. "She's just sleeping for a while."

He let his hand fall back to his side, looking around the room as if seeing it for the first time. "It takes a lot out of her, holding me like this. Can't blame her for needing a little rest from time to time."

The way Jimmy said it, casually, as if the living and the dead became inextricably entwined all the time, chilled Brix.

"Do you know what's happening in the rest of the hotel?" he asked, looking between Jimmy and Virgil.

"Can't say that I do." Jimmy studied the walls, as if searching for something.

It was uncanny. Looking at him now, Brix could hardly see Leonie anymore. His taller, lankier form subsumed hers, his silvery features rising to the surface like a magic trick. Brix could almost believe the real, living Jimmy Valentine was in the room with them. That Leonie was the ghost.

"It isn't just this room," Brix said. "There are other ghosts all throughout the hotel, people who stayed here when they were alive, people who worked here. It's like something is calling them back, whether they want to be here or not. I don't suppose you know why that might be?"

"You know what I miss?" Jimmy ignored the question. He turned, grinning, pulling Leonie's body with him in an uneasy doppler effect. "The piano."

"I thought you were a guitar man," Brix said, disoriented by the sudden change in subject and trying to keep up.

There was a famous picture of Jimmy Valentine alone on a stage in the full wash of a spotlight. Seated on a plain wooden stool, one leg cocked up with a foot balanced on the rung, his guitar slung across his lap and a microphone just at the edge of the light, waiting for the touch of his voice. A crowd gathered beyond, but as far as the picture was concerned, Jimmy was alone in the world against a velvet darkness rife with stars. Brix could see it clearly in his mind's eye. It had been reproduced a thousand times since, on postcards and plates and even coins. Jimmy Valentine was a currency you could use to buy a loaf of bread.

"Sure," Jimmy said. "But the piano was my first love. Before you got here, Mr. Brix, I was telling Virgil and Leonie how my mama made sure I learned how to play. She always said that no matter what anyone took away from me, even if I lost everything else, I would always have music."

Jimmy held Brix's eye as he spoke, like there were words beneath his words. The whiplash change of subject might not be him avoiding the question after all. But whatever Jimmy might be trying to tell him, Brix didn't understand, not yet.

"I even played the piano in the grand ballroom right here in the Peony Hotel a time or two. You think I could find my way back there now if I tried?"

Before either Brix or Virgil could answer, Jimmy and Leonie had already stepped through what should have been a solid wall.

17

They'd retreated to the farmhouse, but it didn't feel far enough. Dee paced, her gaze returning constantly to the kitchen window and the weird light beyond it. The storm hadn't broken yet, but Belle could feel it, electricity crackling along the length of her skin as the evening deepened.

"Why haven't they come after us?" Dee asked. "They know we're here."

"Maybe they want us to go to them." Belle let a sour note creep into her voice. Wouldn't that be just like Clarence, holding court in his new kingdom. He'd forbidden her from returning, but Belle was willing to bet he'd make an exception if she returned on her knees, begging forgiveness.

Belizial turned against her ribs, restless and unsettled. If Belle let them free, she could end all of this now, drive Clarence and his followers from the land.

"If I—" She started to voice the thought aloud, but Dee

spun to face her, putting her back to the sink and bracing her hands against the counter.

"Don't you dare. I won't have that thing in my house."

"You didn't even let me finish."

"No, but I know what you were thinking, and I won't have it."

Belizial shied from the thought as much as Dee had, trying to burrow deeper within her, though there was nowhere left to go. Would they leave her, if they grew frightened enough? Could they?

Her sister continued to glare at her. The grey-yellow light coming through the window behind Dee outlined every hard line in her body. She was as fierce as a storm herself.

"Make tea," Belle said.

She could have gentled her tone, but she didn't. Dee needed somewhere to direct her fear, and it might as well be into anger at Belle. For her part, she needed space, a moment to think.

"While you do what, exactly?"

"Come up with another plan, since you didn't like my first one."

"Fine." Dee made a point of letting each cup rattle as she set it on the counter, opening and closing the cupboard doors with force and banging the kettle onto the stove.

What do you want to do? Belle asked, as gently as she could.

Run. Belizial shuddered. The sick memory of pain returned to her.

Belle grit her teeth. *Not an option.*

Then why ask? The weariness in Belizial's tone hurt more than bitterness would have.

If Dee weren't so opposed to Belizial, they might be able to help her determine what Ava carried within her, whether it was truly a child – Clarence's child – or something else.

Belizial curled and uncurled reflexively, telling her how little they liked the idea. Gods, why did everything have to be so complicated? She longed for the simple feeling of her bones rearranged, Belizial rising around her like a halo, changed and split into two – demon and Belle, Belle and demon, separate yet wound around each other and indistinguishable. Once again, she felt Belizial shy away from the idea.

It stung.

Belle felt the beginning of them reaching for her, tentatively, like an apology, and she pulled herself away. Was it petty? Yes, but in the moment she didn't care. She was tired. Everything hurt. Being here, in this farmhouse, was like pressing down ceaselessly on a bruise. Belizial had suffered – terribly – but so had she. Where was the grace and patience she deserved? Dee didn't trust her, Belizial didn't trust her. Fine. She didn't need them to trust her; she'd figure out a way to save them both, despite themselves.

"Is the phone connected?" Belle spoke to her sister's turned back, amazed at how even her voice sounded, how normal.

Dee shot her an exasperated look. "Just because we don't live in the city, doesn't mean we're completely backwards."

At least if she kept Dee fixed on resenting her, maybe it would keep her mind off everything else. Maybe it would keep her from noticing her sister was falling apart.

Dee made an impatient gesture toward the front room. "You remember where it is."

Belle remembered. Her parents had disconnected it for a time after her "possession". As if cutting themselves off from the world would cauterize their household, sealing Belle away so no other demons could find their way in – and more importantly, Belle couldn't find her way out.

Her mother and father's chairs still flanked the fieldstone hearth in the front room, which had been large enough for her to stand upright in at four years old. She'd burned her hand on the iron pothook there once, not realizing the metal would still be hot over the embers of a fire.

The knick-knacks on the shelves and mantle were different, but the end-tables were the same. The rug was new, the photographs framed on the wall a mixture of those Belle remembered from her childhood and more recent portraits. Clarence and Dee on their wedding day, alongside a few framed sketches Belle didn't recognize. Work her sister had done?

There was so much – too much – about Dee she didn't know. She tried to think how many times they'd actually spoken since their parents' deaths. Not often enough. She should have tried harder.

She hadn't been prepared for how many of their parents' things her sister had kept. She remembered sitting on a different rug between those two wing-backed chairs, one woven from rags and dingy with years of use, listening to her father read from the Good Book, kneeling with her hands clasped in prayer, before climbing upstairs to the room she shared with Dee. There, they'd knelt again at the side of their respective beds to pray once more, as if the Devil might have caught hold of them between the first and second floor.

She searched for a good memory amidst the aching ones and came up empty. Her fingers curled against the lack. She forced them open to lift the receiver. The phone was an ugly custard-yellow, the shade of something spoiled. She dialed the number on the card Gustav had given her.

It didn't ring; a soft click indicating a connection was followed immediately by the sound of voices singing. It was the song they'd heard earlier in the barn. There were other noises too, someone speaking in the background of the music. The words were barely audible, but it sounded like Clarence's voice.

"...land will be cleansed. A new way will open. The light will..."

Belle pressed the receiver hard against her ear, trying to catch the rest of the words as the song rose in volume and washed over them. Then, sharp and clear, as if he was in the room with her, Clarence said the name she'd left behind long ago.

"Jessamine."

Not just Clarence's voice, but her father's voice as well, the two of them intertwined. She was twelve years old again, hands shaking so hard she could barely dial, not even certain who she was going to call. Someone, anyone, to come take her away from this place – but when she lifted the receiver, the line was dead. Grimly, her father told her there would be no calls, prying the receiver from her hand, grasping her upper arm and dragging her back up the stairs. Her parents had already moved Dee to another room by then, so it was easy enough to lock Belle in hers. Alone.

Belle slammed the receiver back into the cradle. It wasn't

enough. She imagined the plastic cracking into a thousand shards, stomping on the phone with her bootheel until it was nothing but dust. How dare Clarence? How dare he?

"Tea's ready," Dee said. Belle startled hard enough she nearly knocked the phone over.

Dee held out a cup. "Everything okay?"

"Set it there." Belle gestured to the table with her chin, not trusting herself to handle the cup without spilling it.

She noted the wedge of lemon set on the saucer, and it cracked her heart a little. Dee remembered.

"I need to talk to Clarence." She glanced past Dee, toward the kitchen window. Twilight had fallen behind the storm clouds. "I want you to stay here."

"You won't—"

Belle cut her off. "I'm a professional," she said, though she felt anything but right now. Dee had made her feelings clear – she didn't want Clarence hurt, she wanted to help Ava, and she didn't trust her sister with either of those things. "I won't do anything stupid."

She kept her tone frosty – not a sister comforting a sister, but an investigator, hired for a case.

Dee crossed her arms, tucking her hands into her armpits like she was trying to get warm. "Fine. Just be careful." Her voice was low enough that Belle almost didn't catch the words.

"What?" Too late, Belle realized the question sounded mocking. It hadn't occurred to her that Dee's concern might be for her, not Clarence.

Dee flinched, her voice rising. "I said be careful. I already lost you once."

"You didn't have to." The words were out before Belle could stop them.

She hadn't meant to be so harsh. She hadn't meant to do a lot of things, but they poured out of her nonetheless, more shaken by Clarence's voice speaking a name that didn't belong to her, that grated against her bones, than she wanted to admit.

Dee whipped around, tears glazing her eyes. "You left me."

"I asked you to come with me. I begged you." Belle let the accusation fly. "Twice." Her throat felt thick around the words, but she was tired of holding back. The conversation was a long time coming, but she still didn't want to have it. She could understand why Dee had stayed as a child, but when Belle had asked again at their parents' funeral... why? Everything could have been different; they could have built a life together.

"Did it ever occur to you, even once, that I'm my own person?" Dee countered. "I want different things. I want my own damn life. This life, not yours."

Oh. Belle pressed her hands to her midsection, as though she'd been struck. She missed the feeling of Belizial there, rising to press their warmth against her touch. They remained distant; all she could feel was a curdled hollowness. As if she had any right to seek comfort from them when they were still hurting, small and frightened within her, absent and present all at once. She took a step toward Dee, but her sister turned again, putting her shoulder between them like a protective barrier. "Just try not to get yourself killed, okay?"

Belle let her hands fall. "Okay."

She kept as much space as possible between her body and

Dee's as she edged to the door and out onto the porch. A square of light from the kitchen followed her, pooling at her feet. Dee closed the door behind her, the soft click worse than a slam.

Dee's trust, her forgiveness, Belizial's – she hadn't earned any of it. In the end, she would be alone. Wasn't that what she'd always wanted, to run away before anyone could leave her, cut herself off before they could tell her she didn't deserve their love?

No.

The voice, so small in her head, was only her own and Belle strode away from it, through the long grass and toward the barn. There was no singing now, just the low hush of wind, the snap of tent canvas. Fires burning in circles of stone. The people gathered here were Dee's neighbors, Clarence's former parishioners. Belle might recognize some of their faces if she let herself. The neighbors who had looked away from what was happening inside their farmhouse when she was a child.

She swung wide around the makeshift camp and reached the far side of the barn where the double doors stood open, looking down over the valley. The ragged shapes of trees reached up toward the lowering clouds, leaving a scant, jagged line of sky between them like a crack in the world.

Like a gap between here and there, where anything might slip through. It had happened once before. Why wouldn't it happen again? A soft light shone from a lantern near the doors. Belle straightened her back and strode inside. She expected the crowded bodies of Clarence's parishioners, their heads turning like a single organism to stare at her, the intruder in their midst. But the space was empty.

"Hello, Jessamine." Clarence's voice crawled along Belle's spine, worse than it had been on the phone, because now it was undeniably real; he was right in front of her.

He stepped into the lantern's circle of light, Ava at his side. A soft radiance emanated from her, nothing so dramatic as the way she'd shone before. He held her hand, but there was something oddly chaste about it. The girl's other hand cradled her stomach. Seeing Belle, her face lit with a smile.

"Sister." It was almost worse than Clarence calling her by that other name.

"Don't call me that. Either of those things."

Ava seemed unfazed. Her smile didn't waver.

"What do you want?" Belle asked.

"To welcome you." Ava glanced at Clarence.

"To help you see the error of your ways," Clarence added. "In the light, all may be forgiven."

Ask forgiveness and the Lord shall grant it. Her father's voice, her mother's voice, overlapping. The smell of her flesh burning as they pressed a heated cross to her skin. The crack of something giving in her wrist as she tried to wrench herself away from the pain, the stripped raw feeling of her throat as Belle finally gave in to the urge to scream.

Spines of bone wanted to push through her skin. Belle's mouth watered. She wanted to devour – as Belizial, as herself, she couldn't tell the difference anymore. Clarence's gristle between her teeth, his blood on her tongue. Gods, it was a disgusting image, and she couldn't stop wanting it.

Belle clenched her jaw, fought to hold herself still. It wasn't enough. Where Ava beamed, guileless, there was something almost slack about Clarence's expression. Belle's skin felt loose and ill-fitting, like it wanted to slide away from her, away from Clarence's words and the way he looked at her. Hunger, without desire. Something in him dug at her like an oyster to be shucked open, to get at the meat inside.

Belizial.

"Don't." She said the word too late, the realizing hitting her past the point she could do anything about it.

She'd walked straight into a trap, not one that Clarence had set for her, but one the thing using him had set for Belizial.

Hunger answering hunger, Belizial pulled toward the surface of her skin, dragged toward the light emanating from Ava. The glow intensified, pale and writhing, casting shadows that seemed to come from nowhere.

Belizial gave an earsplitting shriek only Belle could hear, like a spike of iron driven straight through her skull. Her demon's claws dug into her, fighting to stay as hard as she fought to keep them with her. Something outside of her sought to tear them apart.

"Wait. I don't—"

Pain doubled Belle over, stealing her words. At the same time, Ava let out a soft gasp. Both hands flew to her mid-section now, her eyes widening. She'd looked almost inhuman in her radiance moments ago; now she looked nothing but human – young and vulnerable, a mother frightened for her child.

Clarence touched her back. "What is it?"

Ava shuddered. Belle almost expected to see blood spotting the white of her gown – a miscarriage. None appeared, but Ava's lips stretched as if she fought to birth a scream.

Clarence paled, looking utterly stricken. More than stricken – *haunted*, like his entire world was coming apart, and not for the first time.

"Let me—" Belle fought to straighten, reaching for Ava.

She wasn't certain exactly what she meant to do, but she'd promised Dee she would try to help. She wanted her sister back. She wanted—

Light burst from Ava like knives. Her head jerked back painfully, more light pouring from her eyes and her open mouth. She rose into the air, feet leaving the barn's dusty floor, arms held outward at her side, the strands escaped from her braid swaying in a breeze that touched her alone.

"Ava!" Clarence caught at her hand, trying to pull her back down to his side, but her fingers slipped from his. The alarm in his voice was genuine. He was no longer a man wrapped in a religious fervor, only in over his head and afraid.

Belizial keened. They twisted violently, pulling away from the light, trying to burrow deeper within Belle's bones. Stuttering flashes of pain, broken fragments of memory. It hurt. It hurt like it had hurt before. The knife plied again and again, the whip scouring more than flesh. Tearing them apart. Taking them from themself. Undoing them, unmaking them utterly. The Hollow Queen, watching calmly through the bars of their cell – not with anger or even hatred, but as if their pain was a disappointment.

"I taught you better." The echoing memory of a voice like brittle glass, and the hiss of a beaded hem as the queen walked away. The light, hovering at the Hollow Queen's shoulder, always at her side, as close as Belizial themself had once been.

It trembled and shivered at Belizial's torture, but leashed to the Hollow Queen, it couldn't help but watch, responding to their screams with a soft and mournful song.

"I'm sorry," Belle gasped. Tears slipped into her mouth as she spoke, fighting for breath. "I didn't mean—"

Thunder smashed overhead, the storm choosing that moment to finally break. The concussive sound left her dazed, her head ringing. It was almost like it had been scripted; Belle would have laughed at the sheer absurdity of it all if she wasn't hurting, if Belizial wasn't hurting. The sound lodged in her throat, painful as a fruit stone.

Lightning flickered outside the open door, followed by another percussive crash that Belle felt behind her breastbone. Clarence caught at both of Ava's hands now, but she continued to rise, slipping out of his grasp.

"Please," Belle said.

She wasn't sure what she meant, who she beseeched with her words. Her fingers grazed Ava's foot.

"Don't touch her!" Clarence bellowed, driving his shoulder into her, knocking her sideways.

The last of Belle's reserve snapped. Or she snapped it, stopped holding back and let it happen. She unfurled, Belizial parting her skin, splintering her bones. Flight became fight, her demon lashing out at the pain to tear it apart. Tendrils of darkness streaked through the light, sizzling and hissing. Belizial would not let themself be taken, not let themself be hurt. Not again.

Ava screamed. As if the invisible strings holding her aloft had been cut, she plunged toward the ground with a panicked wail that wasn't anything human. The light tried to arrest her fall – and there was a sickening crack. She hung suspended a scant inch from the ground, her neck canted at a horrible angle, her bare toes brushing the dirt.

Whatever held her let go. Ava folded in on herself, crumpling to the barn floor. The light shot up into the barn's rafters, shuddering, almost whimpering. As it retreated, so did Belizial, folding back into Belle's skin, folding themself so small, she could barely feel them inside her.

Clarence caught Ava, gathering her in his arms like a broken doll. He twisted around, eyes glazed with tears and burning as he glared at Belle.

"What did you do?"

She had no earthly idea. She reached after Belizial and felt nothing, a seed made of ice buried in her heart, shrinking from her touch. She felt so incredibly small, unable to think of anything to do except *run*.

Now. Finally. When it was too late. She gathered her skirts and pelted down the hill, slipping in the wet grass. Rain stung her eyes. She could barely see, the farmhouse an indistinct blur even as she crashed through its door.

Dee jumped up from the kitchen table, alarmed, but Belle scarcely slowed. She seized her sister's hand, dragging her toward the front door.

"We have to go," she said. "Now."

18

"Where did they go?" Virgil asked, alarm making his voice rise.

"I don't know, but we better hurry if we want to follow."

Virgil's eyes widened, but he let Brix take his arm. Brix didn't let himself think about what he was about to do long enough to let doubt set in. He charged forward, trusting in Jimmy's magic and the strength of the haunting and – irrational as it was – they passed through solid wood and plaster.

Brix kept his attention fixed on Leonie and Jimmy, not wanting to let them get too far ahead. He didn't relish the idea of suddenly finding himself trapped inside a wall, but Jimmy seemed to be recreating reality around him as he went.

The surface underfoot changed without warning. Brix lost his balance – only Virgil's hand on his shoulder stopped him from falling. Jimmy had found the ballroom, or *a* ballroom, crafted from memory and desire.

Alternating dark and light wood patterned the floor, until it forgot and became a carpet the color of blood wound with twisting golden vines. Crystal chandeliers dripped overhead, literally in some cases, becoming candelabras installed upside down, shedding wax, flames shivering as they reached toward the floor.

The piano stood against a backdrop of dark red velvet curtains drawn over floor-to-ceiling windows. Jimmy's expression was one of pure rapture.

"Should we—" Virgil started, but Brix held him back. The last thing he wanted to do was startle Jimmy, whose fingers moved lightly, not quite a song yet, but suggesting one. Brix got the sense he was re-introducing himself to the piano, like reuniting with an old friend.

"Who are they?"

Brix turned. Dancers drifted across the floor, wispy outlines drawn by the notes.

"Jimmy's like a beacon right now. It's like I was trying to explain earlier – it's not just him, but a whole mess of hauntings knotted together. More of the dead are coming through, and the longer they stick around, the harder it will be to get them to leave again when this is all done."

Virgil's throat bobbed. Brix wished he had more time to reassure the kid. He was more certain than ever that the boy hadn't meant any harm.

Brix understood. He'd been young and stupid once, too; stupid enough to fall into a duck pond at the sight of a pretty girl. Stupid enough to ask her to marry him a week after meeting her for the second time. Stupid enough to bring her back from the dead instead of letting her go.

Seeing he had an audience, Jimmy's grin spread, slow and golden as honey. His fingers trailing over the keys solidified into the notes of a waltz. As the song crystalized, so did the figures around them. A stray elbow passed through Brix with a chill, the tugging sensation of something caught, and the ghost frowned as if he'd been the one to intrude on her and not the other way around.

Perhaps he had. Brix was struck with the sudden unnerving sensation that Jimmy hadn't merely moved them within the hotel, but he'd pulled the entire Peony out of alignment. Not quite into the fae realms, the realms of the dead, or the hells, or into any one single space, but all of them at once. A liminal everywhere in which anything might be possible.

The sensation only intensified as Jimmy appeared at his side. "May I have this dance?"

Brix startled, hard. Jimmy Valentine stood at the piano, music pouring forth from lithe fingers that belonged more properly to Leonie. And Jimmy Valentine stood beside him, holding out his hand. Both things were true.

He turned to Virgil, lost enough to ask for the boy's help, but Virgil stood transfixed, awake yet dreaming. Lights drifted through the ballroom like rogue stars. Or perhaps they were stars. Nothing would surprise him anymore. A faint, silvery figure stood at Virgil's side – yet another version of Jimmy, leaning close to whisper a private word in his ear.

"How are you doing all this?" Brix asked.

"Can't rightly say." Jimmy's smile didn't waver, but Brix caught the strain beneath the expression and the words both.

Before he could say anything else, Jimmy cut him off. "Dance with me, Mr. Brix. I don't know how much time we have, and I don't know that I can tell you all of what you want to know, but maybe I can show you, if you'll trust me."

Brix felt a kind of giddy abandon, recklessly putting his hand into Jimmy's. "Why the hells not?"

He was lightheaded enough, so caught up in the wildness of it all, that it took him a moment to realize what he'd done. He'd taken Jimmy's hand. He could touch him, which was horribly, colossally unfair. All those months of Abigail, stranded at the other end of the table, never being able to touch her, never being able to hold her like this.

"You know, I heard they made a shrine to me down in Siegleville, outside the Jewel Box Theater where I used to play." Jimmy drew Brix smoothly onto the dance floor. "There's supposedly even a secret room somewhere inside the Flamingo that Bugsy himself had made where they keep some of my bones, like I'm some kind of saint."

He chuckled, like he was just as amazed as anyone at what his life and death had become.

"Virgil and Leonie told me all kinds of things that people believe about me. That I was a secret agent for the government, that I never really died and I'm living safe and sound up on the moon. All those stories and rumors, it's gotten so not even I'm sure what's true or not anymore. Virgil said people still play my music and films all the time, all over the world, so in a way it's like I really did live forever, after all."

The odd phrasing struck Brix. He got the sense that Jimmy was edging up to something, trying to convey more than he could with words. He moved them across the dance floor, and it didn't matter that it was made up of different surfaces – now wood, now carpet, now something Brix was fairly certain was bone – he never faltered. With Jimmy's steadying hand on the small of his back, a touch that also kept him from running, Brix didn't falter either. It didn't matter one bit that he'd never learned to dance, that he had two left feet, and had left Abigail hopeless with laughter the one time he'd tried. Brix danced now like he'd been born to it.

"I'm sorry for losing my temper back in the room," Jimmy said. "And I'm sorry I can't make this easier on you."

Shadows lay across Jimmy's smile. Once again, Brix got the sense he was saying two things at the same time. Like he knew about Abby, and was apologizing for the way he could hold Brix while she could not. Like he was apologizing for a thing that hadn't happened yet but was just about to, and how much it would hurt.

Brix felt himself on a precipice. The drifting lights he'd thought of as stars were under his feet now, inside the floor that was no longer a floor. He was about to fall, only Jimmy's steadying touch keeping him from tumbling inside of everything. The thought made no sense, but at the same time, it was true. Brix was tumbling out of himself, into something else, somewhere else. Those soft-shining stars were inside Jimmy too, under his skin and in his eyes, a vast gulf opening to swallow him whole.

This is what it must feel like to walk the bone road.

The fleeting thought crossed his mind, but he had no time to unpack it. The ink all along Brix's arms tingled. Jimmy hissed in a sharp breath, testing the wards, pushing past them. It shouldn't be possible, but then, nothing that had happened so far should be possible.

"Remember, watch the mirrors," Jimmy said. His gaze pinned Brix, silver as mirror glass itself. Strain showed in the line of his jaw, but he didn't look away. Brix saw someone who'd been taught to endure pain; he wouldn't stop. He felt Jimmy push through the last of his protection, yet somehow, he wasn't afraid.

It was the way he always pictured his own ribs opening to let ghosts step onto the road, only happening in reverse, happening to him as Jimmy pulled him inside and through and he was somewhere else, somewhen else, someone else, entirely.

Jimmy Valentine sits on the tiny stage, washed in overlapping beams of light glowing pale rose and gold. All eyes are on him. No one dares breathe lest they miss a single note plucked from his guitar, lest they intrude upon the rise and fall of his voice as it wends through the crowd and touches each person as if he's singing only for them.

The intimate space is full. Round tables scarcely big enough for one hold groups of three and two so there's no choice but for knees and arms to bump against one another. It's electric and charged, but even in the thrill, there's a dreamy slowness. Up on stage, Jimmy isn't just playing a song, he's weaving a spell. As skin touches skin, heartbeats fall into rhythm. When they finally remember to do so, the crowd breathes as one.

They are so much larger than their individual selves, and no one is alone. They adore Jimmy Valentine. How could they not? They're in love with him, and because he is who he is, he feels the same. Every single one of them is lovely, and he wishes he could give them everything.

The bodies in the room yearn toward him as he lets the final note waver then fade, bowing his head over his guitar and lowering his lashes, smiling his beautiful smile. Between one moment and the next, the attention in the room shifts. It expands. There are other eyes, folded into the shadows. Jimmy sees them in the stillness as he lifts his head just a fraction and peeks up from beneath his lashes. Women with the heads of deer. Men whose cheeks glitter with scales. Soft rabbit ears and feathers, branches and twining leaves. Things neither human nor animal – smoke and bone and storms tucked beneath skin.

Then the moment breaks. Applause sweeps through the room. Someone gasps. He hears a muffled sob, sees faces wet with tears. Whatever else he thought he saw vanishes; the merely human patrons of the club stand and stamp and whistle, and Jimmy allows himself to beam at them. His heart is full to bursting. At the same time, he's lonely, filled with a longing he can't name.

"Thank you." He leans toward the microphone. "You folks go right on enjoying yourselves while I take a short break. I'll be back before you even miss me, I promise."

He stands, ignoring the disappointed groans, the calls for his attention. The two security guards assigned to him for the evening ably do their jobs keeping the crowd away, but Jimmy feels it nonetheless – fingers plucking at him, everyone wanting something from him. He aches to give it to them, all of them, no matter what they want or who they are.

Before the night ends, he will find someone beautiful to take with him. Not home. He scarcely knows where that is anymore, he's lived so many places. But to a hotel. To a place that he can pretend is home for a while, where he will fall utterly in love with the person sharing his bed, before he has to move on again, like autumn folding into winter and melting into spring. Constant restless motion, always keeping going to the next town and the next. He can never stay still.

He'll break the heart of the person in his bed, and he'll break his own in turn, and tomorrow night, it will begin all over again. The promise fills him with equal parts excitement and melancholy. He can't wait to meet whoever it is. He already dreads the thought of saying goodbye. And so, just for now, he needs a moment of quiet, to smoke and look up at the stars.

"Thank you, Rocco. Thank you, Maurice." He makes a point of knowing the names of every handler and bodyguard assigned to him, even if he'll never see either of them again.

He nods at each of them in turn, and they step a discreet distance away to allow him as much privacy as they can. He pats his pockets, looking for the lighter he knows he has tucked away somewhere – a gift from a boy named Aaron with lips like velvet and the shiest, sweetest smile.

"Allow me." The woman melts out of nothing, suddenly there as if she stepped from the shadows into the alleyway holding out her hand.

She wears dark, fitted trousers and a white silk blouse. The soft curl of her auburn hair bounces against her shoulders and her red-black lips know a secret. She looks like every actress who's ever starred opposite him in a film, and so consequently none at all. Her age and features shift every time she moves. Jimmy knows she can't be real, a glamour pulled over something terrible, which only makes him want to know more.

Jimmy puts a cigarette in his mouth. The woman brings the flame closer, cupped directly in the palm of her hand. A brief glimpse of skin the color of new bone and a mouth red as pomegranate juices, teeth like glass knives, a crown rising directly from the woman's skull. There and gone, smoothed over with glamor again; Jimmy Valentine falls in love.

"What is it you want, Jimmy Valentine?" the woman asks. The reflection of the flame cupped in her palm shivers and dances in her eyes. He's falling toward her while standing still.

When he looks side-wise, around the edges of the face in front of him, he sees flickering glimpses of pain. How can those teeth like glass do anything other than hurt her, tucked behind that secret-knowing smile?

"Oh, darlin', I'm so sorry." It's scarcely a conscious thing, pure instinct, when Jimmy reaches out and lays his hand alongside her face.

She startles. The minute fracture through which Jimmy glimpsed her true face widens, running like ice cracking atop a pond. The depths beneath are cold and vast.

Her eyes widen. She no longer looks like every woman who's ever starred opposite him.

He sees a girl whose first lesson was how to starve, sat in front of a feast laced with iron, circled by rowan branches and salt, grown into a weapon, lean and hungry and sharp enough to devour worlds.

He sees her sitting in a shadowed hall, surrounded by the dead, her head bowed under the weight of a terrible crown. Every chair at her table, groaning under its rotten feast, is marked by absence. Their ghosts weigh her down. She can never leave.

She will cut him if he lets her; she will break his heart. This woman whose name he doesn't even know was made for hurting, but he was made for love, and so he doesn't lift his hand from her face.

"What do you want, Jimmy Valentine?" she asks again.

And just for a moment, she leans into his touch, letting her cheek rest in the palm of his hand.

"The better question is, what do you want, darlin'?"

Her hand rises, her fingers ghosting lightly just over his hand where it cups her jaw with something like wonder, then just as quickly she jerks away as if his kindness burns. There's a fixedness to her smile, a dangerous light in her eyes.

"That's okay, you can think on it as long as you need if you don't have an answer for me right now," Jimmy says, undeterred.

He wants to know her, sharp edges and all. He wants to gather up all the quicksilver glimpses of hurting in her and see if he can't fix those broken places, at least for a while. Jimmy lets his hand fall, but steps closer, leaning into her. Smoke from his cigarette threads up between them, but what he smells is animal musk and blood and a river, running fast and wild and cold.

"As for me," he lets the soft burr in his voice stretch like a summer day, inviting and warm, "I reckon I have just about everything I want already, but maybe something will come to me if I think on it for a while."

She lets him kiss her. And for the length of that kiss, he no longer feels like running, and she can almost imagine what it's like to be full.

The queen, no longer looking remotely human, hunches forward in a chair and screams. Her shoulder blades flex and the knobs of her spine press outward against her skin. Her teeth are knives. Her mouth bleeds.

That comes after – but before, she sits with her back against the gnarled trunk of a tree with Jimmy Valentine's head resting in her lap. Fruit, each one like the perfect globe of a full moon, weights down the branches above them. The sky is a cavern, studded with strange-colored stars. The Hollow Queen runs her fingers through the dark of Jimmy's hair and smiles.

He vanished from the alleyway outside the club and stepped into somewhere else. He's been gone for three days. He's lived an entire lifetime here, and it's passed in the blink of an eye, and both stretches – eternity and his too-brief sojourn – are about to come to an end.

From his hair, her fingers trail down to his chest, tracing his ribs, resting lightly over the beat of his heart. She asks the question she's posed to him so many times before, but it's as if she's speaking to herself this time; beneath her touch, he is a puzzle to be solved.

"What do you want, Jimmy Valentine?"

The tips of her nails prick at his skin through the fabric, the faintest pressure applied and in the next moment, removed. As though she's testing him, his solidness, his resolve. He loves her, fully and with all of himself, but he's afraid. He knows better than to answer her by now. If he tells her how he feels, that he only wants to stay with her and make her happy, she will turn his love against him. He's seen enough to know that the fae were not made to love, and her least of all. Yet he still has hope, he wants to believe there is more in her.

"You—" he starts to say, and she lays a hand against his throat, stopping his words.

It might be a mercy, or a warning, he can't tell. She leans closer, her eyes black all the way to the edges.

"So much life," she murmurs. "So much of everything, all inside of you."

Her hand moves lower, splayed across his belly. The sky tilts. The Hollow Queen brushes her lips across his, and her touch is like ice. When she draws back, petals the same moon color as the fruit, drifting down around them, all turn to ash. Jimmy feels it, the moment his queen makes her choice, sets her course, and he goes still beneath her touch, his pulse rabbiting against her hand; he is nothing but prey.

There's a feeling like hunger, only worse, like all he's ever known is starvation and he'll never be happy again. The life he was meant to live, all the songs he was going to write, everything he had left to do, spools out of him beneath the queen's touch.

"What did you do?"

"Shhh." The Hollow Queen puts a finger to her lips. With the other hand, she gathers what looks like a skein of silver thread. Except now it looks more like a flame, or a tangle of roots, or a bundle of feathers. Jimmy sits up, gazing at it in wonder. It's familiar somehow, but he can't for the life of him think why.

When the sound comes, he feels it first in his bones, behind his sternum, across his ribcage, all up and down his spine, filling every part of him. The note shivers, becomes a cry, becomes the awful, lonely sound of a horn blowing far away.

"Now," the queen says, "it's time for you to run."

Jimmy scrambles up, his only impulse to get away from the hunger in her eyes. The long grasses trip him up, but when he falls, it isn't onto the dew-wet ground of a fae orchard, but onto a city street. A car horn blares; the sound twists into something else, a thing that doesn't belong to this world. He hears the thunder of hooves and rolls to the side, narrowly avoids being run over.

Blinking marquee lights assault his eyes. He's utterly dazed until someone says his name.

"It's Jimmy Valentine!"

The cry repeats. A crowd surges around him, hands steadying him and tugging at him even as they help him stand. Wasn't he just outside a club in Port Astor, lighting a cigarette? Now, desert air sears his lungs.

There was an orchard and petals and his heart is broken and it's all too much.

He recognizes the Golden Nugget and the Grand. So, he's in Siegleville, thousands of miles away from where he last stood, and he has no idea how. He desperately wants to go home, but he doesn't know where that is anymore. There's something missing; his chest aches.

There's something terrible following him.

"Mr. Valentine? Are you hurt? What happened?"

He doesn't have any answers. The only thing he knows is that he needs to run.

"I can't. I'm sorry." The words trail over his shoulder as he shoves his way through the concerned press of bodies, wishing he could be gentler, knowing he cannot.

Murmurs turn into voices shouting after him. Beneath the concern, Jimmy hears the clatter of hooves again, and the roar of an engine. His heart is beating too fast, too hard. *Wally*. He needs to call Wally, his manager. He'll know what to do.

"There's a storm coming," Jimmy babbles, clutching at the receiver pressed to his ear.

He's in a hotel lobby, sweat drying on his skin. Lost moments of time have skipped away from him, but Wally's voice is on the other end of the line and Jimmy clings to it like a man drowning.

"What's happening, kid? Where are you? Hang on and I'll send someone to get you."

Jimmy tells Wally as best he can while also leaving out everything that matters. Clouds pile on the horizon. They press against the walls of the hotel while Jimmy waits in the manager's office, shaking. No one else seems to see them; the shadows swarming on the edges of his vision appear only for him.

They make it hard to concentrate, hard to hear when

people ask him questions. Jimmy allows himself to be hustled across the lobby and into a car while curious faces peer at him through the glass. The faces blur and refuse to resolve. They become things with feathers, fur, and horns. He's in the fae lands and the queen is hollowing him out all over again, drawing the very essence of him through his skin. The things he was meant to be, everything he had left to do – she's taking it and spinning it into something new and frightened and Jimmy feels himself stretched between worlds.

It's time to run again.

When he does, it's away from the doctors Wally insists he see. He can't tell them what they want to know, how to help him. There's a thorn pierced through his tongue and all the important words he tries to say taste like blood.

Jimmy cancels his shows and sits in a dark hotel room with a guitar on his lap, picking out notes that he can't quite make into a song. There are trees the color of ash under a sky the color of bone and a road that runs straight between them like an arrow drawn in chalk. He was meant to live forever, but death nips at his heels.

He runs and runs and when he finds himself behind the wheel of a car in the dead of night with engines on either side of him growling like ravening wolves, he isn't at all surprised. It doesn't matter that he can't remember why he's here, or where here even is. All that matters is the horizon ahead of him, a straight shot and if he can make it, he might finally be free.

A flag snaps, or he thinks it does, but he can't tell. Rain slams against the hood of the car as his foot sinks on the gas and he throws wildly between gears. Between each flash of light as the clouds crack wide overhead, he sees them. The hunt. Stags made of stripped bone, their antlers hung with red streamers of their own flesh stitched with chiming bells. Teeth and hunger, blazing embers and billowing clouds of smoke, all of it closing in on every side. The queen rides at the head of it all, a spear, a knife, a bow in her hand.

The gears whine and gnash and he nearly misses the clutch. A bark from the engine becomes the baying of hounds. The tires slip; Jimmy tries to wrestle the wheel back under control, but it spins out of his hands. The horizon is no longer empty. It's full of metal and glass slamming into him, stopping his heart, turning the world upside down.

A long, mournful note calls the hunt to an end. The part of him that is roots and feathers and a tangle of might-have-beens caught up in the long, pale hands of a queen shivers and keens. Even worlds away, it is tied to him. Tying him down to this spot, where he's dying. It will become a memorial, a shrine, flowers piled up across the road so that crews will have to clear them every hour for days just so traffic can flow. All that love and grief will bind his ghost here. It doesn't matter where his bones are buried. He will be a saint, a beacon, a way for the Hollow Queen to find a way into the world.

Unless...

There's a white road beneath his feet, crushed chalk as soft as dust. Jimmy Valentine is dead, but that doesn't matter one bit. He runs.

20

"Where are we going? Slow down."

Dee shouted to be heard as they ran pell-mell through the rain. Belle's boots slipped in the mud, long, wet grass whipping around her legs. Water stung her eyes and plastered her hair against her face, making it even harder to see. She had no answers for her sister, no clear idea of where they were going. Instead of responding, she tightened her grip on Dee's hand, focusing on getting her sister away, not thinking what might be behind them, barreling down the hill from the old barn.

The light, shrieking in pain, Belizial making the same sound, the two of them – demon and light – briefly intertwined. Ava, falling.

"Belle!" Dee shouted. "What happened?"

What happened? (I killed a girl.) Where are we going? (I don't know. Away. Away. Away.)

Dee tried to halt her sister's progress. Belizial wanted to get away as much as Belle did, perhaps more. They weren't simply running from the barn, from the light. They were running from the hells, the sulfur stench choking the air while their skin burned. Past, blurring into the present. Their combined force dragged Dee onward.

Running from the horde of lesser demons that howled in pursuit. Running from the wild hunt. They'd found safety with the Hollow Queen, but it hadn't lasted. She'd used them, she'd hurt them, and always the light had been there, shivering and watching over her shoulder. So much pain and wanting and now it was here and—

"Answer me, damn it!" Dee threw her weight back, digging her heels into the mud, and that – combined with her frustrated curse – made Belle stop.

"What?" Dee held Belle's shoulders and shook her, making Belle look her in the eye.

"I don't know." It hurt to admit it aloud. Since the night she'd run – since the night Dee had refused to come with her – she'd never wanted to look back. She'd never wanted to display the faintest hint of doubt – nothing her sister or her parents could use to prove they'd been right. She knew exactly what she was doing and where she was going.

Except she didn't.

"We need…" Belle faltered.

It was hard to catch her breath. Ava fell in an endless loop behind her eyes: the sickening crack, the boneless slump to the floor. She'd torn demons apart without a second thought and devoured them. She'd defended herself against people who were trying to hurt her.

This was different. Ava hadn't been a threat. She was barely more than a child, caught up in something bigger than herself, something that frightened even Belizial. Ava had been innocent.

"Alright. Here." Dee said. "Let's get out of the rain, for a start."

She turned Belle, pointing her toward a narrow track cutting through the field to their left and shoving her forward. The drive curved around a cluster of trees, revealing a farmhouse smaller than Dee's painted a dusty blue.

"The Kennetts live here. You remember them? They had that old cow you used to try to scare by throwing stones. Anyway, I'm pretty sure I saw them up at the barn with Clarence. We can regroup here, and you can tell me what the hell is going on."

Belle allowed herself to be prodded up to the blue house's narrow front porch. She remembered the cow. She'd never meant anything by her behavior, except for maybe she had, because her parents already thought she was wicked. Why not be the monster everyone thought she was? If they were afraid of her, if she was hateful, it would hurt less not being loved.

Belizial flinched. Belle pushed the feeling away. Her immediate flight instinct had started to fade, and everything felt heavy, shoulders sloping, limbs dragging.

Rain drummed on the porch overhang. Dee stretched up on her toes, sweeping her fingers across the lintel over the door and coming away with a key. She fit it into the lock, ushering Belle inside.

The front room looked much like Dee's: a blue couch patterned with white flowers and draped with doilies, matching wing-backed chairs, polished cherrywood end tables, emptiness stretching through every floor. Presumably, it had only been a few days since the Kennetts decamped to join Clarence, yet their absence permeated the house.

Dee led her through to the kitchen. A ginger tabby seated on the table paused in licking its raised front paw. Golden eyes regarded them haughtily. Belle found herself holding her breath. Absurd as it was, she imagined the cat telling on them, yowling to alert someone to their presence.

Dee made a *pss pss* sound, holding out her hand. The cat dropped heavily onto the floor and sauntered over, rubbing against Dee's legs, butting its head into her outstretched hand and accepting the tribute of attention it was due.

"Morris is a good cat," Dee said distractedly, her voice stretched thin.

"Yes." Belle couldn't think of what else to say, wild laughter just behind her teeth.

Ava fell again and again. She'd killed a girl. She'd killed a girl. She'd–

Did she know for sure Ava was dead? Could she have survived the fall? She wanted to believe so, but the horrid crack as she'd come to a halt, the lifeless glaze in her eyes, made the hope a lie.

"Ava's dead." Belle pulled out the nearest kitchen chair and sat heavily.

Dee straightened, staring at her. "What?"

"She fell." Belle swallowed hard. She couldn't bear to say

the rest, not now, with the way Dee was looking at her. "She was... I don't think she was carrying Clarence's child. There was something... else inside her. I don't know what exactly. It's still there, in the barn, but Ava is gone."

Dee came around to the other side of the table and dropped into the chair opposite Belle's.

"You'd better start over," she said. "Slowly. And tell me all that again."

Belle dropped her head into her hands. Gods, she didn't want to do this, any of this. She tried to dig her fingers into her wet curls, but the pins got in the way and only ended up tangling painfully when she tried to pull free.

"I don't even know where to start," she said.

"Try."

She felt Dee watching her and Belle raised her head. She expected judgement, anger maybe. What she saw was exhaustion and impatience, but beneath it, the will to understand. Her sister was frustrated with her, and rightly so; after promising to help, all Belle had done was push her away.

"You're not going to believe me." Belle lowered her hands, set them flat on the table.

"Tell me anyway, and I'll decide what to believe."

Dee rested her arms on the table, crossed and leaning on them, a posture that was somehow at once defensive and open.

"Belizial, my demon," Belle said, and paused.

She waited for a reprimand, an intake of breath, or lips pressed into a thin line of disapproval. None of that occurred and she let herself relax the tiniest measure before going on, feeling Dee's attention, but directing her words toward her hands on the table rather than looking her sister in the eye.

"Before we found each other, they were imprisoned by someone who hurt them very badly. They trusted that person and she tortured them. The light we saw in the barn is something to do with her, the Hollow Queen. She's one of the fae, maybe the last one, I don't know. She's the reason all the rest of them are gone – dead or deep in hiding. It shouldn't be possible for that light to be here. I'm not even sure what it is exactly – the queen's herald, her fetch? I do know it isn't anything good. I'm afraid it means the Hollow Queen is trying to get through to our world, somehow. Belizial is afraid that whatever else she might want, she'll also try to drag them back with her, turn them into a weapon. When the light reached for them, they lashed out, and... Ava fell."

Belle felt like a coward. Aloud, it was at once too much and not enough, sanitized to omit her role in Ava's death, in failing to protect Belizial, letting things get out of hand. She braced herself, expecting dismissal, disbelief, but when she risked a glance at her sister, all she saw was Dee trying to decide what to say.

It surprised Belle when Dee looked down, considering her hands. Her arms were uncrossed now. Instead of chewing on the skin around her thumb, she picked at it with her fingernail, which looked no less painful.

"I'm sorry," Dee said. It was the last thing Belle had expected. "I didn't know."

Belle opened her mouth, closed it again. How – why – was Dee apologizing to her when Belle was the one who'd broken everything? Again.

"You could have told me, you know, before now." Dee raised her head, fixing Belle with a look that held disappointment, but mostly regret.

"You never wanted to know. Anytime I tried to talk about Belizial, you shut down."

There was the pinched expression she'd been expecting earlier. Dee crossed her arms again, this time hugged around her upper body, her fingers tucked beneath her armpits like they were cold. They were both still soaking wet, dripping all over the Kennetts' kitchen floor.

"I would have told you if I thought you'd listen." Belle caught her voice rising.

It was all unraveling again, slipping through her fingers. Morris rubbed against her leg under the table, heedless of her wet skirt. She flinched at the contact and, offended, the cat stalked away.

"Can you blame me? It took you away from me. Of course I didn't like it or trust it. Why should I?"

Belle stared at her sister, the tight lines of her body. Gods, they were both so stubborn and stupid. She couldn't help it – laughter broke from her.

"How is this funny?" Dee snapped.

Belle shook her head, trying to bring herself under control. "You said almost the same thing to me about Clarence. Or, the spirit is the same. You said I never gave him a chance, and why should I? He took you away from me. We're talking past each other, and we're both idiots."

Dee seemed less amused. Belle understood, beneath the laughter scraping her throat raw, the bruise remained.

It wasn't remotely funny at all. She splayed her fingers on the table, pressed down hard on the wood, and kept them there.

"I was always going to leave," she said. "Whether Belizial found me or not. They had nothing to do with me going."

She felt Dee fuming without having to look at her, and she felt her relent as well, her shoulders slumping.

"And I was always going to stay."

"I know," Belle said softly.

It hurt. It shouldn't, not this much, not still, but it did.

"What do we do now?" Belle lifted her hands from the table and dropped them into her lap.

Damp outlines remained, like ghosts, then faded.

"We try to get some sleep," Dee said. "We're no good to ourselves or each other this exhausted. No one knows where we are. When our heads are clearer in the morning, we'll figure out what comes next."

She stood, a decisive motion bringing the conversation to an end. Belle felt the impulse to grab her sister's hand, but she kept her fingers knotted together in her lap. At some point, she'd taken off her gloves. She didn't remember exactly when she'd done so, and had no idea where they were now.

"I'm sure we can find some clothes to change into while ours dry."

Belle made herself stand, trailing listlessly after her sister as Dee climbed the stairs. She reached for Belizial out of habit. They didn't pull away, but they didn't reach back for her either, curled into a ball so tight she imagined their spine becoming a permanent knot.

A door to the right at the top of the stairs revealed a small bathroom tiled in black and white, with a deep clawfoot tub. The next door on the left appeared to be the Kennetts' bedroom. Dee opened the last door at the end of the hall, and stilled.

Belle peered over her shoulder. Where the rest of the house was pin-neat, haphazard piles of boxes and furniture crowded this space, draped in shadows. Tucked all the way at the back of the room sat a crib. Dee's gaze remained fixed there, her back rigid and her shoulders tight.

Ghosts were Brix's specialty, but Belle knew for certain the Kennetts had never had a child living with them in this house. As the realization settled around her shoulders, she felt a small, cold hand slipped into hers. She flinched, immediately wishing she hadn't as the sensation vanished.

Dee stepped back, and Belle had to move so her sister wouldn't tread on her foot as she closed the door with a definitive click.

"You should take the master bedroom," Belle said quickly. She should have said something else, something kinder, but those were the words that rushed awkwardly to her tongue.

"What about you?" A faint, unmistakable husk roughened Dee's voice, but it was too late; the moment had already slipped away.

No, the moment was years past. If Dee had lost a child, Belle should know, but she didn't, and that was too vast a rift to close. She tilted her head back, blinking. A trap door set flush with the ceiling over their heads dangled a cord down invitingly.

"I'll see if there's anything up in the attic. if not, I'll take the couch downstairs. It's fine."

Running again.

She hurried over the words again, wondering if Dee heard the guilt in her voice. Whether or not she did, her sister didn't protest, drifting back down the hall. Belle followed her into the Kennetts' room long enough to hastily grab an undershirt and a pair of loose undershorts – the first items that came to hand – bundling them against her chest as she retreated.

"Goodnight, Belle."

Before she could respond, Dee closed the door. Belle stood in the hallway a moment longer, staring at the white-painted wood, willing it to open again.

She slunk down the hall to the bathroom, shivering as she stripped out of her wet clothes and hung them in the tub, pulling on the borrowed clothes as quietly as she could. She flinched when the hinges shrieked as she tugged the cord to lower the trap and the attic stairs unfolded. No sound of stirring from behind the closed bedroom door. Belle let out a breath and listened for her sister.

Nothing.

She might as well be in the house alone.

21

Brix's head spun.

He'd been there with Jimmy, closer than his shadow, in the club and in the fae lands. When Jimmy sang, Brix had felt it in his throat and in his lungs. Even now, the notes echoed in his bones.

He pulled himself back with an effort, untangling his thoughts from Jimmy's, reminding himself who and where he was. He ached, wishing he could gather Jimmy up and keep him safe, but everything he'd seen had happened nearly fifteen years ago, though it felt as fresh as a new wound.

"When you make a person for that kind of hurting," Jimmy said, "they can't just stop. You can put a sword on a shelf after war ends, but it will never stop being a sword. Now do you understand, Mr. Brix?"

Silver screen eyes met his, full of sorrow.

Brix let out a breath. "I think so?"

Honestly, he wasn't certain he understood anything at all. They were still in the ballroom, he was still dancing in Jimmy Valentine's arms, which in itself shouldn't be possible, but now his head was full of things he absolutely shouldn't know: the taste of pomegranates from the Hollow Queen's mouth and the feeling of dying in a car crash while being pursued by the wild hunt.

He'd heard stories of the string of broken hearts Jimmy Valentine regularly left in his wake. Now, he felt how every one of those breakings had shattered Jimmy's heart in turn. A lonely idol, always running, finding home briefly, before running again.

Even when he died, some part of Jimmy had remained with the Hollow Queen, keeping him from ever being able to fully rest. That stolen potential, stripped from him, had been made into something new. A link. A queen made of hunger, who could use longing to make holes in the world. And there was so damned much wanting here in the Peony Hotel, in Port Astor, hells, in Arcadia. All of them were skins scabbing over an older, deeper, infinitely patient world.

A rich man who wanted to speak to the dead. Two kids in a hotel room who wanted to say hello to a movie star. And a man who knew far better who wanted his wife back so badly, he'd pulled her through the door that was only meant to be crossed in one direction. Brix had left a wound behind, as sure as John Jacobs Astor had building this hotel; as sure as the fae had leaving the city; and as sure as Virgil and Leonie had, calling Jimmy Valentine back from the bone road.

"How do you stop from wanting things?" He hadn't meant to say it out loud.

"I wish I knew." Jimmy said. "It's the gift and curse of being human, I suppose. But then again, I'm not so sure I'm human anymore." He sighed. "All that time I was with her, I think the Hollow Queen was trying to teach me to become a thing like her. I don't know if she wanted a lover, or a weapon, or both at the same time. Maybe she just didn't want to be alone. Maybe I shouldn't have listened when she told me to run. Promise me something, Mr. Brix? Keep Virgil and Leonie safe. They're good kids, and none of this is their fault."

Just like before, Jimmy was saying more than his words, and one of those things was *goodbye.*

"I know."

Promise.

The word battered against his heart. He felt it loop over and around him, binding him before he even answered.

"I promise."

The colossal unfairness of it all landed on him at once, threatening to crush the breath from his lungs. Not just the unfairness of Jimmy's life cut short, but of the fact that it should be Abby here in his arms, not Jimmy Valentine. He could never kiss her goodnight, never even take her hand. He'd pushed the rules to the limit. Jimmy Valentine had skated past them like they didn't exist.

And the worst of it was, he hadn't even meant to. All he'd ever done was love too much and too deeply.

The truly horrible bit though was that all Brix had to do was step aside and let the haunting continue. He could have everything he wanted here in the Peony. He could have Abigail back. Dancing with him in the ballroom, walking in the greenhouse between fragrant blooms, holed up in a suite as if they were as young as Virgil and Leonie, without a care in the world.

What did it matter that they'd never been married? This could be their honeymoon. Soft sheets rumpled against his skin, champagne and strawberries ordered up from room service, sweet and sparkling on his tongue. That hidden fountain splashing somewhere he couldn't see as Abby walked ahead of him on the winding pathway of mosaic tiles, looking back and smiling her crooked smile, holding out her hand.

It would be so damned easy.

Brix's ribs ached, the chill of the bone road pressed up against him. All he had to do was hold out his hand. Close his fingers. *Pull.*

"Syd?"

A wind blew through Abigail's voice, tattering it. In the torn gaps left behind, Brix heard fear. Just like the first time he'd called her back; just like the first time, he held on. It was selfish and it hurt and every part of him was cold doing it, but he didn't stop. Couldn't. As if she'd ghosted right through him, Abby – his Abby – looked out at him from Jimmy Valentine's eyes.

"Where are... What is this place?"

The mirrored walls, the shifting surface of the floor, the chandeliers overhead all flickered. Brix fought to keep Abby in sight. He'd done it, he'd brought her here, but it was like looking at her through thick glass, or under the surface of a quick-flowing stream. Abby's eyes, when she was alive, had been a warm hazel, brightened by the fresh green of spring. The Abby in front of him now looked back at him through river stones, slick black and wet. Her lips trembled, holding back hunger, hiding pointed teeth, smeared with blood.

"Syd, it hurts." Her voice wobbled, unraveled further.

It wasn't her. She wasn't here, she never had been, but even so, he was hurting her. Brix couldn't seem to stop hurting her. He'd been doing it since she died.

Memory sucked the breath from Brix's lungs. Abby's fear became his own, his pulse running rabbit fast. A hand pressed against the door within him, demanding entry. Hunger that would never stop.

What looked back at Brix now wasn't anything human.

The fae queen leaned toward him, towered over him. Her crown gleamed like ice, leaving Brix just as cold. Her lips peeled to reveal needle teeth. The sound they made as her mouth opened wider, like shards of glass rubbing one against the other, was the worst thing he'd ever heard.

Brix reeled back, tripped over his heels and landed hard on the floor. Except the room was flooding. Waves slapped at him, his face wet with salt spray.

"Mr. Brix?" Virgil blinked down at him.

He'd ended up right back where he'd started, Jimmy no longer at his side, but at the piano, as if he'd never danced with Brix and shown him horrors.

Virgil helped him up. His clothes were sodden, clinging to him. Impossible as it was, the water filling the ballroom was very real.

Shit. *Shitshitshit.* He'd let himself get distracted, let temptation gnaw at him when his defenses were already paper thin. He'd blundered right up to the edge, doing the fae queen's work for her. All because he wanted Abigail back. Because he couldn't let her go.

"We have to get out of here." Brix grabbed Virgil's arm. "I'm dangerous in this place, and I'm afraid you are, too."

"What about Jimmy and Leonie? We can't leave them." The space around them stuttered: a cavern, a forest, a labyrinth, the Peony's own fae-gifted greenhouse. The figures around them changed, too, ignoring the niceties of inconvenient things like gravity, personal space, reality. Bodies overlapped and occasionally sunk halfway through the floor and walls. Clusters of dancers hung from the ceiling. Some unfurled wings. Some had too many eyes, and some had none at all.

"No, of course not."

He'd promised, and even if he hadn't, he couldn't leave them behind. He had to get them all back to the room, somehow, and then... He didn't know. They'd have to figure things out when they got there.

"I'm sorry, Virgil." Gods, he was tired, letting the words slip with more honesty than he intended. "The truth is, this thing that we're up against, it's huge. I don't know how to stop it, not alone. I promise I'll explain as much as I can, eventually, but right now, we need to get Jimmy and Leonie back to the room and once we're there, I'm going to need your help."

"To do what?"

"That's the catch, luv." Brix moved, tugging Virgil with

him as he waded against the tide toward the piano. "I don't know. We're going to have to make it up as we go along."

Virgil's mouth opened, then clamped shut. He nodded, determination in the set of his jaw – a mask pulled over uncertainty.

The music swelled alongside the water, swirling up to their knees. Jimmy's fingers inside Leonie's skin flew over the keys, blurring. He glowed like pale fire, a matinee idol, a silver screen god in danger of burning everything around him. Whatever the fae queen had taken out of him, it tied her to him, left a space inside him that some small part of her could occupy. Brix couldn't imagine Jimmy doing anything to hurt Virgil and Leonie, meaning he wasn't the one currently in control.

As if to prove the point, Jimmy threw his head – Leonie's head – violently back. Flames wreathed the piano, tongues of it whipping outward so that even the water burned.

Brix glanced over his shoulder. "Still with me?"

Virgil's expression was grim and determined. Brix didn't like the seed of an idea growing in him, but it was the only one he had. If he was going to save them, he had to put all of them in danger first.

"If you can get to them, you're our best chance," he said.

Virgil didn't ask him to clarify, and that only made Brix feel worse. He had to look away from the hope and desperate love in the boy's eyes when his gaze found Jimmy and Leonie.

Brix glanced up instead, then immediately regretted it. The dead who clustered along the ceiling yearned toward

Jimmy with pure hunger for the music that swore it would pull them back into the world. The first of them dropped uncomfortably close to Brix, cold brushing against him, through him, his bones creaking and heavy with frost. More and more followed, splashing into the water without a sound.

Luminous shapes swirled in the tide. Brix couldn't tell if they were stars or flowers or the grasping hands of the dead. Ghosts tangled around his legs like weeds, making it even harder to walk.

"I can reach them," Virgil said.

He sloshed past Brix. It was exactly what he'd wanted the boy to do, but that didn't stop Brix's heart tripping over itself. Ghosts caught at his sleeves, his pantlegs, slowing him down and leaving Virgil on his own.

There wasn't a damn thing Brix could do to help him anyway. He'd left his satchel back in the room; he had none of his tools. Salt, iron, nails left to cure by moonlight in a churchyard. He didn't even have the burnt cork he'd used to trace marks of protection throughout the room upstairs.

"Leonie!" Virgil shouted. "Jimmy!"

A fresh swell of water pushed him back, sending him tumbling into Brix. He tried to brace the boy, but his shoes slipped against the floor. He only barely managed to stay upright, hands on Virgil's shoulders.

"Let me go." Virgil shook him off, although Brix hadn't been holding him back.

The piano was a storm now, Jimmy and Leonie its eye. A wave swamped Brix, and he went under, losing sight of Virgil and everything else as the ceiling and the floor exchanged places. He became one of the ghosts, unable to obey the laws of gravity as he tumbled end over end. He'd never learned to swim, despite the duck pond. Something to add to his list, if he survived.

The water was only waist high. He managed to fight off panic long enough to get his legs back under him, gasping and spitting saltwater. He stood, pushing stinging, wet curls from his eyes.

Virgil had nearly reached the piano.

"Hold on to them!" Brix shouted to be heard above the storm. "Jimmy isn't fully himself right now, but you can help him remember."

Jimmy's song rose in volume, shuddering crystals free from the chandelier to drop into the water. Brix ignored the hard rain, fighting his way forward again. He wondered what the guests and staff in the rest of the Peony heard. Phantom hands playing piano keys, or the world coming to an end?

"Jimmy, please," Virgil called from the edge of the storm. "Leonie is still all wrapped up with you. You have to keep her safe."

He paused, glancing back at Brix for reassurance.

"Keep going!"

"Leonie," Virgil called. "I know you're still in there. You have to help Jimmy. You have to bring him back."

Jimmy turned his head, or Leonie turned hers. They blurred, the shuddering frames of a film, a candle wavering.

"She's—" Jimmy's voice ghosted through Leonie's mouth, a poorly tuned radio fading in and out, shot through with static. "I'm trying to hold her. I'm sorry."

Leonie's face rose to the surface again, overtaking Jimmy's, her lips peeled back like a dog snarling over a bone. It struck Brix that Jimmy hadn't just meant he was holding on to the fae queen, or trying. He'd been so focused on his own hurt, on Abigail and his desire to bring her back, he'd forgotten Leonie's pain – how hard she would fight for Jimmy, how fiercely she wanted to keep him here.

The kind of wanting a hungry fae queen could dig into and amplify until it overwhelmed everything else.

"Keep talking," Brix said. "Focus on Leonie. Distract her. And if you can get close enough, put your arms around them. Don't let go, no matter what happens."

Doubt shone in Virgil's eyes. "What do I say?"

"I don't know." Brix wished he had a better answer. "Anything."

Jimmy's hands never faltered on the keys. The music kept pouring from him, his eyes burning. He wore a forlorn expression, as if he would stop if he could, like he would run to Virgil and throw his arms around him.

"I'm here," Virgil said. He drew his shoulders back, licked his lips, and pitched his voice louder. "I'm not leaving you, either of you. We're going to figure this out. Together."

Leonie shuddered, her eyes locking on Virgil. "I can't—"

"I know." There were tears in Virgil's voice as he gathered himself and went on. "Just focus on me. Remember the day we met? The first day of classes. It was pouring rain, and we got soaked looking for Victoria Hall. Eventually, we'd missed so much of the lecture that you took me to your dorm room instead to dry off. You said I looked like a drowned rat, you made us toasted cheese sandwiches on the electric plate you weren't supposed to have and then we—"

Virgil's voice broke, throat bobbing. In the false twilight of the room, Brix was fairly certain he was blushing.

"Come back to me," he said. "Please."

"Virgil."

Just his name, so small and frightened and full of hurt.

It was all the encouragement Virgil needed to throw himself over the last bit of distance between them. His arms went around Leonie, around Jimmy, half tackle, half hug.

Jimmy had been in the dark so long, had spent so long running through the hollow places of the world. Brix wondered if Leonie had, too.

Virgil's lips were at Leonie's ear, whispering to her, whispering to Jimmy. Brix couldn't hear, but the words weren't meant for him. What he heard in their place were the things he'd whispered to Abby at the end, holding on to her hand as it grew colder, no weight to it at all.

Stay, please. Don't leave me here. I can't do this alone.

Brix swallowed, blinked, unable to blame the saltwater – and was startled to see Jimmy Valentine looking straight at him. Leonie remained locked in the circle of Virgil's arms, rigid and shaking. Jimmy was there too, but he was also outside, looking at Brix. Movie star eyes, the eyes of a silver screen god, full of light and pain.

"She's here," Jimmy said. "I'm trying, but..."

"Can you get us back to the room?"

"I—" A flinch, like a spike of pain shot through Jimmy, cutting off his words.

"Your mother was right," Brix said. "No one can take the music from you. But you can choose to let it go."

Jimmy seemed to understand. His expression was sorrowful, but he pulled himself upright, pulling himself back inside Leonie.

"Leonie, darlin', you have to let go, too." The words were soft, but Brix heard them over the tide. "Virgil's got us. It's okay."

"I—" Leonie's voice broke, became a wail.

Virgil's arms tightened around her, and Jimmy's too, inside her skin.

"Now!" Brix shouted.

Jimmy wrenched his hands away from the piano – it looked like it physically hurt him – and the world lurched sideways. The accordion of impossible corridors snapped in on itself. The ballroom that was a cavern and a greenhouse and a forest vanished. Brix staggered to catch himself on the edge of the bed in Virgil and Leonie's hotel room.

Like survivors of a shipwreck, Virgil and Leonie and Jimmy knelt in the center of the bed, sheets rucked wildly around them, clinging to each other, all three of them sopping wet, miserable and shivering. Virgil kissed Leonie kissed Jimmy, dug fingers into her damp shag and his perfect coif, ruined by the waves.

"Come back to me," Virgil begged. "Please."

He pressed his forehead against Leonie's, and she leaned into him in turn. Jimmy ghosted through Leonie's skin, turning to look at Brix even as Leonie and Virgil remained facing each other. It was unnerving in more ways than one.

The eyes meeting Brix's didn't belong to a god, or an idol – just a sad, beautiful man saying goodbye, one more time.

"You'll keep your promise to look after them?"

Brix didn't hesitate. "Yes."

"I don't know if it'll be enough, but I'll hold her as long as I can."

The sorrow in Jimmy's voice was unmistakable. Brix felt the meeting of lips in a dark alleyway, the love and everything it had become afterward. All Jimmy had ever wanted was to hold the Hollow Queen. Maybe in his death and all his time running, he'd finally become enough to soothe her hunger and pain, but regardless, he would try, because he loved Virgil and Leonie too. He would do anything he could to keep them from further harm.

"Thank you." It wasn't adequate, not even remotely close.

Virgil and Leonie either hadn't heard Jimmy's words, or they hadn't registered them. It was one small mercy at least. Jimmy sank back into Leonie so that his forehead rested against Virgil's now too, the three of them together for one last time.

Brix found the charred cork where he'd left it, stepped closer to the bed. His hand shook.

Stay with me, don't go. I can't do this alone.

It wasn't fair to ask this of them. But nothing about death had ever been fair.

"I'm sorry, darlin'. I wish I could—"

"You can't," Leonie snapped at Jimmy, at Virgil, then turned to shout at Brix. "You can't take him!"

Jimmy murmured in Leonie's ear, the way Virgil had moments before. "It's the only way."

Leonie clapped her hands over her ears, as though she could stop the words and make them untrue. Tears glazed her eyes, falling as she squeezed them shut, shaking her head in violent denial. Virgil still held her, Jimmy as well, their arms a circle around her.

Brix wanted to look away from their grief, but he owed it to them not to. Kids this young shouldn't hurt this hard. No one should be asked to choose what day they would let their lover, their best friend, the most important person in their world, go.

"I'm sorry," he said.

They all ignored him.

He used the charred cork to sketch rough symbols across the sheets surrounding the three of them. The candles they'd left burning in the room still flickered, improbably bright. Neither the marks on the walls nor the sheets felt like enough, but it was the best he could do.

It would still hurt. Like ripping a tree from its roots, like physically tearing the lovers on the bed limb from limb.

A thrum ran along Brix's ribs, like a hand knocking, a delicate brush of power along the curve of his bones. The door inside him wanted to open. The bone road wanted to unfurl. He had no idea what would happen when Jimmy crossed over that threshold a second time. He could only hope that it would be enough – that if Jimmy went back willingly, it wouldn't be for nothing.

"It's time," he said. The ink on his arms gleamed wet in the dim light, like fresh blood.

Jimmy broke from the embrace. He was ready.

Leonie was not. "You can't. You can't!"

She lunged within the circle of Virgil's arms, trying to claw her way across the bed. Charcoal smudged on the white sheets, symbols blurred and twisting. Leonie hissed in pain. Her eyes shone red – she was a haunting in her anger and grief, hollow and hungry. The perfect doorway for a patient queen.

"Hold her," Brix shouted.

A wind swept through the room, grave-cold, stirring the pages of the pamphlet Brix had slipped under the door. The paper rattled like birds taking flight. Heavy curtains billowed inward. A glass tipped over and shattered. In the corner of the room, a solid chair scraped a few inches across the floor.

Pain lanced across Brix's side, like Leonie had physically tried to slam shut the opening door. Like she'd tried to destroy it utterly, and Brix with it. His breath caught. He wrapped an arm around himself, half expecting his side to be wet with blood, but there was nothing.

Virgil tightened his grip on Leonie. Brix could see he wouldn't let go, no matter what happened. He almost regretted telling Virgil to do it, but he couldn't think of any other way. Alone, he wasn't enough to save them.

Leonie's eyes went pure white, ghost light shining in them. It reminded him of Abby at the dining room table; she was coming undone. A sound like cracking ice, like snapping bone filled the room, followed by a pained cry.

Virgil's eyes widened. "Leonie, stop! You're hurting him."

Jimmy. Brix felt it too, the shudder that rippled through the ghost inside Leonie as she unwittingly crushed him out of the way, seizing control.

Leonie swung on Virgil, savage, raking her nails across his cheek and drawing blood. Her head snapped back, and she let out another inhuman wail.

"Leonie, please," Virgil pleaded.

The ghosts had her now. Her body shook, bucking and trembling. One of her elbows caught Virgil's midsection, but he didn't let go. Jimmy held her too, both wrapped around her, and still she fought, twisting and wild.

Brix climbed onto the bed, which shuddered beneath him, and he struggled to keep his balance. It rose a few inches before slamming back to the floor, trying to throw him off. Leonie's head tossed from side to side, but he managed to press the burnt cork to her skin long enough to draw a single ragged symbol of protection on her forehead.

Then he threw his arms around all three of them, ignoring the bone-splintering cold of the ghost leeching into him. His heart broke for them. Leonie was right: he was a hypocrite. He didn't deserve the mercy of this working, but he hoped for it anyway.

He closed his eyes, holding as tight as he could, trying to hold them all together one last time. All at once, the fight went out of Leonie. She slumped, Virgil's body holding her up. Brix wished he could take their pain. But the only thing he could do was open a way.

He'd done as much for hundreds of ghosts over the years. It hurt, every single time.

"Time to go," he murmured against Jimmy's hair, against Virgil's hair, Leonie's.

Tears wet his cheeks, but Brix couldn't let go to wipe them

away. He was large enough to encompass them, a doorway for Jimmy to step through. He had to be.

He let the road unfurl, stretching to the far horizon, his ribs an archway. He reached for Jimmy, bound inside Leonie's skin, bound within Virgil's heart, feeling along all the places they were knotted together.

"You have to let go, darlin'," Jimmy said. Words for Leonie, or Virgil, or both. Maybe even for himself.

Brix felt knots loosening, the places where Jimmy had anchored inside Leonie's skin giving way. Jimmy sang as he did it, soft and sweet like a lullaby, a song to say goodbye. A love song. A ballad. It wasn't anything Brix recognized, but he felt it resonating inside of him.

As if harmonizing with himself, Brix heard Jimmy's voice twice, the two versions wound around each other, as close as he and Leonie had been intertwined. One voice was for Virgil and Leonie, saying goodbye. The other was for his fae queen, calling her to him, promising himself to her again. He'd loved her; he loved her still. He loved Virgil and Leonie, and his love was big enough to hold all of them.

The cold hunger Brix had felt in the ballroom drew close, like a hound following a scent. Jimmy caught the hunger inside his song, letting go of Leonie, wrapping his arms around the fae queen instead and pulling her back with him.

The wanting, the ache, was like saying goodbye to Abby all over again. He pressed his face against Virgil's shoulder, feeling more strength there than Brix could claim for himself.

"I'm sorry," he said, his voice muffled.

He meant it for all three of them, maybe even for Jimmy's fae queen as well, and it wasn't enough.

Perhaps without even knowing he was doing it, Virgil braced the door Brix held open. In his mind, Brix saw it as an architecture of silver, gilding his bones, making them stronger.

Jimmy still had to be the one to step through. Brix felt the sole of his hand-tooled leather boot land on that soft white road. The imprint of it would be there forever, like the hand and footprints the living Jimmy Valentine had left outside the Empire Theater in Hollywoodland.

A wind swept over him, wisps of Jimmy still clinging to Leonie, to Virgil, reluctant to say goodbye. The sky over the bone road flipped black. The world lurched, trembled, and strains of music drifted through the air. The hunger withdrew, lulled by the music, held – for now at least – in Jimmy's spell.

Stay with me, darlin'. You can rest now. You don't have to be alone.

Then, he was gone. The door closed, sealing the road.

Leonie keened. The sound echoed in the hotel room – only a room now, the normal dimensions of a ceiling, floor, and four walls. It smelled of unwashed bodies, old cigarettes, and now, improbably, the sea.

Brix drew back. He wanted to keep holding on, craved the warmth of other living bodies where he was freezing cold, but he forced himself to give the two kids their space. Virgil held Leonie as she sobbed, his own shoulders hitching. Brix might as well not be in the room at all. He shouldn't be, but he was too tired to go anywhere else just now.

Picking up one of the three remaining sandwiches from the room service cart, he slumped into the heavy chair in the corner. Tuna on white bread. Simple, but in that moment, the most delicious thing in the world. He couldn't do anything for Virgil and Leonie now, other than witness their grief. He watched over them until they exhausted themselves with weeping and fell asleep in each other's arms.

22

Belle fought the urge to pace, imagining the floorboards bowing with every step and keeping Dee awake in the room below. A small hexagonal window at the far end of the attic, which made her think of an eye, looked out over the fields below. No matter how she positioned herself, she couldn't see anything. The entirety of the land between Dee's house and the Kennetts' might be swarming with Clarence's followers, and she wouldn't be able to tell. Someone would have to be right upon them to be visible, and by then it would be too late, but she couldn't stop herself from checking.

Instead of pacing, she tiptoed back to the narrow, brass-framed bed tucked under the eaves. A trunk smelling faintly of mothballs sat at its foot. The attic was warm, and the undershirt and shorts were good enough for now, but when morning came she would need more. Kneeling, Belle dug a pair of dark brown trousers, matching jacket, and white button-down shirt from the trunk.

The jacket felt oddly heavy. Rooting in the pockets revealed the source of the weight – a revolver. Belle checked the chamber and found it was loaded, which seemed careless. Perhaps Mr. Kennett kept it for shooting at vermin. Or perhaps he liked the weight of it in his hand the way she liked feeling her bones shattered and transformed. She slipped it back into the pocket and hung the jacket from the bedpost.

"Belizial?" She spoke the demon's name softly.

She expected them to pull away from her, but they unfurled tentatively, stretching to fill her now that they were alone. Belle allowed herself a moment to revel in the sensation, like sinking into a hot bath. Except all the sharp edges remained – the edges of Belizial's fear, her own guilt, the two scraping against each other like splintered bone.

Belle spoke as gently as she could. "Talk to me?"

In the barn, Ava was still falling. Would always fall. Even with Belizial filling her, an intense wave of loneliness swept over her. She longed to pull them over her own skin and hide inside of them, but she'd allowed them to be hurt, again, when she should have been big enough, strong enough, to keep them safe.

It was never your burden to carry alone.

The words against her ear were a sigh, reverberating from within. Simple, yet they shocked the breath from her.

Belle pressed a hand against her ribs as if she wore her corset and not a ribbed undershirt. "I didn't—"

I know.

Spiky protrusions pressed against the underside of her skin. She'd experienced Belizial's pain, their memories, but she hadn't felt them, not really. She'd merely pulled their hurt on like armor, girded with their own, letting herself believe they wanted to fight and lash out at the world as badly as she did. It was the same thing she'd done to Dee, insisting that what was right for her must be right for them both, not seeing what her sister needed. Belle had wanted so badly to be fearsome, so she wouldn't be afraid, and she hadn't given Belizial the space they needed to be hurt and small.

She should have held them, curled around them; instead, she'd forced them to transform her again and again. To kill and carry the weight of it every time, so Belle could keep walking, so she didn't have to look back at what she'd done.

Just like the Hollow Queen, she'd made Belizial into a weapon and forced them to keep fighting when all they wanted to do was *stop*.

"I'm sorry." The words were too small in the dusty space of the attic.

Look at me, Belizial said.

Pain gave their voice the hard edge of command. They unfolded from her fully now, and Belle immediately felt their absence. Her flesh goose prickled. She wrapped her arms around herself.

Ava fell in an endless loop behind her eyes. They'd fought demons together, she'd help Brix as he banished ghosts, she'd defended herself, but all of that was different. Ava was innocent. She'd gotten caught up in something so much larger than herself and she'd never wanted to hurt anyone.

Yes, the demon replied. *She died. I killed her.*

"We did," Belle said. "It wasn't your fault. I wanted—" Her voice broke. "But I don't want that anymore."

All around her in the mirror, Belizial formed a halo of darkness, a mantle of spikes and angles and tendrils extending to fill the space, making her big enough to stand when she wanted to fold to the ground and sob.

It hurts, her demon said. *Every time I kill with you and for you, I carry the pain. I still feel it, all of it. I see Ava falling, too.*

"I'm sorry." The words again, and they still weren't enough.

If that isn't what you want anymore, then let go.

It sounded so simple – too simple. It couldn't be that easy, could it? To acknowledge that she'd been hurt, they both had, but that their pain didn't make them weak or lesser. She could share Belizial's burden and they could share hers, feeling all of it and carrying it together, instead of running away.

Let go.

Soothing now, their words whispered against her ear and a part of themself coiling around her throat. Holding her and stopping any response she might make.

Belizial knew her well, too well, better than she knew herself. Belle needed to be hollowed out, to burn through her own pain to make room for theirs. That was what she'd wanted when she first invited Belizial to share her skin: someone she could feed all the worst parts of herself to, leaving her untouched and strong so she could survive, keep walking, and never look back.

It wasn't fair.

Darkness loomed behind her.

She wanted to demand Belizial return and fill up all the places inside of her. She wanted them to transform her, crack her bones into new forms, make her into something large and terrible that didn't have to feel.

Is that what you think? Belizial's voice drew closer, right against her ear, carrying a terrible heat. *That I don't feel?*

"No."

Their darkness tightened around her throat, demanding honesty. Her pulse beat fast, heat building beneath her skin.

Shhh, Belizial said. *Yes, I can be cruel if need be, but that doesn't mean I'm heartless. Look at me.*

"I—" The word emerged a choked whisper.

It would take only the slightest amount of pressure for Belizial to break her neck. They wouldn't, ever, but they could.

They weren't heartless. She'd seen as much in their memories. She'd seen as much in their tenderness. Yet again and again, she demanded heartlessness from them – changing her shape to keep her safe, denying their pain.

Belle felt everything balanced on a knife's edge, a tipping point between them. It wasn't fair and it never had been. They would hollow her out and take her pain, let her be weak and selfish, but after that she wouldn't be able to lie to them and hold back any longer. All these years of sharing one skin, one body, and still she'd held parts of herself in reserve. No more. She would feel Belizial's pain fully; they would feel hers. Together, they would find a new balance, because their relationship could not be sustained otherwise.

She tried one last time to apologize and they cut off her words. She hadn't earned the right, not when she still needed so much from them. She wanted them to take her apart, make her forget herself.

Shhh. Let go.

She knew how the words were meant. The only way past her pain was through it, letting Belizial carry the burden one last time before they started over again. Together. Hot tears gathered at the corners of her eyes. She hated herself for wanting this, for asking them to do this.

I feel everything, Belizial said. *All your pain when you kill with me. I swallow it so you don't have to feel. I do that for you.*

"I know."

I will do this for you now, they said. *And then no more.*

"No more," Belle agreed.

Love was the wrong word. She needed them. They were the only home she'd ever known, and she'd taken them for granted long enough to nearly chase them away. The thought of it broke her, stole her breath. She tried to let all of that sit in her mind, the knowledge and understanding, so they could feel that she meant it this time. She would be the home they needed as well.

Belizial folded themself over her, their darkness extending around Belle's arms, pulling them behind her back. A hint of amusement played at the edge of their being. Of course they knew exactly what she was thinking, feeling; it was Belle and Belle alone for whom the realization had taken so long. Beneath the gloating, she felt the lingering sadness, and guilt wormed inside of her.

They would take this from her too, all of it. They would take her apart and let her put herself back together again when they were done. And she would do better this time.

Belle's head tipped back. Tears slid down the line of her jaw, wet her throat. Belizial licked them clean.

Yes?

"Yes," she affirmed.

Her legs shook, Belizial the only thing holding her up.

The demon pulled her arms back farther, pushed against the space between her shoulder blades. Belle let her legs give way, falling, yet bound so tightly she would never actually hit the ground.

"Yes," Belle said again.

She wanted – needed – control taken from her utterly. Her back arched where Belizial laced themself through her curls and yanked, exposing her throat.

Mine, they said, voice both inside and outside.

Belle shook – half cold, half desire. She'd made and broken so many promises to them. She wouldn't break this one.

She arched into them, pressing backward with all her need. "Yours," she agreed.

Belle shifted her knees against the dust-grit of the attic floorboards, spreading them wider. She was a fever, a star superheating, about to explode.

"Please," she murmured.

She would have begged if they asked, but they didn't. Belizial complied, darkness slicking up her thighs. Her breath stuttered, caught. Another tendril of darkness slipped into Belle's mouth, caressing her tongue, stilling it so she couldn't cry out. Belizial nudged her legs wider still. They entered her, and her entire body shuddered. Pleasure, just on the point of pain, as the demon wrapped around every part of her, holding her tight, holding her on the edge.

Belle surrendered everything. Belizial, in turn, devoured her whole.

23

Jimmy is gone, but his voice remains. Its echo shivers inside her, calling her, wrapped around her. Leonie feels all the places he used to be, like roots painfully ripped free from her insides. It hurts; he's gone, but he's still here – the ghost of a ghost, cradled within her.

She reaches for it and—

Something stops her, pushing her back. There's no comfort to be had, only pain. Only emptiness. If she lets it, the feeling will tear her apart.

When she was lost, Virgil's voice looped around her like a rope and guided her back. Now she needs to do the same thing for Jimmy. She will bring him home.

Still here, still here, still here.

The words repeat on an endless loop in her mind.

He's still here.

How can she leave him when he needs her so very much?

It isn't just a feeling. There's a woman. She puts her lips right up against Leonie's ear and tells her that it's true.

He isn't gone. He's here. Follow the song. Bring him home.

Leonie hears the words directly in her skull, cracking her open and speaking to the deepest part of her. She doesn't know who the woman is, but they want the same thing. To find Jimmy, to bring him home.

If she doesn't...

There aren't words for it. It's a feeling, an icicle lodged in her heart. Her parents put it there with their ugly words and Leonie has never been able to dig it out, no matter how she tries. She isn't enough, she'll never be enough. That's why she ran.

She went as far away as she could afford to go, and she found Virgil. The day they met, the first time they kissed, when Leonie pulled him into the narrow bed in her dorm room and pressed her hands against his skin, everything inside of her thawed. He's never asked her to explain or justify herself; he simply holds her, and they fit together, and she finally feels like she's enough. She wants to give him the world, and for a while, after they found Jimmy, she could.

She held all the love between the three of them inside her – and then Sydney Brix took it all away.

No, not all. There's something. Leonie feels the edges of it, like the hum, the song, a memory of—

The voice is there, sweeping the feeling away and stealing her focus, putting ice back into her heart.

Jimmy is gone. Nothing will ever be right until you find him.

Leonie shivers awake and stands. She looks down at Virgil curled on his side in the bed. The sheets and the pillow are dented in the shape of her body, the memory of her still holding him. She hopes he goes right on sleeping until she gets back, so he doesn't have to miss either her or Jimmy while they're gone.

She needs to follow the song, the thread of it faint, but unmistakable. It holds so many things inside it, and now that she's properly awake, Leonie feels them all. There are fragments of wanting scattered throughout the Peony Hotel, like a trail of breadcrumbs. There's a maid whose feet hurt, who just wants her shift to be over. A boy in the lobby wants to hand out a stack of brochures so he can go back home and play fetch with his dog. This is the farthest away he's ever been; he misses the fence that always needs fixing and the swing hanging from the old oak tree and even the stupid screen door that creaks and gives him away when he tries to sneak out to meet up with his friends. Virgil, even asleep, wants to hold her, and for a moment, the thought of that much tenderness breaks Leonie's heart.

Across the room, slumped in the chair, Brix wants to hold his wife in his arms. Leonie turns away from that thought. Further away, in the direction the song leads, there is a tired woman who wants her life to back to the way it was when she was happy in her marriage. There's a man who wants to burn darkness out of the world. There's a creature Leonie doesn't understand made entirely of hurting who only wants the pain to stop.

Jimmy is there, too. Some part of him.

He wants to be found.

He wants her to bring him home.

24

Ava is gone.

She is gone, but her body remains, haunting him. She put her faith in him, and he failed her. His miracle shivers and keens in the rafters. Clarence failed them both. He feels the loss, sharp and new, but threaded with old pain. His first failure – when the life he and Cordelia made together slipped away from them before they ever had the chance to hold their child in their arms.

This should have been his second chance. The proof he prayed for day and night in the barn, that he was meant for something greater. He was meant to heal his flock and lead them into the light. He was meant to save Ava from her sorrow, from missing her family. He was meant, even, to heal himself. Then Jessamine returned and ruined everything.

Clarence sees now: the shadow of her wickedness never truly left the land. He and Cordelia did their best, planting new crops, building a community, building a life together. But walls built upon a rotten foundation will always crumble. It isn't enough to extract a promise from Jessamine to stay away this time. She is tied to this place; he must tear her out by the roots.

A voice whispers against Clarence's ear. *Yes, see her burn. Tear out the darkness inside of her and leave it nowhere to hide.*

He can have everything he wants. All he has to do is listen.

25

Brix woke with a crick in his neck, folded awkwardly into the chair beside the bed. He hadn't intended to sleep, only watch over Virgil and Leonie, but exhaustion had gotten the better of him. He squinted, trying to work out the hour by the quality of the light, and failed. The curtains had settled back over the windows, admitting only a sliver of the outside world, not enough for him to tell whether it was night or day.

Heaviness pervaded his bones as he tried to stand, not just the raw exhaustion that always followed a quieting, but something more. His eyes kept slipping closed even as he fought to keep them open, like bruising thumbs pressed against his eyelids. The chair held him, sunk deep, while voices murmured close by. He recognized Leonie, but not the other, which had a buzzing quality, like dozens upon dozens of wings beating all at once.

Brix couldn't even turn his head. Straight ahead, in the

narrow slice of room available to him, Virgil lay sprawled on the bed. Leonie stood beside it, on the far side from the chair, and a second figure stood beside her, looming over her.

Jimmy's fae queen.

Brix tried to shout a warning, but spectral hands gagged him, their touch sliding down his throat until he felt like he might vomit.

The scene in front of him jumped, like a mis-spliced bit of film. Leonie, dressed now, gathered her boots from under the bed. Fingers sunk deep into Brix's flesh, hooked around his fibula, his tibia, his radius and ulnar, keeping him in place.

Remnants, scraps of the haunting called by Jimmy's song, clung to Leonie now. Brix could see them all around her like a halo. Mindless things, holding Brix down like an extension of her will.

Hearing the shift in his breathing, Leonie turned, boots in one hand, dark fringe hanging into her eyes. Her gaze shone baleful and foxfire bright. If she could have reduced him to ash with a glare, he imagined she would.

She crossed the room and knelt before his chair, hands braced on the arms, peering into his face. "You never did it, did you? You never quieted her."

One of the phantom hands gripped his jaw, keeping him from answering. All he could do was look back at the terrible youth in her face, the loss shadowing it.

"You took him from us. He wasn't yours to take. You had no right."

Her voice scraped, pained and raw. Brix wanted to apologize. Leonie was right about everything. He was a coward. A good part of this was his fault, and it didn't matter that he was trying to set it right, or that Jimmy had chosen to go. Those truths were nothing against Leonie's pain.

He wanted to explain about the fae queen and warn her, but Leonie would spit in his face if he did. Even with Jimmy holding her, the Hollow Queen was still fighting, her hunger winning out. She couldn't stop.

"They were my home, Jimmy and Virgil both. You took that from me."

Leonie shifted her weight, tightening her grip on the chair. From the corner of his eye, Brix could see Virgil, still asleep under the mound of covers.

"I'm going to get him back." She took a breath, dark eyes like the fingers of the dead hooked around his bones. "She promised me I could have him back. I'm going to bring him home, and this time, you're not going to stop me."

Leonie stood. She was relatively short, yet she towered over Brix trapped in the chair.

"Do you know what it's like to be so close to someone they literally share your skin? To have that taken away from you?" Leonie's voice was barely above a whisper. "To be alone inside yourself, when you'd finally found the parts of you that made you whole?"

She placed one finger against the center of Brix's forehead, the same spot where he'd smeared ash against hers. She pushed lightly, tipping his head back to make sure he was looking at her.

"It's awful, Mr. Brix. I wouldn't even wish it on you. I hope you never know what it feels like."

Except he did. Maybe not the way she meant it, but he did, though he could never explain that to her.

She stepped back, letting his head go so it slumped against his chest. He could only strain aching muscles to no avail as he listened to her pad across the room, the soft sounds made by the door opening and closing, knowing by the time the ghosts released him, Leonie would be long gone.

"Mr. Brix!"

He woke to Virgil shaking his shoulder. He allowed himself the brief hope that his first waking had only been a dream – but Virgil's stricken expression told him otherwise.

"Leonie's gone."

Brix tried to say *I know*, to stand, but his legs went pins and needles under him, and he fell gracelessly from the chair.

"I'm sorry," he managed, pushing himself up, waving away Virgil's attempt to help.

His clothes had dried. He'd fallen asleep with them wet, and now they smelled faintly of ocean brine.

"But where did she go? Where could she go?" Virgil's gaze darted around the room as if expecting to find Leonie folded up in a corner, as if he might have simply missed her.

Where would a frightened girl go? Where would someone hide out after suffering a loss? Brix found himself looking around the room the way Virgil had, though he knew Leonie wasn't there. His gaze fell on the pamphlet, the one on which he'd scribbled his offer of help what felt like a lifetime ago.

The sketched and broken image of the sun hovering above the trees, skeletal branches reaching for it, tugged at him. If Brix squinted, he could almost make the lines look like feathers, roots, a tangled ball of string. If the Hollow Queen was looking for broken places in the world, there were worse places to look than where a young girl had been tortured by her parents and a demon had escaped into the mortal world.

"Shit."

"What is it?" Virgil asked, puppy-dog eyes begging for an explanation.

Brix's heart went out to the kid. He'd lost Jimmy, and Leonie was gone, and baseless as it was, he blamed himself. There was likely nothing Brix could do to talk him out of it. He knew how he would feel in the kid's shoes.

He picked up the pamphlet and flipped it around so Virgil could see the image of the stylized sun.

"I think this is where she might be headed."

"What is this? Why would she go there?"

"It's just a gut feeling."

Virgil snatched the pamphlet, bringing it close to his face as if he could force it to reveal more answers. Brix glanced to where he'd left his satchel in the corner. *Gone.* Leonie must have taken it, perhaps thinking it contained cash or something she could sell.

"I think... someone made her a promise," he said. "Jimmy tried to explain it all when we were in the ballroom, as much as he could at least. There's a fae queen, she did something to him before he died and now she's moving all of us around like pieces on a board to try to get what she wants."

"What does she want?" Virgil lowered the pamphlet.

"If I understand it – and I'm not sure I do – I think she wants to find her way into our world. Jimmy told me that her own people made her into a weapon and now she can't stop. She's still hunting."

"Hunting what?"

"Everything."

Brix tapped the pamphlet. "My partner, Bellefeather, is there right now. It's... complicated, but I'm going to try calling her again. There's a hunch I'm working on, and if I can get a hold of her, maybe she can tell me if I'm right and how it's all connected."

Brix rubbed at his forehead. He wished he could crawl under the rumpled covers Virgil had recently abandoned and sleep for a week.

"I still don't understand," Virgil said. "Why would Leonie think she'd find Jimmy way out in Morganville? I mean, he's gone, right? We sent him on?" He swallowed, pain cracking his voice. His expression pleaded with Brix to tell them they'd done the right thing, that Jimmy was at peace now.

Fuck.

He owed the kid the truth and he was afraid it would break him. He shouldn't have had to go through that pain once, let alone all over again.

"Yes," Brix said. "And no. He's, well, he's holding the door closed from the other side as best as he can, but I don't know how long he can hold out. The doors need to be shut on this side as well."

"Doors," Virgil said. "More than one?"

"Here." Brix tapped his own chest, then did the same to Virgil's. "Here, too, and maybe other places."

Why was this so hard? Why couldn't he just say what he needed to aloud? It felt too final. When he spoke again, Brix found himself skirting around it still, and cursed himself.

"Wanting makes holes in the world. Whether it's grief or lust or missing someone or wishing as hard as you can for a thing to happen. This queen, the one Jimmy got all tangled up with, can use that to make deals, to bind her realm to ours, to bind one person to another. She can slip herself into all those hollow places and then devour the world from the inside out."

"Is that what you meant before, when you said we were dangerous?"

"That, and the fact that you and I are already doors ourselves because of what we can do. It's why we have to be so careful and follow the rules, so—"

"But we didn't." Virgil's expression was stricken. "Neither of us."

He was beginning to see what Brix had, the broken places needing healing. The cracks that just kept spreading and spreading. Putting a foot down on a frozen lake could leave the whole damn thing fractured. Brix had stomped on the ice again and again. Without knowing it or meaning to, Virgil had come behind him on a different part and done the same.

Virgil put his head in his hands, covering his face before dragging them away again to look at Brix. "I can't. I don't know if... It's too much."

He'd been in this room a lifetime. He'd found Jimmy

here – found home, the same as Leonie had. Stepping outside would mean facing the fullness of his loss.

Brix gritted his teeth, hating himself for the callousness of what he was about to say. "Trust me, I know, and you can feel sorry for yourself later. Right now, Leonie needs you."

He hauled Virgil toward the door.

Brix let the phone ring thirteen times. No ghosts clogged the line now, but Belle still didn't answer. Where the hells was she? Had she already left the farm to return to the city? Then why didn't her sister answer either?

Virgil paced in the lobby beyond the booth's glass doors. It felt unfair that Brix had dragged the kid from the room, then left him waiting. He hung up, resting his forehead against the phone's casing.

He was about to do something very unwise.

Brix lifted the receiver. He didn't bother dropping a coin in the slot this time. Just as the Peony had once warranted its own subway stop, it had once operated its very own switchboard. Politicians and businessmen, movie stars and disgraced royals – they all still needed to be reached at any time of the day or night, even when they were holed up in one of the Peony's rooms, hiding from the world. Brix ignored the dial tone whining in his ear, listening to the sound beneath the sound, the remembered click and hum of wires being connected.

"How may I connect your call?" The woman's voice was smoke-roughened, and not just from cigarettes. Brix winced, taking a moment for sympathy. She'd died, and not pleasantly, a carelessly dropped cigarette setting fire to her bed. Before that though, she'd worked at the Peony Hotel, one of the best switchboard operators they'd ever had. Jimmy's song had called her back.

"What's your name, luv?"

A beat of hesitation as the ghost struggled to remember. "Dolores."

"Dolores. I know things must feel a little strange right now, but if you could do me a favor, I promise once I'm done sorting out this mess, I'll help you move on to where you're supposed to go. How's that sound?"

He listened to Dolores breathe, a painful and wheezing sound.

"How may I connect your call?" Her voice wavered, not like a ghost stuck in a loop, but like she was agreeing to his terms.

"I need to speak to Bellefeather," he said. "Trouble is, I don't know exactly where she's located just now." He smiled in a manner meant to charm, for the benefit of a ghost he couldn't see. One who couldn't see him either, but that wouldn't be a problem for her, just as it wouldn't be a problem for her to connect his call.

"Hold, please."

"Dolores, you're a peach."

A shuffling sound came down the line, then a click as Dolores, impossibly, connected him.

"Hello?"

He'd never been happier to hear her voice. "Belle."

"Syd? How did you—"

"No time. I don't know how long this connection will hold. Everything all right there?"

"No. There?"

"Not one bit." Someone knocked impatiently on the glass door and Brix angled his body away, ignoring them. How to explain? "We're dealing with more than ghosts here. The fae are involved, they—"

"The Hollow Queen," Belle interrupted. "Belizial used to be her soldier, willingly, then unwillingly. They felt an echo of her when we first got to the Peony, but I thought she was trapped. I thought we were safe."

He heard the chagrin in her voice and wondered whether *we* meant her and him or her and Belizial, or all of them. The line crackled, Belle's words dropping into the void between them, reminding him of the distance, before it cleared again.

"...girl died."

"Someone died? Is your sister okay? Are you okay?" He gripped the phone harder, willing the answer to be yes.

"For now, yes, but I think you'd better—"

"I'm on my way," he said at the same time, cutting her off. "I'll get there as soon as I can."

She might have been about to tell him to stay away, or she might have been about to ask him for help. It didn't matter; Brix rushed through the next words.

"Look, there's a girl headed your way. Her name is Leonie. I need you to look out for her. This Hollow Queen is dangerous, she uses what we want against us to—"

A fresh wave of static washed the line.

"I'm sorry, sir, the call has been lost," Dolores said.

Brix thumped a fist softly against the back of the booth. Of course it had.

"Yeah, thanks, luv. I'll talk to you soon."

He hung up and stepped out of the booth. Belle clearly knew more about the Hollow Queen than he did; hopefully that meant she knew how to guard herself and stay safe. Not that knowing had helped him or kept him from slipping thus far.

Seeing him, Virgil rushed over. "Well?"

"The call got a bit garbled, but I told Belle to look out for Leonie, and that I'd get there as soon as I could."

"You're talking like you're going alone," Virgil said. "It's Leonie, I'm coming with you."

"I promised I'd look out for you. I can't go putting you right back in danger."

"With all due respect, it's not your decision to make."

"Huh." Brix ran a hand through his hair, feeling bedraggled amidst the lobby's gleam. The Peony had already begun to heal itself. Gustav's doing, no doubt, rushing things right back to a state of profitability. There were still remnants though, loose ends to be tied up – Dolores, for one. All of which would be easier if he had Virgil's help.

"I suppose you're right, at that."

"Anyway," Virgil said, "I can get us a ride." A tentative grin edged its way onto his face. He tucked his hands into his pockets, rocking back and forth from heel to toe. "By the time we wait around for a train, who knows what'll happen? I can drive us straight there."

"You have a car?" Brix couldn't keep the doubt from his voice.

Virgil was beaming now, which did nothing to put Brix at ease. He'd never learned to drive, had never needed to, and as such he'd developed what he thought of as a healthy distrust of cars. Cabs were one thing; the people who drove them were paid professionals who knew the streets of Port Astor better than the backs of their hands. Beyond that, any idiot could get behind the wheel of a vehicle, and he was just supposed to trust them with his life? No, thank you.

Belle called it irrational. It was a ridiculous distinction, according to her. A superstition. Brix didn't care. He felt the way he felt – trains and subway cars rattling through the dark could be trusted because they ran on a track. Cars could not.

"I have a friend who'll let me borrow one. She's got a shop a few blocks from here where she fixes up cars, a lot of specialty and custom work, but she's always got a few spares around the garage. It'll be no problem." Virgil was so pleased with himself that Brix didn't have the heart to turn him down, but he must have looked unsure. "I'm really a very good driver. I promise."

"Fine," Brix said. He didn't have to like it, but Virgil had a point.

"All right. Let's go see your friend."

26

Belle felt raw, bruised as she pulled on Hank Kennett's borrowed jacket, patting the pocket for the gun as if it could have crept off in the night. The shape of it through the fabric was strangely reassuring. Quiet as she could, she crept down the stairs.

The Kennetts' bedroom door remained closed. Belle hoped Dee had found a way to sleep after all.

Dawn was just beginning to pink the sky. She needed to find a way to speak with Clarence alone, a kind of parlay. She would make her apologies for Ava and offer to help if she could. She at least had to try.

A pair of mud-crusted boots sat beside the back door. Belle slipped them on and stepped outside, taking the three wooden steps that led down to a foot-beaten path. A small plot of built-up garden sat to one side, a rusted hand-pump that Belle doubted anyone had used in recent memory on the other.

It wouldn't be a pleasant walk, but if she cut through the fields on a rough diagonal and passed through the trees on the ridge, she'd come out on the edge of Dee's property. From there, she might just be able to work her way up to the barn without being seen until she was ready.

She hadn't made past the garden shed before a blur of motion threw itself into her, knocking her breath free in a startled gasp. She hit the ground hard, too dazed for a moment to react. She registered the weight of a body on top of hers, one that hadn't washed too recently at that. Dust and sweat, someone breathing hard.

Before she could fight, before the first of her bones could twist beneath her skin, rearranging herself into Belizial's form, something cold and metallic clamped around her wrist. There was a rushing like wind, Belizial crammed back inside a part of her that was too small to hold their form. The metal burned. Belle would have howled from pure shock and rage, but a sharp blow landed just behind her ear, knocking her out before she could make a sound.

She woke in the barn, scrambling panic on the inside of her skin. The writhing light shone down from the rafters. She squinted against it. It shed its radiance over her, and hummed softly, just on the edge of hearing.

Her head throbbed, the pain localized just behind her ear. Belle reached to check if she was bleeding, and a chain rattled, arresting the motion. She tried to launch herself up, but the chain rang again, links clattering through a loop bolted into the ground, stopping her flight. The cuff bit into her skin – not just metal, *spelled* metal. More even than that – blessed metal, a complicated knot that tangled Clarence's traditions with ones far older and more terrible. It was the same kind of magic that had been used to hurt Belizial all those years ago, and now it kept them locked inside her where she couldn't reach.

If she'd had any doubt about the Hollow Queen's involvement, Belle shed the last of it now. The same uncaring mouth that had whispered disappointment through the bars of Belizial's cage had pressed itself to Clarence's ear and made who knew what kind of promises. He'd been poisoned into... what, harnessing the wanting of his entire congregation to make a way for the Hollow Queen back into this world? The thought left Belle sick. To what end? Or was hunger its own end? Get Belizial back, because the Hollow Queen hated that something she thought of as hers had been taken away from her, and then carry on destroying everything that lay in her path because that's what she'd been made to do. If any other fae still remained where they could be found, then she would find them out and add them to the collection of ghosts in her hall, and she would burn through the hells and the mortal worlds and the land of the dead to do it.

Even knowing it was useless, Belle twisted her arm, clawing at the cuff until blisters rose over old scars. The more she fought, the more it tightened, popping the blisters and leaving them weeping. She was a child again, bound to her bed, the shadow of her parents filling the doorway. Her throat closed, pinhole tight.

She couldn't reach Belizial. They were locked away from her, but she could still feel them hurting, a black shape with sharp claws, frantic at her ribs and the walls of her skull. She'd promised them safety last night, and she'd failed them again, leaving them a trapped thing with nowhere to go, beating at her to drown out the rhythm of her heart.

Belle struggled to wrest back control, to banish the sting from her eyes. Her throat eased up, letting a shuddering breath through. It hurt, but it was something. She scrubbed her hands over her face and hauled in a ragged breath, clenching her jaw until she feared her teeth would shatter. She shoved the rage down, crushing it into the hollow space inside her where she could no longer touch Belizial.

Fuck Clarence. Fuck trying to reason with him. She would get herself free, and she would tear this whole fucking place to the ground.

The squirming light showed the rest of the barn was empty. If Clarence had left a guard, they were posted outside. Stacked crates and broken equipment cast stark shadows on the floor. Peering into the gloom, an incongruous shape she hadn't noticed before jumped out at Belle. She wasn't totally alone. Ava's body lay at the opposite end of the barn, wrapped in a shroud.

The barn door scraped open, and Clarence entered. "Jessamine. Good. You're here."

"You didn't leave me much of a choice."

He ignored her, producing a key and undoing her chain from the bolt on the floor. He wrapped it around his left hand, using the other to haul Belle upright. He'd cuffed only one wrist, and he hadn't taken Hank's coat. She still had the gun, but Clarence neatly looped the chain around her other wrist, drawing her hands together before she could reach for it. He wrapped the chain around her waist so her hands were pulled tight against her body.

"Come, Jessamine. Let me show you what I built for you."

Belle stumbled in her too-big boots as Clarence led her outside. Her legs felt numb, but the chain gave her no choice except to follow up the slope of the hill.

Clarence stopped. There was no question what he wanted her to see.

A gallows, and beneath it, a pyre. He meant to hang her and burn her at once, and the burning would be done over Ava's body. It was so ridiculous and overwrought, Belle might have laughed in his face, if Clarence hadn't gripped her upper arm, hauling her closer to the structure.

"You haven't even seen the best part yet," he said.

There was a rawness to his voice. She glanced at him sidelong. Stubble shaded his cheeks and chin. How long had it been since he'd last slept? The redness haunting his eyes suggested it had been a while. A man hollowed out by devotion and grief.

Ava, falling and falling—

Belle turned her face, leaning away from Clarence, her only means of resistance. He tightened his grip. Her boots slipped on the grass, still damp from last night's storm. Giving up, she let herself be led, ready to scoff at whatever Clarence had to show her. She would not give him the satisfaction.

The faint scent of char reached her at the same moment she noticed a low hum in the back of her skull. Horror gripped her. It didn't matter that Clarence had a hold of her – she couldn't, *wouldn't,* budge. She knew the wood of the rough structure where she was meant to hang and burn deep in her soul.

Belizial's tree. My tree. Home.

The words rang in her head, drowning out everything else so that it was a moment before Clarence's voice faded back in, like a dial tuned on a radio.

"I had my parishioners help me take it down as soon as you fled. It was a beast, fittingly, but many hands make light work. I mean to cleanse this land once and for all."

He tugged on the chain again. Belle scarcely felt the bite of the metal, scarcely felt her own limbs as they moved her – stiff as if frozen solid – over the ground.

Her tree. The idea of it looped over and over in her head, fueling a rage too big to express, a howl she could not force free. Clarence had no right.

The scent of lightning-struck wood overwhelmed her as they drew right up to the gallows and stopped, filling Belle's senses entirely, making her eyes sting. The whole thing stank of fae magic, too, and she could imagine the Hollow Queen's promises urging the parishioners on as they built this monstrosity with unnatural speed. If her arms hadn't been bound by the chain's loops, she could have laid her hand against the wood. Even with what had become of it, she ached to lean her cheek against it, let it take the weight of her body.

Clarence touched the structure where she could not. If she still had the ability to transform, she would have ripped him limb from limb. As it was, Belle considered launching herself at him – even chained – and tearing into him with her all-too-human teeth.

Where his fingers touched the gallows, she felt it like they rested against her skin over a cluster of nerves, promising pain. Her name – the one she'd been born with and shed like dead skin when she left – was written there. She'd carved it into the wood after her parents' "cure" so she could leave it behind, a thing that was outside of herself and had nothing to do with her anymore.

"She told me," Clarence said, eyes shining, "how you lured your devil here and made a pact, willingly letting yourself be possessed. The proof of your guilt and wickedness is right here, your name signed in your own hand."

She. The words landed sharp as a strike, leaving Belle dizzy. Did he mean Dee? Would she? *Could* she? The slope of her sister's shoulders last night, the weariness in her as they'd tried one more time to fix all the things that were broken between them said otherwise, but doubt remained, a sliver in her heart. She didn't really know Dee, not anymore, and perhaps she never had.

Belle's jaw ached with clenching it so hard. Her entire body ached in fact, nothing to do with being struck, with being chained. She wanted desperately for Clarence to mean the Hollow Queen, whispering in his ear, convincing him that somehow Belle had cursed the land. The need for it to be true sang in her bones like hunger, a dangerous resonance. Here, within reach of the writhing light that was every color and no color at all, wanting was a terribly dangerous thing.

The expression on Clarence's face could almost be mistaken for a smile, but his words themselves were passionless and cold. "For your sins, Jessamine, you will burn."

27

The car Val lent them was a pick-up truck she'd been restoring as a favor between paying jobs. She'd just about managed to scrub all the rust from the wheel wells and had even found a match for the original paint – a powdery robin's egg blue. It was a practical vehicle for where they were headed, but sitting beside Virgil as he navigated through Port Astor's streets left Brix clutching the leather bench beneath him with both hands.

True to his word though, Virgil was a very good driver, taking it slow and easy until they reached the limits of the city proper and got onto Rockefeller Bridge. Once the hum of tires settled after the metal grating however, he sank his foot on the gas. Brix tried not to think of Jimmy Valentine, wrecking his car at the meeting of two lonely roads. He'd been there, seen the sleek, awful shapes that moved between the drops of rain. He'd heard the lonely sound of a horn being blown as the hunt was called. He remembered dying, and his skin prickled as if the protective wards inked there were trying to crawl off on their own.

Brix simultaneously wanted to roll down the window for fresh air and crank the truck's heater. To distract himself, he did his best to fill Virgil in on what Jimmy had shown him, giving him the sanitized version. The kid had been through enough. He didn't need to know about the heart-broken expression on Jimmy's face in the moment the Hollow Queen had told him to run. He didn't need to know what it had felt like for Jimmy to have the promise and potential of his life spooled out from him and wound between the queen's hands. Brix wished he didn't have to know those things either.

Through it all, Virgil kept quiet, nodding occasionally to show he was listening, but he didn't interrupt. Brix could only guess what he was thinking, but even the kindest version he could think to tell still clearly hurt. Virgil was too damned good, he loved too much – like Jimmy himself. Just hearing what Jimmy had been through wounded him, deepened the lines around his mouth and the shadows around his eyes.

"I wish..." Virgil's throat bobbed, an audible clicking sound as he swallowed before he tried again. "I wish Jimmy could've told me all this himself."

I wish Jimmy was here. The kid didn't have to say it aloud; it was written all over his expression.

The infrequent lights of cars passing in the other direction did strange things to the planes of Virgil's face. The lines on his cheek where Leonie had scratched him were pink and shiny.

"Or, maybe he did," Virgil said. "I don't know. Sometimes while you were talking it was like I already knew everything you were going to say, but it's all muddled in my head. Nothing sits right. All the details keep sliding around and getting lost."

"I know what you mean," Brix said. "This whole thing is... a lot. I'm used to garden-variety haunts, accidents, natural deaths, even tragedies and murders, cases where ghosts don't want to move on. I've never seen a death quite as complicated as Jimmy's."

Brix scrubbed a hand over his face, tried to run a hand through his hair, but it got lodged in his curls and he gave up. He fished the pack of cigarettes from the hotel out of his pocket and held them up. Virgil nodded. Brix lit two and passed one over.

"Once we deal with whatever we find at the farm, there'll still be work that needs doing back at the hotel. A haunting like that is messy." He glanced at Virgil sidelong. "I could teach you, if you want, or try at least. If you want to learn."

"You mean I could do what you do?" Virgil's grip flexed on the steering wheel, making the leather creak.

"Call the dead, help ease their pain, help them move on. All of it."

Silence filled the cab for a moment as Virgil thought it over. Brix rolled down the window on his side, letting the night air spill in.

"Where do they go, when we help them move on?"

From the way he asked the question, not taking his eyes off the road, Brix could tell Virgil was thinking of Jimmy.

Again. Still. Always. And he would be for some time. He cursed himself. He should have expected the question and been prepared for it.

He'd made a point of never giving too much thought to what lay at the end of the bone road. His job was to open the way, make it possible for ghosts to step through. The rest was none of his business, as far as he was concerned. It was easier not knowing.

Except one day, soon, he'd have to help Abigail onto that road. One day, presumably, he'd have to walk it himself.

"I wish I knew. The way I see it, we don't get to know that answer until it's our turn, so all we can do is help folks move on in the kindest way we can. That matters. And in the end, they aren't alone."

"I suppose," Virgil said, but his shoulders slumped. "You know what I want to be true though? Something my grandmother used to say – that when we die, we become stars."

"I like that idea," Brix said. "If any of us are fated for the sky, it's Jimmy Valentine." He could see it, a tree made all of silver light; Jimmy Valentine, loose-limbed, his back against the trunk, legs stretched out in the grass. His guitar lay beside him, picked out in silver too, just waiting for him to pick it up again and play.

Virgil's chin wobbled, but he lifted it, setting his jaw as if he could place Jimmy where he deserved to be by sheer force of will. Etched in starlight forever, glittering across the sky.

"I wish I had better answers for you," Brix said. "I really do. But I don't know what comes next. None of us do until it's our turn. For all we know, it's different for everyone."

"Is that why you haven't sent Abigail on yet?"

The words, innocently spoken, stung. It was a fair question, though. Why did it all have to be such a mystery? The uncertainty settled, an itch he couldn't scratch, a bruise on the wrong side of his skin.

"Probably." He turned to look out the window at a small town, just visible as it slid by. "I never claimed to be anything but a coward. Abby was always the strong one."

"I didn't mean—" Virgil started to apologize, but Brix waved his words away.

He lit them both another cigarette, and after a moment Virgil spoke again.

"Did you really propose after just a week?"

"That I did." Brix chuckled. "I was an idiot, but luckily Abby set me straight. What about you and Leonie? Are you going to marry her someday?"

He wanted to keep Virgil talking, but more than that, he didn't want to sit with his own thoughts, worrying on them like a dog with a bone.

A faint blush colored Virgil's cheeks. "I'd like to, but we haven't really talked about it. It probably sounds silly, but I knew right from the start I wanted to spend the rest of my life with her."

"It doesn't sound silly at all, luv."

Virgil's thumb jigged restlessly on the steering wheel.

"Leonie wasn't ever happy where she came from. She doesn't like to talk about it much, but things weren't good for her. But the two of us are good together. It's not that I don't think she can take care of herself – I know she can.

I just hate the thought of her being out there somewhere alone, not knowing if she's okay."

"We're going to get her back," Brix said.

He needed this one thing to be true. If he willed it hard enough, maybe it would be, especially if Virgil believed it as well.

They stopped once for gas, once to get food, but other than that, they drove straight through. The sun wasn't up yet, but the sky looked like it was thinking about turning from deep blue to grey, the stars paling and fading. Brix's muscles were stiff; he could only imagine how much worse Virgil must feel.

He hadn't been able to share the driving, not to mention that all his cash was in the bag Leonie had stolen, leaving Virgil to pay for everything. Virgil didn't seem bothered. Likely, he was thinking only of Leonie and would give whatever it took to get her back, but it made Brix feel like a bum.

"This should be the turn here."

The truck's tires splashed into puddles left by a storm. "Looks like we're in the right place," Brix said, as Virgil slowed.

Trucks and cars were parked at odd angles on either side of the road, some of them half-mired in mud. Up on the hill, Brix could make out the shape of a sprawling farmhouse, backlit by an intense source of light that had nothing to do with the rising sun. Between the farmhouse and the road, the lesser glow of fading campfires and lanterns illuminated tents scattered across the damp field.

Virgil put the truck into park, and Brix climbed out, his back protesting. The stump of a tree that had been cut so recently Brix could smell it stood just to the side of the drive. A few scattered chips of wood decorated the grass, and long marks showed where the rest of the tree had been dragged away.

"What do we do now?" Virgil asked, coming to stand beside him.

"Now," Brix said, "it's time for your first lesson. I'm going to see if I can't call us up a ghost, get a lay of the land. I'd rather not go into this completely unprepared, with no idea what we're up against."

He flipped open the pocketknife he'd found in the truck's glove compartment, crouching and gesturing for Virgil to join him. Wind stirred the grass around them as Brix went to work gouging a linked circle of symbols into the dirt.

"This is a protection circle. I'm guessing you and Leonie didn't use anything like this in the hotel?"

Virgil blanched. Brix held up a hand. "There's no way you could have known. Get closer now, and make sure you don't touch the edges. The first thing is to center yourself, and act with intention. You want to be calm, so you don't startle the ghost, and you don't want to just start yanking on threads the moment you feel them, or you might end up with more than you intended."

Brix focused on his breathing, the movement of blood in his veins, the things the ghosts might want from him if the situation got out of hand. He let his awareness extend past their circle, feeling the small deaths of the field – mice and birds, shrews and voles. Nothing immediately tried to pull him apart. He moved deeper, scratching past the surface to cows and horses; a rabbit startled by a hawk, ripped up into the air. Below all those, he found something human, just as baffled by death as the rabbit, just as lost.

Brix took hold as gently as he could, not letting urgency and unease make him rough. The shape of the death told him it had been relatively peaceful, as they went. A laborer, struck by a sudden heart attack. His body had lain in this very field for hours, baking in the hot sun before the birds gathering overhead alerted the farmer.

Even now, years later – years being academic to the dead – the man still didn't understand what had happened to him, tying him to the place where he'd passed. Someone was meant to bring a pail of lunch out to the field soon. He would sit under the shade of a tree, rest his aching back and have a sip of cool water.

"Shhh," was the first thing Brix said as he opened his eyes.

Virgil started to protest that he hadn't been speaking. Brix indicated where his attention was directed without looking away. Virgil's eyes widened.

"It's okay. I know all this is frightening and you likely have many questions. My name is Sydney Brix. I can help you, but I was hoping you might be willing to take a look around for us first."

He kept his gaze fixed on the laborer, pale against the rising sun. If he looked away, the man might fade. He was already thin, barely there. Brix focused on the threadbare, dirt-smudged fabric at the knees of his overalls. A hole hadn't developed yet, but the material was working on one. They would need to be patched soon.

Narrowing in on that small detail made the rest of the man easier to see – the fraying hems of his pantlegs, the kerchief tucked into his pocket to wipe sweat from his brow, and the precise angle of the hat he wore to shade his eyes from the sun.

"Can you tell me your name?" Brix asked. Not every ghost knew who they'd been, lost along with what had happened to them and where they were.

"Nedry." There was a syrupy, slow quality to the man's voice, the words lagging a moment behind the movement of his mouth. "Folks around here call me Big Ned."

He paused, scratching the back of his neck, then looked at his hand, perhaps realizing the sensations didn't feel quite right. That he wasn't, in fact, itchy, or hungry, or anything at all. The corners of his mouth turned down. "I wish they wouldn't. I don't like that name."

"Okay. Nedry, then."

The corners of the man's eyes crinkled. Brix tried to guess what color those eyes had been when the man was alive. Gray, maybe, like light coming through a cloud. The way light would look from the *inside* a cloud. Not sunlight though, not exactly. The flicker of lightning, still and steady.

"I don't... What's going on?"

"I'm sorry to say you died," Brix said. "Quite some time ago. Seems like you've been waiting. I can help you move on. But first, I'm hoping you might head on up to that barn and see if a friend of mine is there."

The ghost turned his head. Brix was afraid the motion would disperse him, focus lost, tearing him apart. But he remained. Someone had waited on Nedry once, and he'd never come home. Mary – the name sat in Nedry's mind, a prickling wound. She'd never called him Big Ned, always Nedry. When she said it, it sounded like home.

"It would really mean a lot to us, sir," Virgil broke in.

Nedry slowly turned back to look at them, interest in his eyes. Brix tensed, ready to intervene, but he held himself still and let Virgil talk.

"The person we're looking for," Virgil went on, "is called Leonie. She's in trouble."

Virgil's open, hopeful expression had the same effect on Nedry as on Brix. It was damned impossible not to like the kid, not to want to protect him from anything and everything that might try to hurt him. He was just so earnest, innocent, unaware that the world might crush him. Looking at him made Brix want to keep it that way.

Virgil went on, "She has dark hair, wearing trousers, suspenders, and a white shirt. She's…" Virgil faltered a moment, looking down and whispering the last bit. "She's everything."

In place of an answer, Nedry moved across the field, not quite walking or drifting, but something in-between.

Virgil made a move as if to leave the circle. Brix caught his arm. "We should probably stay put."

Nedry returned, not taking the time to physically cross the distance, simply appearing before them, hovering in the air.

"Nedry?" Brix could feel the ghost's distress. Virgil crowded at his side; Brix didn't nudge him away.

Nedry's eyes focused, but his mouth opened and closed a few times before words emerged. "The light up there is bad."

"Is Leonie there? Did you see her?" Virgil moved right up to the circle's edge.

Sunrise ate at the edges of Nedry, leaving him tattered and raw. "The light was like a song. It wanted to take me apart. It made me hungry. I saw your girl. In the barn. She looked sad."

"We have to—" Virgil started forward; again, Brix put a hand on his arm, addressing Nedry even as Virgil quivered with the urge to run.

"Thank you for your help," Brix said.

He stretched his hand past the circle's barrier. It was a risk. A drowning man might pull his rescuer down and doom them both, but he couldn't ask Nedry to trust him without offering trust in return.

"When you're ready, just take my hand. You won't be able to actually touch me, but it's the thought that counts."

Doubt sparked in Nedry's eyes, but after a moment, he tentatively lowered his hand over Brix's. It was cold, like dunking his arm in a bucket of ice. He felt it all the way up his bones, right to his shoulder.

"Your hair," Virgil said.

"Yeah, it'll do that." Brix had only seen hints of the oil sheen effect, like a sunrise with the colors all wrong, stirring lightly in a breeze of their own. "Yours does it too, I'm afraid. You'll get used to it"

The tug of the protective circle around him was an anchor keeping him from falling into Nedry.

"It's just a quick step through onto the road, then you'll be on your way," Brix said.

The chill stretched to his lungs, but he didn't let go. Then, all at once, Nedry stepped through him. Brix caught himself with his hands braced against the ground so he wouldn't fall on his face.

Virgil touched his shoulder. "Are you okay?"

"Perfectly all right, luv. I promise it's not as bad as it looks."

He straightened, offering what he hoped was a reassuring smile.

Now, we clean this up." Brix gestured at the circle cut into the grass. "Then we go help Leonie."

28

The interior of the barn was overly warm, crowded with too many bodies, and cacophonous with voices speaking to be heard over each other. The open doors at either end did nothing to relieve the closeness, the smell of humans crammed shoulder to shoulder. All the people who'd once come to hear the word of God in Clarence's church had now come to worship something else.

The Hollow Queen. They were feeding her their want, their need, without even realizing it. All their wishes and hurts, big and small – hope for good growing season, for a call from a daughter moved away with a family of her own, an end to the aches and pain keeping sleep at bay, forgiveness for not being there for a father when he died.

Belle could almost hear them, or at least imagine them strongly enough – the thoughts that consumed these people's lives. She recognized friends and neighbors of her parents, people who had lived in this town all their lives and had never been anywhere else. None of them looked at her directly, occasionally glancing at her from the corners of their eyes, then quickly away again. As if *she* were the unclean thing. If they looked at her too long, they might see the child she had been and be forced to reckon with the fact that they'd been complicit in what had happened to her then. And what was about to happen to her now.

"Please," Belle said. "If you'd just—"

She lifted her hands, chains clinking. A man who'd strayed too close to her ducked his head, hurrying away. No one was willing to listen to her. Why should they? She wasn't one of their people, never had been, despite being born here.

But Belle wondered if it was more than that, even. The light, the song, made it hard to think, clouding people's judgement. They were all under a spell of sorts, the way Dee had described Ava and Clarence. Belle felt it herself, the song working on her, pulling her attention. It plucked at the strings of her own desire to hurt Clarence for what he'd done to her, for what he still intended to do to her. It sought to build her want into something irrational, something strong enough to tear through worlds.

Belle shifted her hands. The digging of the cuff and the chains helped, gave her something to focus on besides the light.

Sturdy crates had been repurposed as seats for some, while the rest of the congregation sat on the floor. She'd been chained in a spot that all the parishioners now faced. A sham trial, like the witch-burnings of old. Clarence had already decided her guilt. The light humming and rippling in the rafters was like a scythe, ready to be swung, not caring what it cut. Its presence had only drawn Clarence's worst impulses to the surface, turning him into something she doubted Dee would even recognize.

As she scanned the crowd again, Belle's gaze caught on an unfamiliar young woman huddled up against the wall at the end of a makeshift row. Brix hadn't had time to describe Leonie. This could be her, or any other young woman drawn away from the city, recruited by Clarence's followers.

No one else paid any attention to her, suggesting she'd come alone. She radiated a hunched-over misery strong enough to make the people in the barn instinctively draw away. Belle couldn't get a clear look at her face, covered by the shag of her dark hair. The faint sliver of her face that was visible looked drawn and exhausted.

Belle wondered if she could catch the young woman's eye. She wasn't from here; maybe she'd be willing to listen. It was a desperate hope, but these were desperate times. Belle raised her hands as far as she could, trying to signal the girl without drawing anyone else's attention.

A hush fell over the crowd, and Belle lost her opportunity. Her skin crawled as Clarence entered, everything in her wanting to lash out. She reached for Belizial by habit, but the cuff around her wrist burned, slamming her backward and separating them. Even without being able to feel them, she imagined Belizial drawing back from the hurt as well, made even worse by the memory of what had been done to them before. She needed to school herself not to reach for them.

Clarence spread his hands, smiling. Without a word, he

tilted his head back to bathe in the light roiling across the ceiling. Belle had the unnerving impression that his face was a mask, his smile carved and laid over an empty space.

"Brothers and sisters, we are here in the presence of a miracle both to mourn and heal. Our sister, Ava, was taken from us and I am to blame. I have sinned. I have allowed a shadow to exist in our midst for too long out of misguided loyalty. Jessamine, who stands before you now, is my own sister-in-law."

A gasp rippled over the crowd, as if half of those gathered didn't already know exactly who she was. As if Clarence had ever felt any kind of loyalty to her, even through Dee. Belle wished she could spit at all of them, him most of all. More people had crowded in to fill the spaces between the makeshift seats. Through a scant gap in the bodies, she could just see the miserable young woman leaning against the wall, eyes closed.

"Brothers and sisters, with your help, I will purge this sin from myself and cleanse this land. Once Jessamine's wickedness is gone, we will enter a new age together, a new dawn. Together we will step into the light."

Belle ground her teeth. The Hollow Queen played upon them all, dozens of strings to be tested, plucked to see which would be the first to break.

Even as the thought crossed her mind, the young woman leaning against the wall looked up, as if just now realizing where she was. *Shit.*

If she shouted a warning, surely Clarence would silence her. What would she even say? *Whatever is hurting you, pretend it isn't there. Stop wanting what you want.* Belle had done that very thing, and look where it had gotten her.

The young woman's head tilted back, eyes widening as she took in the rippling light. The expression of awe she wore was different from the others around her. It looked like recognition, like hope and longing. Her lips moved. Belle couldn't make out the words she mouthed. Using the wall as support, she climbed unsteadily to her feet, swaying slightly. Her face shone with tears, reflecting the light, but she didn't move any closer.

"Let us begin by hearing testimony first," Clarence said, drawing Belle's attention as he swept his arm to indicate the door at the far side of the barn.

Dee, flanked by two men holding her arms – to keep her from fleeing or to support her, Belle couldn't tell. She moved when they did, head down, feet shuffling across the dusty floor. When she drew close, Belle caught sight of her face: pure misery.

Idiot. Belle couldn't stop the thought from flying through her head. Why hadn't Dee run, stayed hidden? Unless she'd come here willingly, to speak against Belle.

She watched as Dee was jostled into place at Clarence's side. Her head remained lowered. Perhaps it was just as well. She wasn't sure she could bear to look her sister in the eye.

"Cordelia." Clarence turned to Dee. Her head rose like a string had been pulled.

"You know better than anyone your sister's wickedness. You were there at the beginning. Will you testify now, tell us of the dark pact she made?"

Belle tensed. The smug satisfaction on Clarence's face spoke of certainty. He thought he knew how Dee would answer.

There was a swooping sensation in Belle's chest, like missing a step. She wasn't so sure. The chains holding her sang as she leaned forward. She was sixteen again, sneaking into Dee's room, filled with desperate hope that Dee would take her hand, crawl out the window with her, and run across the moon-dark field.

"I don't..." Dee faltered. Tears glimmered in her eyes. She turned her face away from Clarence, but she didn't look at Belle either.

The crowd shuffled restlessly, a murmur passing among them. Clarence's mask slipped a fraction – annoyed, caught off guard. Dee hadn't followed his script. Belle felt a flickering moment of triumph.

Clarence recovered quickly, smooth and cajoling. "Come now, Cordelia—" He reached for her, and Dee twitched her arm away. It was only the faintest of movements. The breath ached in Belle's throat.

"It's him." The young woman who'd been leaning against the wall spoke, drawing all eyes to her. She took a step away from the wall, closer to Clarence. To Belle.

Belle looked around. Who was the young woman talking about? She couldn't see what the girl meant, but at the far end of the barn, she caught sight of a familiar face.

Brix.

Belle tried to shake her head. If he had a mind to stage some stupid rescue, he was going to get himself killed. She raised her hands a fraction, trying to draw his attention to the chains, hoping he would understand. She'd been cut off from Belizial; she was alone.

She couldn't tell whether he'd even seen. There were so many bodies crammed between them. Too many people for the two of them to take on.

"Enough!" Clarence's voice thundered.

The murmuring fell silent. Clarence took a step forward. Dee shrank back, but he ignored her completely. He gestured to the two men who'd led her into the barn, pointing them to Ava's wrapped body instead.

"Bring our fallen sister. Jessamine's influence has spread far enough. Even my poor wife is corrupt, confused. We cannot delay any longer."

Clarence grasped Belle's chains, unlocking them from the bolt in the floor and gathering them into his hands.

"Come, brothers and sisters. We will see this darkness ended." Clarence turned on his heel, giving the chain a sharp tug.

Belle caught an exchange of confused glances. After a moment, those seated began to rise, making their way toward the barn door. Even if Belle had been able to resist the drag of the chain, the sudden press of bodies would have washed her forward.

Brix was trying to reach her, struggling to keep his eyes on her above the heads of the crowd. A young man at Brix's side caught hold of his arm, pointing at the young woman who'd interrupted Clarence's trial. Belle's guess had been right, then – that was Leonie. She had no idea who the young man was. He peeled away from Brix, fighting the crowd.

Another sharp tug on the chain caused Belle to stumble. Clarence increased his pace, striding up the hill. The boots she'd borrowed from Hank Kennett, too big for her feet, sought to trip her. If she threw all her weight backward, could she pull Clarence off balance, get the chain around his neck? Belle twisted around as far as she could while keeping her feet under her, but she'd lost sight of Brix and Dee.

They reached the gallows above the pyre. The two men bearing Ava's body had gotten there first and laid her out atop the piled wood. Clarence grabbed Belle's upper arm and yanked her into place beside him as he turned to face the crowd.

The fear she hadn't allowed herself to feel before made itself known. "Whatever you think this is, Clarence, you're wrong. She's using—"

"No more from you."

He shook her hard enough that her teeth clacked together, then spun her around, shoving her forward. Belle wound up pressed against the scaffolding.

Clarence's voice was pitched loud enough for the gathered mass, though his words were directed at her.

"Is that not your name right there, your pledge to serve the darkness?"

It was flimsy as evidence went, but that didn't matter to Clarence or the assembled worshippers, not anymore. The light, and the Hollow Queen inside of it, had a hold of them. They'd given themselves over willingly, wanting to be part of something larger, seeing the faith they'd been told to have all their lives rewarded.

Even if it meant Belle's pain, her life in the end. It was her parents' thinking all over again.

Clarence pushed Belle's cheek against the gallows, the smell of lightning-struck wood filling her nose. It smelled like loss, like home. It didn't matter what she said, what she denied or admitted.

She thrashed in Clarence's grip, trying to knock him off balance. His hold tightened; for a moment, Belle thought he would forgo hanging and simply bash her head in on the scaffold.

"Clarence!" Dee called.

His grip on Belle loosened. Her legs went watery with relief. She fell, catching herself painfully on one knee. Dee had a hold of Clarence's shoulder, her full weight dragging at him. He couldn't push Dee off and keep hold of Belle at the same time.

Suddenly, Leonie was in their midst. This wasn't part of Clarence's script either. All her attention was on Ava's body, moving like someone in a trance. Dee continued to hang off Clarence's shoulder, but they were no longer grappling, their attention on the young woman as she stretched her hands out toward the shroud-wrapped corpse.

"I hear it," she said. "It's him. It's Jimmy. No, not here, he's—"

She turned away from Ava, her hands patting the empty air as if searching for something.

"I can't..." Leonie's hand drifted briefly to her midsection, then she turned in a circle, eyes wild and searching. "Where is he?"

Belle had no idea what the girl was talking about, but if it kept Clarence distracted...

"Leonie!" The young man who'd arrived with Brix pushed his way through the crowd, Brix on his heels.

Too much was happening at once.

Leonie turned toward Clarence. Belle was startled to see that even away from the barn, her face glowed with the same rapture as when she'd looked up at the squirming light, an echo clinging to her skin.

"You have to give him to me," Leonie implored, grabbing at Clarence's sleeve. "She said I would find him in the light. She promised."

Clarence looked baffled as he tried to shake off Leonie's grip.

"Leonie!" the young man called out again.

With dream-like slowness, Leonie turned her head. "I found him," she said, her expression rapturous. "It's going to be okay now. We can all be together again."

"Virgil, wait—" Brix said.

"Who—?"

Dee got no farther. Clarence shoved her away with enough force that she staggered. Belle's chain slithered through his hands and thumped heavily to the ground. Belle held her bound hands out to catch her sister, but Dee steadied herself, staring after Clarence as he took Leonie by the shoulders.

"You see, don't you? You recognize the light?"

Each of them clearly saw something completely different in the other – the light, the Hollow Queen, promising them what they wanted. They might not even be hearing each other at all, talking past each other, wrapped in their own private worlds.

Belle moved to her sister's side. While Clarence's attention was elsewhere, she nudged Dee's shoulder.

"Jacket pocket," Belle murmured. She turned her body to put the pocket in question closer to her sister. Dee stared, uncomprehending. Clarence tightened his grip on Leonie's upper arms, pulling her away.

"She is the one. I see it now. She is sacred and will bring our miracle into this world."

An uncertain, ragged cheer went up from somewhere in the crowd. After a moment, other voices picked it up. Its volume and certainty grew.

Belle's patience snapped. "Dee. Pocket."

Her tone jolted Dee into action. She reached into the jacket pocket – and recoiled.

"*Dee.*" Belle made her voice hard, a desperate warning.

Dee pulled Hank Kennett's revolver free, but held it like it might bite. Belle glanced at Clarence, to be sure he hadn't noticed

"Leonie," Virgil tried again. "Whatever you think, whatever she promised you, it's not really him. Jimmy left to try to help us. We can't bring him back without undoing all that he's done to keep us safe." His voice wavered, uncertain.

Doubt clouded Leonie's features. Virgil reached for her – and Clarence's face twisted in rage. "She is a holy vessel. You will not touch her," he thundered as he tried to wrench Leonie away.

Dee said, "Don't." Her voice was small, almost lost under the sound of the gun firing.

Belle jerked instinctively to the side and Clarence did the same, but too late. The bullet grazed his arm, and he howled, in surprise as much as pain.

"I didn't—" Dee's hands shook so badly, Belle was certain she hadn't meant to fire. With no safety catch, it would be far too easy to accidentally pull the trigger. "Belle?" She looked utterly stricken and lost.

As the echo of the shot died over the field, all hell broke loose.

29

Virgil lurched toward Leonie. Brix reached for Virgil. They both seemed to be falling away from him, impossibly distant. A woman – Belle's sister? He could see the resemblance – dropped to her knees, shoulders heaving. She let the gun fall from her hands. Belle reached toward her, but her wrists were bound.

The man who'd been shot – Clarence, Brix assumed – clutched his arm. Blood seeped between his fingers, staining his shirt. Not a mortal wound. Why in the hells had Cordelia shot him? Why was Belle in chains?

The echo of the shot became a song, rising and falling without words. It reminded him of struck glass chiming, or a choir. It reminded him of Jimmy Valentine playing the piano in the ballroom.

Clarence straightened. One hand was still pressed to his wounded arm, but he moved toward Cordelia as if he meant to knock her down. Belle stepped between them, throwing her shoulder. Meeting an immovable object – an apt description of Belle – stole his balance. He staggered back. When he tried to approach again, she lowered her head and smashed it into his nose.

"Get these chains off me." Belle twisted around, holding her hands out to Brix. She tried to keep an eye on Clarence, whose nose Brix suspected she'd just broken. When Brix didn't move, Belle thrust her bound hands forward impatiently. But it wasn't as though he'd packed a bolt cutter or a lockpick.

Virgil had Leonie by the arm now, trying to lead her gently away.

"It's Jimmy," she insisted, her voice cracking. "I can feel him."

The hell of it was, she wasn't wrong, not entirely. But he couldn't tell Leonie that; it would only make things worse.

"Syd!" Belle shouted and his attention snapped back to her.

"Right, luv. Any ideas about the key?"

"He's got it." Belle tossed her head to indicate Clarence, who'd let go of his arm to cradle his bleeding nose instead.

"Your brother-in-law, I assume?"

"Unfortunately." Belle grimaced, dodging as Clarence made a clumsy swipe at her with one bloodied hand.

Brix edged toward Clarence's other side, trying to shut out the ringing in his head, the sounds of chaos. Voices rose in prayer from the slope between the gallows and the barn. At least the crowd hadn't physically joined the fray.

Clarence made another feint toward Belle. Cordelia threw herself at his legs, wrapping her arms around him and bringing him crashing down. Brix took the opportunity to dart forward, reaching into his pockets. Belle took her chance as well, retrieving the pistol her sister had dropped, holding it awkwardly in her bound hands.

"You have to help him." Cordelia's voice was breathless as she tried to keep hold of her husband.

"Dee." Uncertainty shone in Belle's eyes. "He's not... He isn't himself anymore. I don't know—"

As if to prove Belle's point, a thrashing kick from Clarence caught Brix behind the knee. He hadn't even been the target, but it dropped him halfway. Another wild blow caught him in the throat. His vision spotted as he gagged for breath. His hand closed on metal. He stumbled back, tripping over his own heels and going down with the key in his hand.

"Clarence!" Cordelia yelled.

A hand caught Brix's ankle, trying to drag him backward, but it was just as quickly removed. He heard the sounds of a struggle, then flesh striking flesh. When his vision cleared, Cordelia was sprawled on the grass, cheek pressed to the earth, eyes closed. She breathed, but Brix couldn't tell if she was conscious.

Brix tried to push himself up and failed. There was something wrong with the light falling over the hillside. The sun had turned strange – or it had gone altogether, and the light shining over them was something else.

He looked up, squinting. The light from the barn writhed, drifting closer, lashing tendrils down toward the congregation like a tree, planting itself in the men and women who stood with their faces upturned. The same light he'd seen the

Hollow Queen pull out of Jimmy, but grown to a much larger size, feeding on the desires of the gathered crowd. Whatever it was exactly – Brix still didn't fully understand – he knew it being here couldn't mean anything good. The Hollow Queen would use it as a weapon, or a doorway, a way into this world – following her nature and devouring everything until nothing remained. Not this world, not her own realm, not even the hells, of the realms of the dead. Just nothing, forever.

He shielded his eyes. Looking at the light slantwise between his fingers made it easier to bear. There was a raggedness to it, like a crack into another world. Brix glimpsed the hall from the mirrors in the ballroom, cold and dark. The perspective was wrong. He couldn't tell if it was above or below him, but either way, he felt poised to fall.

He tore his gaze away. He had to make sure Virgil and Leonie were safe. He'd promised.

They stood only a few paces from him, but their edges blurred. The light around them was ice, the palest lilac, the surface of the ocean, a gathering storm. Virgil's arms wrapped around Leonie, his face buried in her neck as if trying to sink into her skin or pull her into his, sheltering them both.

Brix's knee throbbed where he'd been kicked. The pain was good, keeping him centered, keeping him from slipping. He glanced up again.

A figure stood silhouetted against the light, drawing closer. He'd seen her in the hotel room, whispering to Leonie; he'd seen her in Jimmy's memories.

The Hollow Queen with her crown of glass, her mouth full of bloodied teeth.

She reached for him, fingers like ice dragged across his ribs. "*You can have her back.*"

Abby wasn't hers to give, but even knowing as much didn't stop the promise from slithering against his ear, winding its way into him. Brix took a step back, away from the light, or tried, but it was everywhere. He stumbled – and fell into a duck pond.

It was impossible. Rationally, he knew nothing was there besides the grass of the hill, but soaked clothing still clung to him as he sputtered to the surface and a hand grasped his own to pull him free.

"I've got you."

Abby. Sunlight caught in her hair, illuminating her gentle smile as she tried to keep from laughing at him and failed.

She steadied him, hauling him from the pond that wasn't there. Her hand was warm. She hadn't yet let go, and Brix could feel her. He could actually feel her. His heart turned over behind his ribs, gilded with frost where the Hollow Queen had touched him.

"I'm okay," Brix said. "You can let me go."

"I don't have to though," she said, and as she spoke, her mouth blurred – the lips he knew so well bleeding into a mouth the color of pomegranates. The warmth of her touch turned to frost all at once, creeping up his arm.

Brix wrenched himself away. The Hollow Queen shrieked, lunging after him. In the same moment, he felt the dust along the bone road stir, a polite request without words brushing against his mind. The notes of a song shivered down the length of his spine. The familiarity of it made Brix acquiesce before he'd even fully processed what was going on. Just before the

Hollow Queen reached him, Jimmy appeared at her side.

"There's no need for all that, darlin'." The honey of his voice matched his sweet, sad smile.

Jimmy glowed, the vision in starlight Brix had pictured. It was hard to look at him straight on, the same way it was hard to look at the light. Brix squinted, and when he did, Jimmy looked like a door – a burning outline that he could step through into another world.

"I know it hurts," Jimmy went on. He hadn't even looked at Brix, all his attention for the Hollow Queen. "It's never stopped hurting, and I'm truly sorry for that. I never should have left you, but I'm here now. I'm hoping you'll trust me and take my hand."

Brix felt the sincerity of the words, the regret, the weight of everything that had broken between Jimmy and his queen. Jimmy held out a hand. The Hollow Queen didn't move, but for a moment, she looked lost and small.

It was enough. Jimmy stepped close, put his arms around her and rested his forehead against hers. Brix imagined the chill of the crown seeping through his skin, but to his credit, Jimmy didn't move. He went right on holding on to her, and this time, he wouldn't let go.

"It's okay, darlin', you can rest now."

The words were soft, barely a whisper. They sounded like all of summer in a day, they sounded like hope, which could be just as dangerous as wanting, but nonetheless he chose to believe they were true. Then, like a hand had been pressed to his chest, he felt himself pushed gently away. He hadn't moved, but distance now existed between himself and

Jimmy and the queen, and the hillside with all its chaos came rushing back.

"Clarence." Belle's voice broke through the haze and the lingering sense of melancholy in Brix's mind.

He turned in time to see her lift the revolver, pointing it square at her brother-in-law as best she could with bound hands.

"Belle, luv, you don't—" Brix began, but Clarence's voice drowned him out.

"You. Will. Be. Cleansed." He bit off each word, advancing toward Belle, heedless of the weapon pointed at him, of the blood slicking his chin from his broken nose. The light bolstered him, let him ignore the pain.

He only slowed as he nearly tripped over Cordelia, still sprawled on the ground. The look he gave her was cold and devoid of compassion, as if he saw not his wife but an obstacle. He grasped the back of her neck as if he meant to shake her roughly, or simply haul her out of the way. Cordelia whimpered softly, but didn't struggle.

"Don't," Belle said.

Clarence ignored her.

Belle didn't warn him a second time.

She fired, and there was no doubt she'd meant to pull the trigger. The bullet caught Clarence between the eyes, throwing him back, spattering Belle in red.

The light stuttered, fragmented. Clarence fell backward in a series of still frames captured by its flashes until he hit the ground. No longer held upright, Cordelia slumped bonelessly alongside him.

The light howled, the same sound as it had in the hotel room – the shriek of hunger denied. Clarence had been taken away, and even now, Virgil coaxed Leonie out of its grasp. Jimmy had the Hollow Queen distracted. They were winning, but they hadn't won yet.

Brix clapped his hands to his ears, but the sound was already inside him. There was no shutting it out. He ducked, as if he could escape, but it was below him too, shaking the earth. He lurched toward Virgil, trying to get his attention.

"We have to push it back," Brix shouted. "Get the door closed."

The very air around them vibrated and roared, a storm bent on tearing up chunks of ground, scattering grit and tiny rocks into the air to pummel at them. Brix raised an arm, trying to shield his face.

"Like we did in the hotel," he said. "We have to untether it, make it let go."

Virgil raised his head from Leonie's neck. His face was splotched red and pale from crying, but he nodded. He kept one arm around her, and she leaned into him, slumping with exhaustion.

"I'm sorry," Brix said.

A muscle in Virgil's jaw twitched, but he set it in determination, meeting Brix's eye. "Tell me what to do."

"This goes against everything I'm going to teach you later, but right now, I need you to lean into the fact that you don't know what you're doing. Follow your instinct. Don't think about it, just do what your gut tells you and help me stitch this thing closed."

Brix reached toward the light. It hurt. Gods, but it hurt. Not just the burning, freezing sensation, but the torrent of images. The hall and the queen with her terrible crown. A dark place under everything where something had been bound, pain drawn from its skin. Trees flashing by in a headlong flight from a horrible pursuit. A feeling like being split in two, then knit together again. A stage in a club. The world ending and beginning in the lonely baying of the hunt being called. One step on a bone road. A chord strummed softly, a voice like velvet singing.

Jimmy held the Hollow Queen in his arms. Hers remained slack at her sides, allowing herself to be held, but not holding Jimmy in turn. That didn't seem to matter to him. He went right on singing, a song meant only for her. In her stillness, eerie as it was, Brix had the sense that she was crying.

Virgil braced the doors of Brix's ribs the way he had in the hotel, holding open the way to the road between worlds. Brix concentrated on the light, even as its brightness stung tears from his eyes. It had been a part of Jimmy once, but it was so much more than that now – bound up with the Hollow Queen, with all the hopes of Clarence's followers gazing up at it from below.

He would treat it like any other ghost. What else could he do? Brix reached, slow and steady, then felt something catch and hold. He pulled the light toward himself, offering it his own need. Abby taking his hand and pulling him from the duck pond. Walking with her in the sun the day she'd agreed to have coffee with him, and all the walks they'd taken together since. The darkening like bruises around her eyes when she first got sick, and the weightlessness of her hand when he held it for the last time.

He couldn't imagine exactly what the queen felt, but he knew what it meant to be hollowed out by pain that would never end.

The light moved toward him, through him, yearning toward Jimmy's song as he called to it from the other side. The bone road wasn't just unfurling within him this time, but as if he actually stood astride it, one foot in either world. He shuddered, but Virgil steadied him, speaking words of encouragement. Brix couldn't hear exactly what he said, but he got the gist. He could do this thing. He could hold it all.

Then Jimmy was there too, a boy leaving his hometown with his head full of dreams and a guitar slung across his back. An idol, up on the screen, holding the audience rapt with the spell of his words. A singer, surrounded by the velvet dark, lips next to the microphone. A man who loved deeply enough that it might even heal the hurts of the Hollow Queen.

Jimmy turned his head, looking straight at Brix. "I think it's time you came home now, too."

His pulse lurched. He couldn't, not yet. He hadn't sent Abigail on; he couldn't leave her trapped and go on without her to the bone road. Panic scrambled through his mind; it took him a moment to understand that Jimmy wasn't talking to him, but the light. All Brix had to do was be what he'd always been: a door.

With Virgil bracing him, he stretched, reaching for Jimmy on one side and the light on the other. It felt like he would snap, pulled to his breaking point, but he forced himself to hold on.

Abby still needed him, and so did all the people on the hill.

Roots tore, threads broke. The light rushed toward Jimmy and his song, hungering for all that it had lost, two halves longing to be whole. Brix let go and slammed the door closed.

A howling implosion. The sky turned a strange silver-slate color, like a lid clapped down over the world. Thunder followed, mingled with the cries of the parishioners as the light went out. Brix staggered sideways, the land itself trying to buck him off. At the bottom of the hill, the barn collapsed as if flattened by a gigantic hand. A great rushing wind sent a shockwave outward, bowing the grass.

Useless as it was, Brix curled in a ball, arms over his head. The wind washed over him like the slap of a wave. After a long moment, when the only sound was the thud of his own pulse, he lowered his arms and risked looking around.

Belle had lowered the gun, but other than that, she hadn't moved. She looked incredibly tired. Virgil and Leonie slumped against each other, holding each other up. The world had ended, or maybe it had just begun, and it had all happened within the blink of an eye.

Brix unfolded and stood. Several parishioners lay on the ground. Some wept openly, the sounds of their grief joined by murmured prayers, while others knelt to tend the fallen or tried to lift them. Still others wandered in listless circles, or brief jags in one direction before changing their minds and wandering back the other way.

Chains rattled; Brix remembered the key. He stepped over Clarence's body, unable to stop himself from looking at the ruin of his face.

"You'll want to stand back as soon as these are undone," Belle said. The faintest tremor marked her voice – the strain of holding herself back, the force of her rage, her exhaustion, all of it together.

Brix fitted the key into the lock, stepping back swiftly as the shackles fell. Belle's demon burst from her skin. He turned his face away, instinctively giving her privacy – but Virgil gasped, and he looked back despite himself.

Belle had half transformed, a mass of tangled blackness rising from her skin. Belizial surrounded her, holding her, and she held them too, clinging together like a storm had swept over them.

It lasted an eternity, and it lasted only a moment. Belle and the demon together stepped over Clarence's form and knelt beside Cordelia, one hand outstretched, as if afraid to touch her. Her fingers found the space beneath her sister's jaw to feel for a pulse. Brix saw the relief, strong enough that she would have collapsed on top of Cordelia if Belizial hadn't been there to hold her up.

Brix used his sleeve to wipe the pistol Belle had dropped clean before setting it back down next to Clarence's foot. He began to guide Virgil and Leonie down the hill. "Let's give them some privacy, shall we?"

He glanced back. The sky was just the sky now – grey clouds backed by sun that struggled to break through. The gallows stood ugly against it. Below, Belle and her demon were a single, twisted form crouched over Cordelia, crouched beside Clarence's body, silently emptying themselves of all their pain.

30

Belle closed the bedroom door softly, leaving Dee to sleep. A bruise darkened her jaw where Clarence had struck her, but other than that, her wounds were not physical. Belle had put her in their childhood bedroom, the one they'd shared for a time.

It seemed kinder than leaving Dee in the room that had belonged to her and Clarence. Belle had tried to keep Dee from seeing his corpse, but of course Dee had stopped. She'd spent a good long time looking down at him before pulling free of Belle's arm and continuing down the hill alone.

She'd loved him, regardless of what he'd become. He'd been her home in the way Belizial was Belle's. Finally, she understood what her sister had been trying to tell her. A life in the city, a life away from the farm where she'd been born, weren't things Dee had ever wanted. Belle had simply wanted them so badly that she couldn't fathom someone else not wanting them as well.

She returned to the kitchen where Brix, Leonie, and Virgil sat around the table. The remaining parishioners had scattered, limping back to their homes, sore in body and spirit. How much would they remember of what had occurred, of the fae power that had pulled them here and held them briefly under its sway? Those who'd come from the cities had either returned to their vehicles or found someone to take them in for the night. The makeshift tents remained, fluttering in the wind beside dead campfires. The gallows stood, for now. Clarence and Ava's bodies lay side by side on the pyre.

After everyone else was asleep, Belle would return to the field. She and Belizial would give Ava a proper burial, at least. They'd let Clarence and the gallows burn.

Brix stood hastily when she entered, chair scraping over the floor. He moved to the stove where pans sat over two of the burners. She smelled eggs and bacon.

"It's not much, but it's hot. I even rustled up some bread if you want toast." Brix looked so hopeful that she felt guilty refusing, but her stomach roiled.

She'd have to find somewhere for them all to sleep. They couldn't possibly be expected to return to the city in their current state. Leonie and Virgil, she could put in Dee's room. Brix might have to make do with the uncomfortable sofa. It was too short, but at least there was enough bedding. All she wanted to do was be home in her own bed with Belizial twined around her, but Belle didn't anticipate sleeping tonight.

"Not right now," she said, then remembered to add, "thank you."

She waved Brix back to the table, trying to ignore his

disappointed look. Belizial coiled beneath her skin, making their disapproval known. She spoke to appease both of them. "I promise I'll eat something later. I would take tea if there's a pot."

Brix hurried to get a fresh mug. Belle dropped heavily into the remaining empty chair. Virgil had cleaned his plate, Leonie picking at hers. They both watched her with wide eyes.

"I'm Bellefeather. Brix's partner. I gather you're Virgil and Leonie."

Brix set tea in front of her and resumed his seat. Belle tried not to picture her own family here. Had they ever been happy together, shared a pleasant meal? All she could dredge up in her mind were hands joined, heads bowed in prayer, always a requirement before they were allowed to touch their food. Then, the awkward scrape of forks and knives over plates. She couldn't once remember her mother or father asking her or Dee any questions beyond whether their chores were done.

She remembered eyes narrowed in suspicion, being watched like a hawk after finally being released from her room. Dee's eyes red and puffy, refusing to look Belle's way. She remembered her own hand just under the table, clutched around the hilt of a knife so dull it could barely cut the roast that had been softening in the oven for hours, let alone living flesh, but she couldn't make herself let go.

"Are you alright?" Virgil asked.

Belle shook herself, about to answer, when she realized the question had been directed at Leonie. She was still pale, the way she'd been in the barn, but instead of misery, Belle saw uncertainty in her face. She glanced between the three of them like there was a question she wanted to ask, but didn't know how.

Virgil took her hand, and Leonie ducked her head, speaking quickly. "Before I left the hotel, I felt like... like I was trying to remember something important but she wouldn't let me. I think I remember now."

Leonie glanced up quickly and away again. She seemed almost... embarrassed wasn't quite the right word, but as if she doubted everything about herself, and was afraid of what the rest of them would think of her. Belle didn't consider herself particularly good at judging people's ages, but just now, Leonie looked very young.

"I think... I might be pregnant," she said.

Virgil's mouth dropped open, struggling for words, and his voice cracked when he finally found it again. "A baby?"

"I don't know," Leonie said. "I know Jimmy's gone, really gone. I think the part of him I still felt with me isn't really him but... someone new. It's just a feeling. I could be wrong."

She sounded on the verge of tears. Belle didn't know everything they'd been through before the barn, but she could recognize exhaustion, loss. Virgil put his arm around Leonie's shoulders, pulling her to him.

"Belizial could tell if you are," Belle said.

Virgil looked at her. "Belizial is your..."

He let the words trail, clearly uncertain how to finish the sentence. She had no idea what Brix had told them about her, but they'd all seen her change on the hill. Her wrists itched. She had no idea where her gloves had gone. She still wore

Hank Kennett's clothes, his white shirt spattered with blood, the sleeves pushed up far enough that her scars showed.

"Yes," she said. "Belizial is mine, and I'm theirs."

The demon's warmth spread around her bones, more comforting than the tea. There were things that needed to be worked out between them, but for now, they were being kind. She didn't deserve it, but she would take the grace offered to her.

What she'd said was true: they belonged to each other. Belizial hadn't left her, wouldn't leave her.

"And they could tell if Leonie is...?"

Leonie sat up, pulling Virgil's arm from her shoulder so she could hold his hand instead.

"Yes," Belle said.

Leonie released a breath. "I'd like to know."

Brix shifted his gaze to Belle. His expression was doubtful – not of her, but of her choice to do this for Leonie and Virgil. After all the times she'd asked him to turn away while she changed, he wanted to protect her privacy. A complicated knot untangled itself inside of her.

"It's okay." She'd never been ashamed of Belizial. She'd been... protective? Jealous? What exactly was it that she hadn't wanted Brix to see?

Her. All of her. If he saw, if he knew all of her, then he might leave.

Belle swallowed, putting the thought away. She laid her hand on the table, palm up. After a moment, Leonie took it.

Belizial uncoiled from her skin, a tendril of darkness circling Leonie's wrist. No one flinched. Belle felt herself relax a little more.

Leonie was entranced, her features slack with wonder. Brix's expression was more complicated, something like gratitude. He'd understood all along – better than she had – what this meant about the way she trusted him. The urge rose in her to apologize – but there would be time for that later, too. She turned her attention fully to Leonie.

Belizial spread further, flaring about her. Belle's awareness flowed through them as they extended themself. Leonie, but again, she didn't flinch or pull away. She kept her hand in Belle's and let Belizial examine her.

Leonie's pulse, her heartbeat, the breath in her lungs. A second heartbeat, the fluttering of new life. But a life that straddled two worlds. Interesting.

Belizial withdrew, sinking back comfortingly beneath Belle's skin. She found herself smiling and brushed her thumb lightly across Leonie's knuckles before withdrawing her hand.

"Yes," she said.

Leonie stared at Belle a moment longer before turning to face Virgil. The world narrowed between them. She and Brix should give them their space, but she was too tired to move.

The look Brix gave her implied she'd done a good thing. She wondered again what the two across the table had been through.

"Are we okay?" Leonie asked Virgil.

Virgil's mouth opened, like he was surprised she'd even asked. Slowly, his expression became a grin.

"We're better than okay." He leaned closer until his forehead touched hers. "I love you, and I'm going to love our baby. I mean…" He faltered briefly. Belle noted the scratches marking his cheek. "If you… want it, that is, and if you don't, it's okay. I'll love any baby you might want to have, whether it's this one, or whether you want to wait until we're a hundred years old or—"

Leonie stopped him with a kiss. Belle wasn't sure where to look, settling on Brix, whose expression was both proud and somewhat melancholy.

Virgil was breathless when she finally broke it off.

"This baby," Leonie said.

Virgil's grin returned, doubled now.

"You're going to be a heck of a mom," Virgil said. "And I'm going to be a heck of a dad. I can't wait to teach him everything and tell him all about his other dad. Do you think he'll be a singer, too? What do you think about naming him Valentine?"

Belle couldn't draw an ounce of sense from Virgil's words, the rush of them, but she understood the excitement shining in his eyes and the hectic blush coloring his cheeks.

"What if it's a girl?" Leonie's mouth crimped in amusement, caught in Virgil's infectious excitement and baffled by the magnitude of it. Under all of it, Belle sensed a lingering sadness, held at bay.

"It works either way." Virgil didn't miss a beat, squeezing Leonie's hands. "Valentine. But it's going to be a boy. I can feel it."

"Well." Brix pushed his chair back from the table. "This calls for something celebratory, I'd say."

He disappeared into the front parlor and returned a

moment later with a bottle sealed in red wax and a layer of dust. He worked the wax off the cork with a knife from one of the drawers, which he also used to dig the cork free and poured a small splash into each of their empty mugs. More, Belle noted with approval, for her and him than Virgil or Leonie.

"To new beginnings." Brix raised his mug. Belle didn't miss the catch in his voice, nor the troubled expression beneath his mask of cheer.

She obediently raised her mug. "New beginnings."

The sound of clinking ceramic filled the room. Brix leaned close, properly careful with his words this time, so only she would hear. "It's not quite all done yet, is it, luv?"

She knew what he meant. Not just the possibility of legal trouble that might fall on them, the bodies waiting for disposal. She owed it to Ava to try to find her sister and give her some kind of explanation. Freed from the Hollow Queen's spell, the parishioners might not remember what had happened, but Dee wouldn't forget that she had shot her husband, or that Belle had finished the job. But Brix also meant Abigail and Belizial, wounds that needed to be healed, doors that needed to be closed.

"The baby..." Belle let the words trail.

A life straddling two worlds.

"I promised to watch over them," he went on, dropping his voice farther still. "We'll talk about it later, but this is a good thing, and they deserve some happiness."

Belle heard the uncertainty in his voice. He had his doubts, but he was right – they could figure things out later; for now, they had all earned a break. Still, she wondered what pasts Virgil and Leonie were leaving behind, what kind of future they looked forward to, and what kind of future she herself, and Brix for that matter, could expect.

She sipped, warmth spreading over her tongue and through her empty stomach. Belizial nestled around her spine, sending a gentle reprimand and reminder of her promise to eat something. She tried not to think of the past or the future, to exist only in this moment. Tried, and failed.

The truck Virgil had borrowed wasn't designed to hold four, but Brix crammed in beside Belle long enough for the drive to the train station. The roads had dried out after the storm, and the truck kicked up dust as they drove. It felt like a lifetime ago that Brix had met them in a hotel room, and now Virgil and Leonie's gazes drifted to each other repeatedly, as if neither could quite believe the other was real, that they'd survived.

Virgil pulled in next to the platform. Brix climbed out, Belle following him. Virgil surprised him by jumping out as well, crushing him in a hug that stole his breath.

"Thank you, really, for everything," Virgil said. "And if the offer still stands, I would like to learn properly, once things have settled down."

He'd glanced back at Leonie in the passenger seat. Brix wondered if he should try to say something to her, attempt to apologize again, but she looked away, ducking her head so her hair covered her face, an effective curtain between them.

"She'll come around," Virgil said. Brix hoped he was right. "Promise you'll be in touch?"

"Of course, luv." Brix tried to keep the worry and weariness of out of his voice. "After all, I still owe you for that meal on the road, and the gas. You've got a nest egg to build now."

Virgil's face lit with a grin, and he glanced back at Leonie again, glowing.

"Oh, I'm not worried about that."

Before Brix could ask, Virgil fished in the pocket of his shirt and drew out two folded sheets of paper. He unfolded them, turned the top sheet around so Brix could see.

Brix recognized stationery from the Peony Hotel, bearing the three trademark flowers and the hotel's name. Beneath them were chords and lyrics written in plain pencil, but which seemed to shimmer faintly with the silver of foxfire and ghost-light.

"Is that...?"

"Jimmy gave it to me in the ballroom." Virgil's smile took on a note of sorrow. "I almost forgot all about it until we were going to sleep last night. He said it was a gift for me and Leonie, and it ought to be worth a fair bit if I took it to a man named Wallace Statler. He used to be Jimmy's manager. He's in his eighties now, but Jimmy said he's still sharp as a tack and can get things done. He gave me a letter with a whole bunch of stuff in it that only Jimmy and Wally would know, said it'd prove the song really came from Jimmy, and that the money from selling the rights ought to go to me and Leonie. I don't know if Jimmy knew about the baby, but either way, it seems he did his best to set us up for life."

Virgil folded the pages carefully back into his pocket, his eyes glazed with tears. Brix squeezed his arm.

"Take care of yourself," he said. "Take care of each other, and whenever you're ready, give me a call."

Virgil nodded, blinking, and climbed back into the truck. Brix watched them pull away, his heart going with them.

Belle returned from procuring tickets. While they waited, Brix launched into an update, filling her in as best he could on everything that had occurred at the Peony Hotel.

"Jimmy Valentine," he'd told her. "*The* Jimmy Valentine. In the flesh. Well, not in the flesh exactly, but still, can you believe it?"

Belle returned a blank look. Wind swept the platform, tugging at her skirt and her hair. She'd regained her own clothing, burning the borrowed suit. The man she'd borrowed it from wouldn't miss it, and besides, she couldn't return it stained with Clarence's blood.

"Seriously, you've never heard of Jimmy Valentine?" Brix asked. Belle shook her head.

Brix didn't let that daunt him, going on about the idol, his songs, his movies, as they settled into their carriage, ignoring Belle's air of distraction.

She rested her head against the train window, ostensibly watching the scenery roll by, but Brix suspected she was thinking of her sister, and of Belizial. Belle filled him in on some of what had occurred at the farm, but she kept her account brief and left him to do most of the talking. She'd been cut off from her demon for a short enough time, but it couldn't have failed to open old wounds, dig up a past she would rather forget.

By the time the train pulled into the Grand Plaza Station, he was exhausted, but even so, Brix wished the journey would last even longer. He didn't want to go home. He followed Belle under the station's vaulted ceilings, past the massive Tiffany clock that made him think of the glass mural in the Peony.

She hailed a cab, and too soon, they pulled up in front of his brownstone. There was nothing left to say to delay the inevitable. He couldn't talk past this moment any longer. He needed to let Belle get home. And he had work to do.

Belle touched his wrist as he reached for the door. He paused, the meter ticking, the cabbie professionally ignoring them as he'd done throughout the ride.

The unspoken offer was clear in Belle's eyes; she would do this thing for him if he asked. She would be by his side if he needed her. She already knew his answer, yet made the offer anyway, and he appreciated it. But he needed to do this alone.

He patted her hand where it rested on his wrist. "Thanks, luv."

She gave a near-imperceptible nod and withdrew, but kept watching him for a moment longer. If she asked whether he was sure, he would crack.

She didn't. She folded her hands back into her lap and he slid out, closing the door behind him.

Before the cab pulled away, Brix said, "Tomorrow night, you're coming around for dinner. No excuses."

"Why?"

It was a sign of Belle's own exhaustion that she'd let the unfiltered question slip – he was certain she hadn't slept at the farmhouse. Brix couldn't stop a smile lifting the corner of his mouth. Belle had the grace to blush, or as close as she got to it, anyway.

"Because we're friends, that's why." He let it go unsaid that after what would happen next, he didn't want to be alone. "Tomorrow, seven. You can bring wine."

Belle nodded, and the car pulled away. The weight of the house settled against Brix's back. He patted the satchel at his side, a half-compulsive gesture. Leonie had returned it; she hadn't gotten around to selling anything, not that there was much to sell.

He turned and faced the house. It was five short steps from the sidewalk to the door, yet it loomed – the brick façade imposing, the windows watching him in silent judgement.

Brix dragged himself up to unlock the door. He lifted the strap of his satchel over his head and set it down. He toed his shoes off, removed his coat and hung it up. It felt like he'd been gone for years. The house breathed silence around him. He imagined he could smell dust and time and beneath it, waiting.

He paused with his hand on the newel post, his foot on the first stair and glanced toward the dining room, the empty chair at the end of the table. If he squinted, he could imagine Abigail's form, a smudged absence sketched upon the air.

"Soon, love," he murmured. "I'm going to do things right."

Upstairs, he shed his clothes while he waited for the

bathtub to fill. He tipped in a measure of lavender-scented oil and climbed in, wishing the dread settled against his spine didn't insist on following him. He sank below the water line, trying to soak the stink of death from his hair, and wondered briefly if he could stay below until his lungs ran out of air.

He surfaced, scraped a razor over his cheeks and chin, rubbed soap into his skin.

Once he'd dried himself off, Brix dressed in his best suit – one of his only suits, the one he would have worn to their wedding one day. He ran a comb through his hair, doing the best he could to tame it, and returned to the dining room. He wished he'd thought to buy flowers from one of the vendors outside the train station, one last romantic gesture before saying goodbye.

He spread salt around Abigail's chair, around the table, and as an extra precaution, trailed lines across the thresholds between the dining room, the hallway, and the kitchen. He marked the windowsills, then dropped his ring into the shallow bowl beside Abigail's and moved to stand just outside the circle surrounding her chair.

He'd barely closed his eyes when he felt her presence, rushing like a wind through an open door. She'd been waiting, just on the other side, eager for him to keep his promise and let her go.

"Hello, love." Brix opened his eyes and made himself smile, despite the thickness in his throat.

Abigail's glance flicked from the chair at the far end of the table where he normally sat, to where he stood. He saw her register the table's emptiness: no meal, no plates, no candles.

"Sydney?" She turned his name into a question that held multitudes, including barely contained hope.

It hurt. It hurt worse than bloody anything, but Brix made himself keep smiling against the tears filling his eyes.

"It's long past time," he said. "I know that. I've been horribly unfair. But I'm wondering if you'd do me one last honor before you go?"

Doubt flickered in Abigail's eyes, the color of the moon, and that hurt too. She expected him to go back on his promise. Brix took a breath, focusing on her eyes, which he could almost imagine were the shade they'd been when she was alive.

"Will you marry me?"

"What are—"

"Please say yes." Brix reached for the dish on the table, palmed both rings and held them out. "I know it doesn't change anything about what we are and were to each other, but it would mean something to me to say it all out loud before the end."

It was only a moment before she spoke, but it felt like an eternity. "Yes."

Brix had been holding his breath. He let it go, every part of him bruised. He let the tears go too, wondering why he'd ever bothered to fight them. As Abby watched, he dragged a toe through the line of salt surrounding her. She opened her mouth, but he shook his head and reached for her hand.

"I trust you," he said. More than he trusted himself. "Trust me?"

She hesitated only a moment, then lifted her hand. He couldn't touch her. Not the way he wanted. He thought of

Leonie and Jimmy Valentine, entwined. That could be him and Abigail, if he let it happen. He wouldn't, even though it was the most gods-damned unfair thing in the world.

He slipped his own ring back onto his finger, then held his hand under Abigail's upturned palm. Her hand rested just over his, a scant, chill space between them. Yearning toward each other, but not making contact. Not sinking into each other, as much as he wanted to.

Brix met Abigail's eyes, kept his gaze there, and rushed through the words he wanted to say before he lost the ability to speak altogether.

"Abigail, I hereby take you as my wife and give myself as your husband." Brix paused, and regretted it, breath stuttering. Fuck formality. He smiled at her, tears sliding into the corners of his mouth. "We've been through better and we've been through worse and I'd do it all again, given the chance. I'm yours, Abby. Always have been, always will be. Death doesn't mean a bloody thing. I don't intend to ever stop loving you."

He moved the ring to approximately where the tip of her finger would be. The air shivered where Abigail stood; he could feel the tension of her holding back, holding on.

"Sydney, I don't know... what I can say." It sounded like the words pained her, like she wanted to stay and needed to be gone.

"*I love you* will do."

"I love you."

He knew she meant it, too.

"Time to go," Brix said.

He slid the ring over nothing, closed his eyes again, and leaned in to brush a kiss over nonexistent lips. Frost spread over his skin, digging into him like he would never be warm again. He didn't care. He wanted to hold the moment as long as he could, but he'd already been holding on too long.

The door was open, ready for Abby to step through, the bone road stretching to wherever it went. He couldn't know, not until it was his time.

Brix opened his fingers. The silver ring dropped onto the dining room floor. It spun there a moment until it came to a rest in the silence and emptiness of the room.

32

"I don't know the first thing about wine, so I hope this is okay," Belle said.

She held out the bottle for Brix's inspection, feeling suddenly shy. She'd never been across the threshold, never actually set foot in his house before. Brix took the bottle from her and dutifully turned it, his expression serious in a way that let her know he was gently mocking her. She'd let the clerk at the shop pick it, trusted it would be good, and trusted Brix to be kind enough not to say anything if she'd chosen wrong.

"Perfect," Brix said finally. "It'll pair nicely. I did duck, roasted mushrooms, whipped potatoes, and greens. I hope you're hungry."

Brix's sleeves were rolled to his elbows, a wash towel slung over one shoulder. At the scents coming from the kitchen, Belle realized she was starved. Belizial rumbled beneath her skin, both encouragement and more gentle mockery.

Told you so.

She didn't deign to respond.

Brix gestured for her to follow him. "I thought we'd eat in the kitchen. I hope you don't mind. The dining room is so formal."

He tossed the words casually over his shoulder, but Belle didn't miss the hitch in his voice. Nor did she miss the places he didn't allow his gaze to linger, even for a moment – the chair at the far end of the table with its back to a tall, stained-glass window.

"Sit," Brix said as they crossed into the kitchen.

He gestured to one of two tall chairs side by side at either end of a long counter, close enough for comfortable conversation, far enough to give them each their space to navigate into this new stage of their friendship.

Brix was right; the kitchen was cozier. Copper pots hung from the ceiling. The bottom half of the walls were white-painted wood paneling, the upper half a warm, dusty blue. Belle draped her coat over the back of the chair and sat. She'd foregone her gloves, which felt monumental. She fought the urge to tug at her sleeves.

Brix poured two glasses of dark red wine, which Belle accepted gratefully as he handed her one.

"I'm ready to serve up if you're ready to eat," he said.

He touched the rim of his glass briefly to hers. It chimed, a pleasant sound in the warmth of the room. Belizial turned within her like a cat settling in for a long nap. They liked Brix, always had, and they liked him even more now that he'd insisted on feeding her. She'd have to watch out for the two of them getting too close; if she wasn't careful, they'd end up conspiring against her.

"By all means. It smells wonderful."

Belle watched with fascination as he plated and served. She'd never seen Brix look more comfortable, more in his element, than he did moving around his kitchen. He took the second chair, angling his body slightly so that he could watch her.

"It's been a long time since I've cooked for anyone. Tell me what you think." His eagerness bordered on ridiculous; Belle wished she couldn't also see the sorrow lying just below the surface.

She tried to ignore her self-consciousness as she cut a slice of the duck and put it in her mouth. She nearly choked from sheer surprise at the perfect crust of spice crisped into the seared fat, at the delightful juice of the pink-red center. When she remembered to chew, it was ravenously. Belizial chuckled again. It was just as well her mouth was full, otherwise she would have told them out loud to shut up.

"Syd, it's incredible." She couldn't keep the awe out of her voice and hoped it wouldn't come off as rude. She'd never doubted his skill, but she'd also never eaten anything like this in her entire life.

"Of course it is." Brix flashed her a grin as she speared a mushroom and dragged it through the cream of the potatoes. "This is what food is supposed to taste like. Not dry toast or store-bought tinned biscuits."

She took the comment with good grace, too enraptured by the meal to care. Brix turned his attention to his own food.

"Thank you, really," Belle said after a moment. "I'd offer to return the favor, but I'd likely give us both food poisoning."

"It's alright, luv. It's just nice to have someone to cook for again." Brix paused. She heard the way his throat tightened. He covered it with a sip of wine. "A friend."

She did him the courtesy of not asking if he was okay. She knew the answer, but hoped in time that he would be. Just like she hoped she would be okay in time, as well.

Belle turned her attention back to the food. Silence stretched between them, but it felt easy, companionable. For now, this, spending time together over a good meal, was enough to keep everything else at bay.

She still didn't know where things stood with Dee. She'd left her sister with an open invitation to visit whenever she wanted, to call if she needed anything. She'd offered to stay, to do whatever Dee needed to get through the next day, the next week. Finally, in the face of Dee's pallor, the way she pressed her lips together telling Belle without words she just wanted to be alone, she'd stopped.

Dee had promised to call if she needed anything. She'd left unspoken that whatever she needed, she didn't *want* anything from Belle, not right now. Whatever she'd felt about Clarence at the end, he'd still been her husband. She needed to process her pain and decide the way she intended to go on. Belle wasn't a part of that. Maybe she could be, one day. But not now. Belle could only hope that they would find their way back to something that felt like family eventually, whatever that might mean.

"So, I'm going to be a mentor," Brix said, lifting his glass.

His elbow was braced on the counter, his plate clean. Belle realized she'd completely demolished her meal.

"I promised to show Virgil a thing or two. Who knows, maybe I'll even end up an honorary uncle while I'm at it."

"I'm sure you'd be a great one," Belle said. "Teacher and honorary grandfather both." She sipped her wine, held the liquid on her tongue behind her smile before swallowing.

"Watch it, luv. I said uncle. You're the same age as me, you know."

He rose to retrieve the wine and refill both their glasses before settling into his chair again.

"You could help, if you wanted to," he said. "You know far more than I do about nearly everything, and Leonie might want to learn some of this stuff, too. They're good kids, even if they made some bad choices."

"I'm sure they are," Belle said. "I'll think about it."

Worry sat just on the edges of the circle of warmth and camaraderie Brix had created, like he'd cast a spell of duck fat and whipped potatoes. Belle took another swallow of wine and tried to let it mellow her. She'd never seen herself as a mentor, but then, she'd never imagined she'd have a partner – a friend even – either.

"The baby..." Once she'd started the sentence, Belle wasn't sure how to finish it. If she'd understood what Brix had tried to tell her on the train, one of the fathers was a ghost, and just trying to hold that impossibility in her mind made her head hurt.

"It's complicated. But I mean to keep my promise to watch over all of them, and I have a feeling that kid is going to want for nothing once they're born." Brix's grin faded into something more troubled for a moment, but determination overrode it, and he fixed his expression into one of hope. "We closed at least some of the doors. There are probably others out there, but we'll work on them where we find them. That's all we can do. There's also a chance, even if it's only a slim one, that the Hollow Queen has what she wants now."

"Which is?"

Belizial stirred behind her ribs, the first pricklings of alarm. Belle tensed, protectively. If whatever they'd done on the hill wasn't enough, if the Hollow Queen was still out there hunting...

"To rest," Brix said. "To stop being what she was made to be, which won't be an easy task."

He picked up his wine, contemplating the dark red liquid as he swirled the glass. It wasn't like in the Peony, when she'd seen him fade before her eyes, but Belle still had the impression that he'd gone somewhere far away for a moment before he spoke again.

"It remains to be seen whether love is stronger than hunger. But if anyone can help the Hollow Queen change her nature, it's Jimmy Valentine."

Belizial settled within her, only the faintest edge of tension remaining. She reached to soothe them. No more promises or apologies; she would speak with actions now, not words. Their own door, the physical one at least, had been obliterated. The rest, well, they needed to work on that, healing the hurt between them, finding a balance where they could help carry each other's pain without it overwhelming either of them.

Trusting each other to build something new and strong, no longer a thin place where a hungry queen could work her will.

"Right." Brix jumped up. "Dessert, then."

Belle groaned, an undignified sound. She couldn't remember the last time she'd eaten so much. "I'm stuffed."

"You'll change your mind." Brix returned with two plates, presenting one to Belle with a flourish. "Flourless chocolate torte."

A perfect triangle of cake so dark it seemed to drink the light sat atop a swoop of raspberry sauce alongside a scattering of whole berries.

"Trust me." Brix dug his fork into his own dessert. "It's worth it."

Belle used the edge of her fork to cut the point from her slice of torte, lifting it to her mouth. "I do."

The cake melted in her mouth, and she let out another undignified groan. He beamed, proud. Once again she saw the sorrow just below the surface, lingering in his eyes. When she left, he'd be faced with the emptiness of the house, the emptiness of everything that came after letting Abigail go. Belle had the emptiness of her apartment waiting for her as well, but she also had Belizial.

"You know," Belle said. "I was so tired on the way home yesterday, I'm not sure I really absorbed everything. Tell me again about Johnny Valentine?"

"Jimmy," Brix corrected with a flicker of gratitude, a flicker of guilt, all the hurt he tried to hold inside.

"Jimmy, right. You'd better start from the beginning," Belle said. "And pour us some more wine."

"Your wish is my command, luv." Brix swept a theatrical bow as he rose to oblige.

Belle took another bite of cake, chasing it with a mouthful of wine. She let the cadence of his voice wash over her. Even grieving, he had the natural flair of a storyteller.

"It begins," he said, "in a hotel room."

ACKNOWLEDGMENTS

What's your book about? Oh, it's about 80,000 words. Terrible jokes aside, the point is, it takes a whole lot more than a single author to turn a messy collection of several thousand words into an actual novel. Especially when the author in questions is me. To that end, there are several people I need to thank here.

First off, a huge thank you to my fabulous editors Katie Dent and Esme Dennys for their insightful comments, feedback, and their patience with me throughout multiple rewrites. The entire team at Titan did an amazing job turning my words into a novel, so thank you to everyone who had a hand in making this book look and feel gorgeous – the copyediting, the cover, the type, the design, all of it.

Thank you to my agent, Barry Goldblatt, for early feedback on the novel, general encouragement throughout the process, random bakery recommendations, and tolerance for my insistence on genre-hopping and occasionally switching projects midstream.

On a related note, thank you and apologies to A+S. The novel I was originally writing, the one they were supposed to be in, went so disastrously wrong that I had to cheat on it by writing this one instead. Maybe their story will still get told someday, or maybe not. We'll see.

As always, thank you to Siobhan Carroll, Stephanie Feldman, A. T. Greenblatt, Sarah Pinsker, and Fran Wilde for their friendship, feedback, and encouragement. Best critique group ever! I'm likely to egregiously leave someone out if I start trying to list too many names, so thank you to all the writers who hung out with me in various coffee shops while we stared at our laptops and occasionally cursed quietly at them. Thank you to all the folks who hung out with me at conventions and bookstore events, talking shop, sharing meals, commiserating, and celebrating victories. Thank you to the writers and editors I've only met and interacted with online but hope to finally meet in person someday. You are all amazing and your words keep me going.

Thank you to my family, by blood and by choice, including the four-legged members who are involved in the writing process more directly than the rest, supervising, judging, wishing I would pay attention to them instead of the computer screen, and even occasionally just keeping me company.

Last, but absolutely not least, thank you to everyone who read this book for picking it up and giving it a chance. I really hope you liked it!

ABOUT THE AUTHOR

A. C. Wise is the author of *Wendy, Darling*, *Hooked*, *Out of the Drowning Deep*, and *Ballad of the Bone Road,* along with the short story collection, *The Ghost Sequences*. Her work has won the Sunburst Award for Excellence in Canadian Literature of the Fantastic, and has been a finalist for the Nebula, Bram Stoker®, World Fantasy, Locus, British Fantasy, Aurora, Lambda Literary, and Ignyte Awards. In addition to her fiction, she contributes a review column to *Apex Magazine* and *Locus Magazine*.